THE BLACK DWARF

It may seem strange to take a small weight-increase pill so seriously. However, not only is the story of this pill a recorded fact from the end of the Second World War, it is also a pill whose formula, were it discovered, would be worth a great deal of money. For it manages to produce opposite effects from those intended.

In his search for the missing formula, Lewis Horne meets the lovely dietitian, Dr Hanna Pearce. They travel from London to New York and from Oxford to West Germany to the heart of the Black Dwarf Mountain.

THE BLACK DWARF successfully combines human interest with a dynamic and racy plot to produce a first class thriller as exciting and compelling as it is perceptive and highly readable.

About the Author

Michael Molloy was born during an air raid in December 1940; after that he took no further part in the war. Since leaving Art School, where he studied painting, he has worked on newspapers and has been the Editor of the *Mirror* since 1957. He contributes regularly to *Punch* and lives in Ealing with his wife and two daughters.

The Black Dwarf

Michael Molloy

CORONET BOOKS
Hodder and Stoughton

'The Man Who Bought New York'
© King and Green
'I Can't Get Started'
Composer: Vernon Duke. Author: Ira Gershwin
© 1935 Chappell & Co. Inc.
Used by permission of Chappell Music Limited London

'East Side, West Side' © 1894 Howley Haviland Pub Co.
now Shawnee Press Inc USA. Reproduced by permission
of EMI Publishing Ltd

Copyright © 1985 Michael Molloy
First published in 1985 by Hodder and Stoughton
Coronet edition 1986

British Library C.I.P.

Molloy, Michael
   The black dwarf.
   I. Title
   823'.91 [F]   PR6063.0484/

   ISBN 0-340-39984-8

*The characters and situations in this book are
entirely imaginary and bear no relation to any real
person or actual happening*

Printed and bound in Great Britain for
Hodder and Stoughton Paperbacks, a
division of Hodder and Stoughton Ltd.,
Mill Road, Dunton Green, Sevenoaks,
Kent (Editorial Office: 47 Bedford
Square, London, WC1 3DP) by
Richard Clay (The Chaucer Press) Ltd.,
Bungay, Suffolk

Prologue

It must be remembered that Hazlitt is carried away by a theory he has hit on – a theory that Scott only marshalled facts and comments, and let them fight their own battle . . . "All that is gossiped in the neighbourhood, all that is handed down in print, all of which a drawing or an etching may be procured is gathered together, and communicated to the public; what the heart whispers to itself in secret, what the imagination tells in thunder, this alone is wanting . . ." His mind "does not project itself into the world unknown, but mechanically shrinks back as from the edge of a precipice". Scott would have behaved foolishly if he had tried to write fanciful romances of the unknown future. But he did gaze steadily over the edge of the precipice, and, as his Life and his Journal show, in the future he saw anarchy. Was he wrong?

The Black Dwarf
Sir Walter Scott
From the Editor's Introduction,
March 1983.

Of all the leaders of the Third Reich, perhaps the strangest was Reichsführer-SS Heinrich Himmler. Timid and modest in his private life, this former chicken farmer and music lover had a reputation for kindness to his subordinates. He also personally arranged the extermination of more than six million human beings.

The instrument he forged to carry out this stain on humanity was the SS, an organisation which was truly a state within a state. The SS was in effect a private army that owed total allegiance to Adolf Hitler: it also controlled large sections of the German economy and the wealth and resources of the territories that it overran.

Hitler had no interest in money and at one point was quite poor even though he was Dictator of Germany. The problem was solved by embarrassed colleagues who arranged for a royalty to be paid for the portraits of him which appeared on postage stamps and all newly married couples were presented with a copy of his book, *Mein Kampf*, which was purchased for them by the state.

Himmler worshipped Hitler and sought to justify his Führer's lunatic racial theories through mysticism. Astrologers were consulted, Nordic legends exhumed and pre-Christian religions researched in an effort to support Himmler's belief that Hitler was the Aryan Messiah who was destined to lead all the Germanic people in a crusade to subjugate the lesser races.

Leaders of British Intelligence became aware of Himmler's murderous eccentricities and desperately sought for ways to exploit them. Agents in Sweden, Switzerland, Spain and Portugal were instructed to contact SS representatives and create the impression that Churchill was ready to break with his old foe, the Bolsheviks, and join in the crusade against the Soviet Union.

Himmler was delighted, for he knew from his own reading of *Mein Kampf* that Hitler approved of the British Empire and had always favoured the idea of an alliance with Britain. Finally he decided to test the validity of the reports by making a 'special' request to the British Prime Minister.

In the first week of June 1942 Dr David Whitehaven, an open-faced, fair-haired young Englishman, was instructed to take part in a documentary made by the Crown Film Unit concerning his job as a nutritionist at the Ministry of Food.

During the filming, Whitehaven struck up an acquaintance with the assistant director, a slim, languid man called Paul Sheridan, and on the fourth day, while they were waiting for a complicated lighting arrangement to be set up, Whitehaven confessed to him that he found the filming almost as tedious as the work he was normally engaged on. Surely there had to be a more active role he could play in the war? After all, he was in robust health, had no near dependants and spoke excellent German, thanks to the three years he'd spent doing post-graduate work at the University of Heidelberg.

Later that same evening, after the filming was done, the assistant director offered him a lift. There was someone he'd like him to meet. Intrigued, Whitehaven accepted and Sheridan took him to a block of flats in Baker Street where, to Whitehaven's amazement, he was immediately interviewed by two men he took to be senior members of British Intelligence. After an hour's exhaustive questioning they asked him if he would be prepared to go back to Germany. They wanted him to resume working with his old head of department at Heidelberg University on a project concerning research into the nutritious value of food.

At first Whitehaven was suspicious. How could such a thing be arranged? And to what end? His questioners assured him that the enterprise had the full approval of the Prime Minister, and that the request for his services had come from no less a person than Heinrich Himmler. There were to be no heroics connected with his task; he was simply a decoy, a hunter's bird set to lure the wild game into a sense of false security. Whitehaven was given a stiff whisky and told to think it over. For the past two years he had grown used to the slow plodding pace of Whitehall where decisions, even in warfare, were reached only after painful deliberation. Now he was asked for instant reaction. For a moment he heeded a distant voice that told him to be cautious. Then he finished the drink in two swallows and agreed to take the job.

Thirty minutes later Whitehaven found himself being driven to 10 Downing Street. He was hurried along a corridor with a black-and-white chequered floor and shown into a large office which he recognised from photographs as the Cabinet Room. It was packed with equipment and the same technicians that had been filming him at the Ministry of Food were setting up for a scene. When they were satisfied with the arrangements Sheridan nodded to a hovering figure who hurried away and returned a few minutes later with Winston Churchill. Whitehaven was presented to the Prime Minister who shook his hand and gestured for the bewildered visitor to stand beside him. Churchill was handed a piece of paper which he studied for a moment before casting it aside.

"Begin," Churchill boomed and the camera began to turn. He then held out his hand to Whitehaven and shook it warmly. As he did so he said: "My dear Dr Whitehaven, I am delighted that you see fit to undertake this vital work. I am sure that future generations will look back on your efforts and bless you for this venture." The Prime Minister then turned and scowled around the room. "Sufficient?" he asked. A muttered chorus of "Yes, sir" came from the technicians.

Churchill was about to go when he glanced at Whitehaven once more. "What is it like to be my personal traitor?" he said gruffly.

The next morning a dazed Whitehaven, still accompanied by Paul Sheridan, left Poole Harbour in a flying boat for Portugal. After a short sojourn in Lisbon, where he was given a canister of movie film and approached by an unknown escort, he was taken to an airfield some miles outside the city. Whitehaven was told to board a twin-engined Lufthansa aircraft, which took off moments after his arrival – as if the crew had been instructed to wait specially for him. Some hours later the air hostess announced that they were beginning their descent on Berlin. For the first time since his adventure had begun, he allowed himself to feel scared: his next appointment was to be with Heinrich Himmler.

Sixty minutes later, Whitehaven stood facing him. Himmler looked immaculate, but there was something grotesque about the squat, black-clad figure. Despite the brilliant tailoring, the body looked short and plump. His chin was weak and there was a puffiness about his face. His hair was shaved close to his skull at the sides of his head so that at the top it looked almost like a toupee. The overall image was of the bad goblin in a fairy story, the fantasy figure from a child's nightmare.

"Reichsführer, I was instructed to present you with this," Whitehaven said as he handed over the canister of movie film that he had been given in Lisbon.

Himmler turned to a leather-coated figure standing a few feet behind him. "Werner, I believe you are waiting for this?" The man took it with a salute, and uttered a few curt commands to a soldier at the door. A moment later, to Whitehaven's surprise, the same film crew that had greeted him on his arrival at Berlin airport filed into the room and began to set up their equipment.

"How long will you be?" Himmler asked the crew.

"Just a few minutes, sir," one of the men replied.

"Then we will take the opportunity to explain to Dr Whitehaven just what he is doing here," Himmler said, his voice suddenly filled with good humour. He nodded to another officer in the room. "Schneider, will you be so kind?"

"Certainly, sir." And then he began his narrative.

At the beginning of the war, Schneider explained, it immediately became clear to Reichsführer Himmler that food would be as vital as ammunitions in the coming struggle. "With great foresight, the Reichsführer assembled the best nutritionists in the Reich and ordered them to produce a drug that would enhance the value of food. Only last winter did it become apparent how important this work was when our Waffen SS Units in Russia lost an average of fifteen per cent of their bodyweight due to the intense cold. When the Führer saw these figures he demanded to know from the relevant Ministries what was to be done to maintain the fighting efficiency of our soldiers. Only Reichsführer Himmler was prepared. Our Führer ordered that an all-out effort should be made to perfect the drug, and personally named the project Operation Hermann.

"Professor Carl Raeder, the head of the research programme, was summoned and the Reichsführer asked him whom he would like to recruit. Without hesitation Professor Raeder named you, Dr Whitehaven."

Himmler had begun to chuckle. "Professor Raeder's face was quite a picture when I told him that I would arrange for you to join his team, wasn't it, Schneider?"

"It was indeed, Reichsführer."

Himmler then took Whitehaven's hand and began to speak to the camera: "On behalf of the people of the Greater German Reich, I greet Dr David Whitehaven, a loyal subject of His Britannic Majesty King George VI, and welcome him to the struggle against Bolshevism. *Heil Hitler!*"

As the lights were dimmed and the camera packed away Himmler sat down behind his desk once more and turned to Whitehaven. "I must not keep you any longer, Doctor. You have a long journey to make, but you will not lack company. Werner and his men are going with you." Whitehaven nodded and left the room as Himmler smiled benevolently after him.

Whitehaven was fascinated by Werner and his crew. The four-man team wore battered uniforms, carried sidearms and they handled their equipment with the careless professionalism of master craftsmen. All bore the stamp of seasoned troops. Once they were away from the 'brass' upstairs and waiting for their transport in the coverway of the headquarters they slumped down with their kit, lit cigarettes and looked with cynical contempt at the guards who stood each side of the doorway.

"This is a nice cushy number for us, Doctor," Werner said as he took a pull from a silver hip-flask. "I suppose I ought to thank you."

"I'm afraid I don't understand."

"We're to go with you to these new headquarters to make a documentary about the research you'll be doing. It seems they've got all the facilities there: cutting rooms, recording studios, everything. It's going to be an official SS film archive." He patted two large canvas bags beside him. "We've got to process this lot and store it." He took another swig from the flask and gently kicked one of his companions. "After all, it's got to last a thousand years, eh, Klaus?"

"What is it?" Whitehaven asked as their truck arrived.

"Oh, just some stuff we shot in Russia," Werner replied.

Whitehaven and the film crew arrived at the Alpine village of Vosbach after dark, having spent the whole day travelling from Berlin by a relay of aircraft and military vehicles, the last of which deposited them at the tiny inn run by Herr Scholl and his wife Rosa. Whitehaven was so tired he could hardly manage to eat the bowl of soup they gave him before he stumbled to the bedroom.

The next morning he sat in the minute bar of the inn, drinking fresh coffee, when he heard a familiar voice speak his name.

"I understand that Dr Whitehaven is here," he heard Carl Raeder say in his soft courteous voice. David rose as his old friend entered the bar. "My dear fellow," Raeder cried as they shook hands. "How wonderful to see you!"

"You look exactly the same," David replied.

Raeder had one of those spare athletic bodies that seemed to form in late youth and remain unaltered for life.

"How is Hanna?" David asked lightly.

The question fell like a blow on the older man: "She was killed last year, David. An air-raid."

"I'm so sorry, Carl. I had no idea."

"How could you?" Raeder said. "According to Reichs-marshal Goering it was impossible. You know he gave a personal undertaking that Berlin would never be bombed!"

David could think of nothing to ease the man's grief. They stood for a moment in awkward silence.

"Come," Raeder said, breaking the silence. "I will show you the Wagnerian laboratory our masters have built for us."

There was a small half-tracked military vehicle parked by the entrance to the inn; Werner and his men were loading their equipment on the back as Whitehaven and Raeder squeezed into the front seat. The *kübelwagen* ground away past the church and immediately began to climb a fairly narrow road that had evidently only recently been completed. "This used to be a mountain track until a few months ago," Raeder shouted over the noise of the engine. David nodded and watched as the scenery revealed itself. After a few kilometres the *kübelwagen* passed the high Alpine meadows where cattle were grazing, and the road started to hug the mountainside.

The view was breathtaking. Great ragged rock faces and pine trees were contrasted by splashes of sunlight, and occasionally a mountain stream would gush white water down the side of the rocks, creating grottoes of fern and lichen. To the left, the road fell away into a deep gorge so that they were level with the tops of the pine trees growing

13

there. Then the angle of the road began to level out as they approached a checkpoint built into the side of the rock face.

A guard waved the vehicle on and they swung around the corner past the pillbox into a huge semicircular area at least seventy metres in diameter. Several army lorries and small personnel carriers were parked under camouflage netting to one side. In front of the lorries a squad of soldiers were exercising vigorously to the instructions of an NCO: the huge peak of the mountain rose above them. Two great doors stood open in the mountainside marking the entrance to a massive bunker.

"The area was blasted out," Raeder explained, sweeping his arm to encompass the semicircle on which they stood. "But the bunker is constructed from natural caves. However, there is one charming feature. Do you feel like stretching your legs?"

"Happily."

Raeder led David towards a pathway that climbed in a zig-zag pattern up the side of the mountain. Eventually they reached the top and Whitehaven found himself looking over a beautiful Alpine lake.

"Feel the temperature," Raeder said.

David stooped down by the edge and dipped in his hand. He had expected it to be icy cold but instead found that it was pleasantly warm.

"Amazing, isn't it?" Raeder said. "At this altitude one would expect it to be freezing, but there appears to be some Artesian principle involved so that it is fed by a warm underground spring from deep in the earth, as well as by the melting snows from up there." At this he gestured to the snow-clad peaks rising from the far side of the lake. "There we have the happiest feature of this place, David." Then he shrugged and turned. "Well, we'd better get you settled in and explain the work," he said more cheerfully.

Conversation was easier on the way down. "So you see it is a question of stability," Raeder was saying as they reached the base once more. "The formula seems to be effective. The fat

14

cells expand and the weight is maintained, but only for a limited time. Then the reverse effect occurs. The creatures are perfectly healthy but they suddenly experience a dramatic weight loss, which then stabilises with a corresponding increase in appetite. In fact, we have achieved exactly the reverse effect to the one that we desire. Instead of increasing the bodyweight of the animals they became extremely thin whilst eating large amounts of food."

"What can I do?" asked Whitehaven. "My experience hasn't prepared me for such a project."

"I need your unorthodoxy, David. My people here are thorough and devoted but I worry that they may have missed some oversight of mine. They tend to take my work as gospel. Just go over everything we've done. Use your discerning eye. If anyone can spot where we've gone wrong it will be you."

For the next few weeks Whitehaven's work consisted of poring over the contents of the filing cabinets and reading the mass of notes that the team had produced since first starting the experiments; he had also volunteered to feed the animals, a job which had to be done with scrupulous care, as variations in their weight were the very basis of the experiments. Sometimes Werner would film him at work, but for some reason unknown to Whitehaven the German seemed to be drunk most of the time.

Gradually he became used to the bizarre quality of life inside the giant caves that lay beyond the great steel doors. The laboratories took only part of the space that was available inside the mountain. The first massive chamber had a rough domed roof that merged with the walls, that in turn had been dressed with concrete. When Whitehaven first entered the chamber he was filled with awe. Its size reminded him of the dome of St Paul's. But although the conditions were pleasant enough in the bunker Whitehaven found the constant proximity of others tiresome: it was as if he were back at boarding school. He tried to spend an hour each day in his cubicle alone, then every evening, at about six o'clock, he would leave his room and make his way through a labyrinth of passages to the main laboratory, where the rabbits and rats were kept in clinical comfort.

One afternoon Carl Raeder came and asked if Whitehaven felt like a walk. He readily agreed, and they set off. After they stepped through the small door set in the giant steel shutters, Raeder led them to the furthest edge of the perimeter, where they could look over the valley to the mountains opposite, bathed in the last rays of the day's sunlight.

"You know, people always think winter is the saddest time," Raeder said after a few minutes. "But autumn can be just as melancholy."

"Do you miss Hanna very much?" Whitehaven asked as casually as he could.

Raeder shrugged and kept his eyes on the distant mountain peaks. "I miss both of us. One often hears people say 'a part of me died'; now I know exactly what they mean. There is no grief; just a lingering numbness." He paused and then spoke again. "The part of me I liked is with her." They walked on slowly before Raeder added, "She was an American. Did you know?" Whitehaven shook his head. "Oh yes. We met at university. Her family were very strict. They did not approve of her studying science. And when Hitler came to power she wanted us to leave and go to the United States. But I said no; I am German. I will not abandon my country to these creatures. Look at me now! The lackey of a chicken farmer."

He turned and stared into Whitehaven's eyes. "You should not stay, David. All this is wrong." He gestured towards the bunker. "Something terrible will happen here, I know it. Switzerland is just beyond those mountains. Your place is in England, not in this madhouse. I feel it deeply. They are rehearsing Götterdämmerung, and eventually those clowns in Berlin will ask for a live performance."

"If I should ever go, will you come with me?" Whitehaven asked.

"Yes," his friend replied after a time. "I brought you here with a chance remark. I owe it to Hanna to take you home."

Later that week Whitehaven was standing, with a few other spectators, at the edge of the great dome listening to a young soldier playing Bach on the violin. Because of the magnificent acoustics the music sounded magical. Whitehaven was lost in thought when he suddenly became aware that Werner was standing beside him. He could tell from the way the German swayed that Werner was very drunk. "What do you think of this German culture?" said Werner in a thickened voice as he gestured towards the young soldier.

"I think it is very beautiful," Whitehaven said quietly.

"Yes," Werner said, "beautiful; art, music, philosophy. We are truly a gifted nation." He slapped Whitehaven on the back. "Come and have a drink with me."

Not allowing Whitehaven a chance to refuse, Werner led him through the usual maze of passages to the part of the bunker where the film laboratories were housed. He unlocked a door and switched on the lights. It was a long room with racks of film canisters along one of the walls, each carefully labelled. At the far end was a screen and next to the door a small table, some chairs and a film projector.

Werner went to a cupboard and produced a bottle of brandy and two glasses. He poured a tumblerful for Whitehaven, ignored his own glass and took a long pull from the bottle. Then he slowly walked along the racks of film. He reached up with the bottle of brandy and rapped one of the gleaming silver canisters. "That's *you*, Doctor. You and Churchill and Himmler and all the brilliant scientists. My God, wouldn't Comrade Stalin like to see that film!"

Whitehaven took a sip of his brandy and waited. He was feeling distinctly nervous.

Werner turned and focused on him. "What do you think of the soldiers here in the bunker, Doctor?" he said in a quiet voice.

Whitehaven shrugged. "They seem much the same as any other troops. Why?"

Werner took another pull from the bottle. "Because they're Einsatzgruppen." He paused. "Do you know what that means?"

Whitehaven shook his head.

"The Einsatzgruppe doesn't fight the enemy, Dr Whitehaven. It exterminates civilians of the 'wrong' sort;

mostly Jews – men, women, children – all are killed. Whole villages are shot, hanged, herded into buildings and burned to death."

As he spoke Werner massaged his face with his hand. "This is official policy?" Whitehaven said with disbelief in his voice.

Werner nodded. "The orders come from Himmler himself. It is going to be the final solution to the Jewish problem and the SS will be the organisation honoured with carrying out the act. Let me show you." Werner took down one of the canisters, threaded the film into the machine and snapped off the lights.

For the next half an hour Whitehaven sat numb with horror as he watched one of the films that Werner had shot on the Eastern Front. Finally it came to an end and the only sound in the room was the tack, tack, tack of the loose end of the film striking the empty spool. The light from the projector shone brightly against the blank screen and reflected back on to Werner's face. It was rigid with grief.

Whitehaven could not speak. Silently he got up and left the room. He made his way back to his own quarters and lay down on his bunk. He closed his eyes but the terrible images from the film played over again in his mind's eye. They were a record of unbelievable horror: the kind of savagery that seemed to mock a thousand years of civilisation. He knew as long as he lived that he would never be able to purge them from his mind. A wave of nausea and weakness passed over him at the memory of the bestiality he had witnessed. He felt helpless and drained by the evil he had thought modern man incapable of committing. Then suddenly he knew what he must do. He had to escape and warn his people of the horror that was loose in the world.

1

The more high spirited among the youth were, about the time
that our narrative begins, expecting, rather with hope than
apprehension, an opportunity of emulating their fathers in
their military achievements.

The Black Dwarf
SIR WALTER SCOTT

Lewis Horne was late for work. For the last fifteen minutes
he had faced the front-page headline, SUMMIT TALKS
SAMBA, as the figure opposite read the contents of the
newspaper until Lewis had grown to loathe the words and
the parts of the body that showed around the edges of the
page. The manicured hands were plump and pink and the
chubby legs that jutted from beneath the page strained the
chalk-striped trousers so that only the faintest crease showed
in the worsted cloth. Silk socks crossed at the ankles with the
polished Oxfords resting on the welts among the detritus
of discarded sweet packets, cigarette ends and cellophane
wrappings. The train stopped with a grunting sigh and the
newspaper was lowered to reveal a face so stamped with the
cares of mortgage and matrimony that Lewis felt a stab of
remorse for the angry passion his fellow passenger had so
recently conjured in him.

Lewis sat for a few seconds as the rest of the people hurried
to leave the stuffy womb of the carriage, and contemplated
the desirability of Prohibition. He had to admit that if a
referendum had taken place at that moment on the banning
of alcohol he would have gone with the ayes.

As the last of the occupants shuffled impatiently off the
train he made a reluctant effort and hauled himself to his feet.

On the platform things were worse. Diffused white light streamed through the glass roof of Liverpool Street station and made his eyes smart despite the cheap sunglasses he had bought at the beginning of his journey.

By the time he reached the ticket barrier he felt as though someone had sprinkled sand next to his skin. As he walked across the concourse of the station towards the Underground entrance the ground beneath his feet seemed to pitch like the deck of a ship in a gentle swell, while the joints of his body ached and squeaked as if he were a badly stuffed teddy-bear.

Lewis had The Hangover: the definitive, cosmic benchmark for drinkers. He felt about as tough as a light bulb—extraordinary, he mused, as yesterday he had been pronounced perfectly fit by government-appointed experts.

But yesterday had been his birthday.

At 5.20 p.m. the previous evening he had waited at the gates of the camp for the car that was to take him to the station when a voice with a Belfast accent had called softly to him, "Captain Horne, sir, you may be an officer and a gentleman but you stand about as straight as the seams on a whore's stockings."

Lewis turned and looked down into the grinning face of Sergeant Sandy Patch. "'Allo, Lew," he said in his usual South London voice.

"Christ, Sandy, I thought you were still in bandit country."

"Naaah, I've got a new number, dead cushy. Cowboy instructor at Lambeth. I come down here now and again to give the lads a demo in gunfighting. What are you doing here?"

"30,000 mile service. I've just passed my MOT."

Sandy clicked his fingers. "It's today. Blimey, thirty. I never thought you'd make it. What the hell are we standing here for? I'll buy you a big one in the sergeants' mess."

And when they got there Lewis, of course, had to buy him one back . . .

With the slow, deliberate actions of a deep-sea diver he raised his wristwatch to eye-level and concentrated on the time. 9.51 a.m. on the first day of his thirty-first year. The languid image of Charlie Mars swam into his mind and he groaned as he thought of the sardonic banter he would have to endure from his civilian superior. A shower and a cold lager, he decided. That would be armour enough for Charlie's barbs about the licentious soldiery. With the start of a spring in his step he followed the late crowd on to the Central Line.

While he waited for the westbound train he took off his sunglasses and was about to throw them into a rubbish container until he looked at them again. Their obvious vulgarity would be sure to offend Charlie Mars: he would shy away from them like a racehorse confronted by a totter's cart. Lewis placed them carefully in his top pocket. He was feeling better every minute.

When the train arrived, he squeezed into a compartment and noticed that he was entirely surrounded by young women.

The doors parted again at St Paul's station and a grotesque figure entered the packed carriage. The fresh chorus of girls made a considerable amount of space for the new passenger so that Lewis had no difficulty in studying his fellow traveller.

Matted hair in greasy strands framed a creased and blackened face. The burly body was clad in two filthy raincoats that hung open over dungarees that were short enough to reveal sockless feet. These were encased in ancient, cracked army boots. Clutching a handrail the tramp mumbled to himself for a few moments then looked up at Lewis and grinned, revealing a mouthful of ruined teeth.

"It's me mother's birthday and I've got to buy her some flowers. Can you spare a pound?" he pleaded in a hoarse growl.

Lewis had encountered beggars all over the world. Some had angered him and some had made him feel ashamed. This one amused him. As the train pulled into his stop he reached into his pocket and placed a crumpled note into the grimy outstretched hand.

A cool breeze blew down High Holborn as Lewis emerged from the north-west entrance of Chancery Lane tube station and walked briskly towards Warwick Court. He turned into the narrow street and nodded to the plaque dedicated to Sun Yat-Sen that was set into the wall before the entrance to the Inns of Court.

Once he was into the maze of alleys away from the main thoroughfare the warm summer day reminded him of his earlier discomfort and he walked even faster towards Lamb's Conduit Street. Lewis unlocked the front door of the flats that were located above the Old Times Antique Shop. The sparse marble-floored entrance hall was cool and silent as he checked the wooden shelf and picked up the advertising circulars addressed to Flat Two. When he reached the first landing on the staircase he was confronted by a large sign stuck to the wall next to the front door of the flat. The legend read:

> There's a girl inside all trim and perty,
> Lookin' for a lad who's thirty,
> If you're that man be glad you're born,
> Just come inside and blast! you're Horne.

Underneath was a caricature of Lewis which emphasised his black tousled hair and pale blue-green eyes.

The door was slightly ajar. He leaned towards the crack but could hear nothing, so he climbed the next flight of stairs to his own flat.

It was the kind of place people often told him he could make something of, unaware that he had deliberately chosen the bleakness of his surroundings. He liked to know that he could pack all his worldly possessions in forty-five seconds; besides, it saved hours of housework. To his surprise and pleasure he had discovered that women found the flat seductive because of the total lack of the feminine touch. He had bought nearly all the furniture from a second-hand dealer in Gray's Inn Road one Saturday afternoon for twenty-two pounds; most people thought he had been cheated.

Inside the living room the air was flat and stale. Lewis opened the two sash windows and paused to look up at the sky. The white haze had broken up and bright sunlight shafted down into the street. The area below had been turned into a pedestrian walkway and people strolled aimlessly as they window-shopped in the morning heat. He watched one girl in a short summer dress that clung to her body as she made her way towards The Lamb public house. Then his appraisal was rudely interrupted by the ring of the telephone.

"Captain Horne?"

He recognised the voice of Sergeant Hillary.

"Yes."

"Mr Mars is anxious to speak to you, sir."

"What's the problem?"

"I don't know, sir. Shall I put you through?"

"No thanks, Sergeant. Just tell him I won't be long." Lewis hung up.

The condemned man had a hearty shower, he said to himself as he stripped off his clothes. There was an old-fashioned set of chemist's scales that the previous tenant had left in the bathroom. Lewis stepped on to them and adjusted the weights. Eleven stone, nine pounds: six pounds down since he returned from Milan a month ago. He ran his hand down over the scar that was now just a white weal over his stomach. *"Bellissimo,"* he muttered and thanked God that Latins were so in love with gleaming steel. Had his opponent used an old-fashioned revolver his navel would have been deep enough to serve as a fountain-pen holder.

He showered, then shaved quickly, to deal with the tiny parts that he'd missed earlier that morning. Next he went to the wardrobe to get a suit. Like most people in his line of work Lewis tended to buy his clothes abroad. The day was so warm he selected a dark blue lightweight that he'd had made in Hong Kong two years before. As he dressed, he recalled Charlie Mars's advice when he was leaving on the job.

"When you get to the colony someone will offer to make you a suit in twenty-four hours for fifteen pounds. If you take up the offer that's exactly what you'll have: a suit made in twenty-four hours that's worth fifteen pounds."

He emptied the pockets of his discarded jacket and just in time remembered the sunglasses. Then he consulted his watch: ten forty-five. What the hell. He decided to pop into the flat below and say hello to his sister, Janet.

Lewis glanced at the sign on the wall again as he pushed open the door. They'd certainly celebrated his birthday in style. Bunting, streamers and the sad, shrivelled corpses of burst balloons decorated the hallway. Every tabletop had its share of empty glasses, scattered peanuts and overflowing ashtrays. He wondered for a moment why pictures on the wall always managed to end up askew after a party so that even the room had a drunken appearance.

Walking slowly around he read the guest list from the spoor they had left. To the right of the sofa cigarette ash was scattered in a semicircle. Obviously Roland Perth had sat there and held court.

He looked over at the bookcase and saw that a copy of *A Passage to India* lay face-down and out of its usual place. He could imagine the conversation. At one end of the table, where the food had been, stood a cluster of empty Perrier bottles. A couple of glasses held the dregs of Campari. He looked into the ashtray and found four minute butts of marijuana. This was where the art department from the advertising agency that Janet worked for would have set up shop.

The sleeves on the record player told him that someone had been selecting modern jazz records until a younger person had taken over and insisted they play some old Sinatra. He was sorry he'd missed it all. He had been to the same party before but he had enjoyed it the last time. One clue was missing. He paused for a moment, thinking. Last night it had been warm. He moved to the open window and looked along the ledge outside. There was a bottle of Glenfiddich whisky with about four drinks gone from it and a cut-glass goblet. Charlie Mars had been there, but not for long.

Lewis looked into Janet's bedroom and found it empty, with the bed neatly made. He smiled. Despite the chaos elsewhere the room looked as crisp and tidy as a matron's uniform. Next to the bed was a photograph in a silver frame of their parents – his father in dress uniform and his mother in a ball gown. But for the hairstyle of the Fifties she could have been Janet.

He pushed open the other bedroom door and looked into the dim light that filtered through the white roller-blind.

The supine figure of Gordon Meredith blinked at him blearily and said: "You missed your party, Lewis."

Horne frowned down at him. "What are you doing in my sister's flat, you cad?"

"Fat lot of good it did me," Meredith grumbled. "She wouldn't let me touch her. Just my bloody luck to fall in love with a girl who's never heard of the permissive society."

Meredith sat up and massaged his face, then looked at himself in the dressing-table mirror at the end of the bed.

"I can't understand it, Lewis. You don't have any trouble with women and I'm much better looking than you."

Lewis had to admit the statement was true. He'd always had a slightly battered face even as a boy – nothing to compare with the Grecian regularity of Meredith's features.

"It's my age, Gordon. When you get to be thirty they'll start throwing themselves at you."

"They already do," Meredith said sadly. "But I don't want anyone but Janet." He added wistfully, "She's so beautiful and she's talented too. Did you see the drawing she did of you?"

Lewis nodded. "The grace of Aphrodite, the skill of Titian."

"Titian was a man, wasn't he?" Meredith asked suspiciously.

Lewis nodded again. "Venetian. Probably good with a knife," he said and his fingertips fluttered to his stomach. "Come on, get up. Charlie Mars wants me at Gower Street."

Meredith sprang to his feet at the side of the bed and all six feet two inches of him stood quivering to attention; he threw up a perfect guardsman's salute and barked out the word, "Sah!"

Lewis waved a languid hand as he left the bedroom and in the hallway bumped into Janet, her arms full of groceries.

"Wotcha," he said and gave her a brisk kiss on the cheek.

"Hello, Lulu," his sister said. "You missed your surprise party."

"Nobody told me I was having one," he said, following her into the kitchen.

"That would have rather defeated the idea of a surprise, wouldn't it?"

"As ever, your logic is irrefutable."

She went to the sink and began to fill a kettle. As she did so she studied him. "You've lost weight," she said matter-of-factly. Lewis broke the end of a piece of French bread that was sticking out of the carrier bag and began to chew it without relish.

"That's the idea of a health farm," he said with his mouth full.

"Why didn't you take any luggage with you?" she said, trying to keep the interest out of her voice.

"Oh, they supply everything there, even down to a tooth-brush and spare socks. That's the great thing – you're not supposed to worry. Just sit about all day in a dressing-gown listening to your stomach rumbling."

Janet made some space on the littered table and set down two mugs of instant coffee.

"Haven't you got a beer?" Lewis asked.

"We drank it all last night, I'm afraid. Anyway, it's too early," she said sharply, and with that went into her bed-room.

"It's never too early for a drink. Do you know who said that?" he called out.

She re-emerged with a package wrapped in gift paper. "I don't know. W. C. Fields?"

"No, Denis Thatcher during the 1983 election campaign. You don't often get the absolute truth from someone con-nected with politics."

She placed the package before him. "Happy Birthday," she said. "Incidentally, why *didn't* you come home yesterday?"

Lewis sipped the coffee and studied the package. "I ran into Sandy Patch and we had a few together."

Janet looked at him closely. "Sergeant Patch?"

"Yes, you remember him. After the army we both joined the firm together at the same time. He's been in the Dublin office."

"I'd have thought he'd had enough of Ireland after Belfast."

"Oh, Dublin's a long way from the Falls Road. Anyway, he's back in London now."

Lewis attacked the wrapping and was soon holding a beautifully carved and painted figure of an eighteenth-century rifleman.

"It is the right regiment, isn't it?" Janet said.

"Yes," he said after a moment. "That was the way we used to look. Thanks, Jan."

Meredith came into the kitchen adjusting the knot in his tie. There were two pieces of lavatory paper stuck to his chin.

"That's an awfully blunt razor in the bathroom, Janet," he said reproachfully.

"Good heavens," she said in a shocked voice. "And last night you told me I was perfect. Were you toying with my affections, Captain?"

Meredith glanced across at the electric clock on top of the refrigerator and gasped: "My giddy aunt, is that the time? The God of War will skin me alive."

Like Lewis, Meredith worked for Charlie Mars.

"By the way, why aren't you at work this morning?" Lewis asked his sister.

"Guy Keneally gave me the morning off as a special dispensation," Janet said. "Only fair, really, as his ghastly girlfriend caused most of the mess."

"Was that the woman who kept complaining to us all about how frightfully mean somebody's wife was to her?" Meredith asked.

"That's right," Janet said. "Actually it's Mrs Keneally that's being so mean to her."

Meredith took another anxious look at the clock. "I'm going now, Janet," he said in a mournful voice.

"Goodbye, then," she said briskly, ignoring Meredith's moonstruck appearance. She turned to Lewis. "Will you be home tonight?"

"I'm not sure. Why?"

"I thought we could have a drink to celebrate your birthday."

"What time?"

"About seven o'clock."

"All right. I'll do my best. Anyway, I'll ring you later."

Meredith lingered a moment longer to give her a final

smile until Lewis tugged at his sleeve. When they reached the pavement they set off at a cracking pace towards Gower Street so that after a few minutes Meredith, in a heavy flannel suit, was sweating. "Christ, Lewis, slow down. We weren't all light infantry, you know."

Lewis eased his pace and smiled. "I forgot you guardsmen trained by dancing with debutantes."

Meredith took out a red spotted handkerchief and mopped his brow. "Well, you've obviously got over that Milan business. Henderson said you would probably be away for months."

"Henderson is a peanut," Lewis said pleasantly. "The only wound he ever saw was on a pox doctor's chart."

Meredith looked at him with admiration. "That's a particularly vivid piece of imagery, Lewis. I don't think I've heard it before, even at the depot."

"I picked it up from an old friend I met yesterday," Lewis said as they approached the entrance to their offices in Gower Street. "Sergeant Patch. We did our last tour in Ulster together."

In the hallway he waved goodbye to Meredith, crossed the chequered floor and climbed the stairs towards the attic rooms where Charlie Mars worked.

It was like walking into his past. The room was exactly as he remembered another from his undergraduate days at Oxford, when Charlie Austen Mars had been his tutor. Sometimes when he was there he was forced to raise himself on tiptoe to peer out of one of the high dormer windows, half-expecting to look down on the Cotswold stone walls of their old college.

Inside the room everything was the same. Books, pictures, furniture, even the ratty Persian rug kept faith with Lewis's memories. Occasionally he wondered if Charlie himself was an artefact that had been transported there when he left the academic life for his new career as a civil servant, so little did he change.

His six foot three inches of bony slimness lay stretched from sofa to coffee table where his handmade brogues nestled among the usual piles of files and books that barricaded the room. Charlie took his glasses from the tip of his nose and laid them on a table by his side.

"Ah, my Achilles at last," he said acidly. "I learned from your clownish companion last night that you have been sulking in your tent."

Lewis took a pile of books from the chair opposite the sofa, dumped them on the floor and flopped down. "Gordon Meredith passed out of Sandhurst top of practically everything including dressage," he said easily. "I do wish you'd drop this affectation that he's almost a half-wit."

Charlie sighed deeply and passed a hand across his eyes. "Forgive me," he said, "I forget that you possess this absurd loyalty to your brothers-in-arms." He studied Lewis for a moment. "How are you? Fit? Did they issue you with those hideous sunglasses? What have you been doing at that ridiculous establishment? Practising killing people with knitting needles and doing press-ups, I suppose."

"Something like that," Lewis said with a grin and removed the sunglasses.

"What a waste," Charlie sighed. "When you first left me you had the beginnings of a fairly promising mind. They've blunted you, Lewis. How much is left of the edge that I so carefully honed?"

"If I remember correctly, we spent most of the time listening to your collection of Billie Holiday records. It's a bloody miracle I got a degree at all."

"Did we?" Charlie said. "Surely I taught you something?"

"Yes," said Lewis after some thought. "You taught me how to do the three-card-trick. Very useful. I won a lot of money doing it in the army."

"Nonsense. You can't surprise me anymore."

Lewis grinned. "Tell your beggar I want my pound back."

Charlie raised his eyebrows questioningly.

"Come on, I know that tramp was one of your wunderkinder."

Charlie put his fingertips together in donnish fashion. He only did that when he was annoyed. "Very good, Lewis. How did you spot him?"

"His eyes were as clear as spring water. Apart from that, he was excellent."

Charlie sighed. "Showed that much, did it?"

Lewis nodded. "Looked like Al Jolson."

"Dear me," Charlie said. "Still, he managed to pick you up even though you were a day late."

"I wouldn't say walking up to me in an Underground carriage was a good way to practise surveillance."

Charlie nodded. "I'll have a word with Claude Henderson. He's really one of his trainees."

"In that case you can tell him if he's going to dress up like an Arab beggar he's got to smell like one. Claude's boy was wearing deodorant."

"You must have been very popular with the locals in the Middle East, Lewis."

"To some people I was a little ray of sunshine."

Charlie Mars nodded. "You must show me *your* Arab disguise sometime. Did you look like T. E. Lawrence? He was always a boyhood hero of mine."

"No, I used Rudolph Valentino as my model."

"Well, I have a more mundane task for you today. I want you to check on something the readers have turned up."

He handed Lewis a Xerox sheet of paper initialled by Victor Smight.

"Isn't Victor retiring soon?" Lewis asked. Charlie nodded.

Lewis read the cutting and paid special attention to a paragraph underlined in red ink. The article, from *New Society*, was by a Dr Hanna Pearce and explained the research she was doing into a drug that would alter people's metabolism so that the food that they ate had more calorific value. The underscored paragraph mentioned a conversation she had once held with a Professor Carl Raeder who had done research into the same subject during the Second World War on a project called Operation Hermann.

Lewis put down the cutting. "So?"

Charlie recrossed his legs and gazed up at the ceiling. "According to Victor Smight, Professor Carl Raeder has been dead since 1943. Victor did a complete trawl through the records and the only Raeder doing this kind of work was killed in an air-raid on Cologne. The Americans were quite specific. It seems they wanted to interview him after the war so they made a thorough search in 1945. They even have a copy of his death certificate on file."

"I still don't understand," Lewis said.

Charlie could not resist a dramatic pause.

"Hanna Pearce is only twenty-five years old. What was she doing holding a conversation with somebody who was killed sixteen years before she was born?"

2

"Did you, then, know my parents, and do you know me?"
"This is the first time you have crossed my waking eyes,
but I have seen you in my dreams."

The Black Dwarf
SIR WALTER SCOTT

Sergeant Hillary glanced up from the book he had been reading when Lewis entered his office and managed to sit rigidly to attention. Charlie Mars had instructed that protocol should be kept to the minimum at Gower Street, but despite his comparative youth the sergeant found it difficult to overcome the deeper instincts instilled in him by his training. He was regular army to the polished bottoms of his shoes. The civilian clothes he was forced to wear in his present post bore mute testament to his preference for uniform: white shirt, blue blazer and grey slacks with razor creases. There was a military quality to his office that stood in stark contrast to Charlie Mars's creative disorder. Plain brown linoleum, trestle tables instead of desks, a row of filing cabinets, their tops as uncluttered as a barracks square, and a noticeboard filled with instructions about fire drill and duty rosters. The only splash of colour came from a photograph cut from a magazine that showed the Prince of Wales as Colonel-in-Chief of Sergeant Hillary's old regiment, carrying out a ceremonial inspection.

It was a regular army room all right, the army that Lewis had left a long time ago. Now he was used to sergeants to whom the Queen's Commission was a mere technicality.

Lewis picked up the paperback that Hillary had been reading. The illustration on the cover showed a Waffen SS private about to attack a Russian tank with a potato masher grenade. *The Devil's Blood Brothers* the title proclaimed.

"Good book, Sergeant?" Lewis asked, forcing his voice to be friendly.

"Yes, sir."

Lewis put the book down. "I understand you made me an appointment for this lunchtime."

"Yes, sir. Mr Mars told me to book you a table at the Snapper's winebar in King Street for one o'clock. I took the liberty of reserving one under the picture of Raquel Welch."

What made him think of Raquel Welch? Lewis wondered. James Mason as 'Rommel, Desert Fox' would have been more in keeping with Sergeant Hillary's mental processes. Perhaps Raquel Welch was a deliberate act of provocation. Dr Pearce the Nutritionist somehow brought forth the picture of an angular woman with hair drawn back in a bun and mouth tight with disapproval. Lewis sighed.

"What did Dr Pearce sound like when you spoke to her?"

"Sound like, sir? I'm afraid I don't quite follow you."

"Well: young, old, gruff, smooth, hostile, enthusiastic?"

"Hard to tell, sir, she didn't speak much. She had a funny accent but I couldn't place it from the little she said."

Lewis sighed again. "Sometimes we perform harsh duties for Queen and country."

"Yes, sir," the sergeant said in a flat monotone. Lewis left him to the Waffen SS private and made his way to his own office.

All the rooms at the top of the house had been servants' quarters. Once two chambermaids had lived in the room Lewis shared with Meredith and the bells that summoned them to duty still hung over the door. It was pokey and dim with a tiny grate in which Gordon burned handfuls of smokeless fuel during wintertime. There was one high attic window that looked over the rooftops. The old whitewash on the walls had mellowed to cream and brown. Meredith loved it. During his last golden year at school he had occupied a room that was similar, and as Charlie Mars had recreated Oxford in Gower Street so Meredith had fashioned a study straight from Tom Brown's Rugby. Gradually he had filled the room with his possessions so that now there were trunks of tin and leather, a corner piled with squash racquets, fencing foils and fishing rods, heaps of books. Group photographs with Meredith in a variety of uniforms marking his progress from prep school to Sandhurst covered the walls. Lewis's only contribution was a stuffed owl in a glass case that he had bought from his furniture dealer in Gray's Inn Road. It fitted the decor like the bolt in a Lee Enfield rifle.

Meredith didn't look up when Lewis entered. He was sitting in a wickerwork chair with his hands in his pockets in front of the fireplace, his legs stretched out comfortably so that he could rest his feet on the mantelpiece.

Lewis sat down at the small wooden desk they shared and began to work his way through the pile of paperwork that had accumulated during his absence.

The first circular was from Special Branch to all security departments, saying Petra ben Azziz, the terrorist who had led the recent massacre of a busful of tourists in Haifa, was believed to be in Britain. A Member of Parliament thought he had recognised her at a recent Embassy reception. The memo ended with a note saying: known associate of KRONSTADT, see other reference. Pinned to the memo was a gossip-column cutting with the headline: DRESSING TO KILL. Underneath was the picture of a blonde woman trying on a coat. Lewis's stomach gave a tiny lurch as he studied the picture. The copy read:

Susan Armitage, 30, heiress to a £350 million fortune went shopping yesterday and bought a £4,000 coat in the shop top people go to stay chic, but she couldn't ask her husband, Patrick Armitage, also 30, for his advice. He prefers to keep a low profile as he is wanted in most countries of the West for his activities as Britain's most notorious revolutionary. Asked whether her husband would approve of such an extravagant item of clothing she replied: "I'm here privately to visit my family. My husband's political beliefs are nothing to do with me. Anyway, Lenin had a Rolls-Royce." In fact so will her husband when his grandfather the Duke of Spada dies. Armitage will inherit Castle Spada and the world-famous collection of vintage cars although he claims that he dissociates himself from his family and prefers to be known by his revolutionary name: Kronstadt. Susan Armitage is of course the only daughter of Mark Alberici, the financier who has recently been stricken by a heart attack.

Lewis sat for a moment, his mind going back ten years to a conversation he had held with Charlie Mars when he had returned from the summer vacation and told him that Susan Alberici had broken off their relationship. "That's definitely the last I shall be seeing of her," he'd said with an attempt to keep the bitterness out of his voice. "Don't be so sure," Charlie had replied as gently as he knew how. "In my experience the people we meet at Oxford have a way of turning up throughout our lives."

Lewis sat there for a moment longer then folded up the cutting and put it in his pocket.

After a few moments he came to a circular from Claude Henderson. It was headed 'To All Departments'. Lewis read it through twice before he reached for the telephone and dialled Henderson's internal number.

"Lewis, give me the first line of a good love poem."

" 'Last night, ah, yesternight betwixt her lips and mine,' " Lewis intoned as the telephone rang monotonously in his ear.

"Thanks," Meredith said and got up and took down *The Oxford Book of English Verse* from the bookshelf. Henderson finally picked up the receiver.

"Horne here," Lewis said. "About that memo you circulated dated the 21st."

"Yes?"

"Let me read you the relevant paragraph. 'Once again I must draw attention to the danger of field operatives using automatic weapons. Just this week Captain Horne was almost killed due to an automatic pistol jamming at a vital moment. Were it not for the quick thinking of his companion he would have been despatched by an assailant armed only with a knife.' "

"I fail to see your point," Henderson said. "Surely there's nothing inaccurate in what I stated?"

"It's what you left out, Henderson. You sent me on that job after persuading Charlie Mars that it would be good for the firm if we army types got to know one or two of your civilian field operators. No guns or thuggery, just a good old-fashioned piece of spying. So I went off with nothing but a ball-point pen. Your dummy, Valcini, took me into a restaurant in the middle of Milan and the psychopath he was supposed to be observing went for him with a steak knife. Valcini was armed with a Luger, Henderson. It wasn't even a Second World War Luger; it had been manufactured in 1911. Your man is a gun collector. Did you know that? It's his hobby. He even makes his own ammunition. We would have been safer had he brought along one of his flintlocks, because the pride of his collection indeed jammed, as you so accurately state. Not only did his pistol jam but he slipped over on a piece of calamari and lay on the floor for the rest of the action."

"All this was in your report," Henderson said stiffly.

"I know it is, but reports don't go in your personal file. This kind of memo does. I wouldn't want someone to read my file in the future and gain the wrong impression. So be a good fellow and withdraw the circular. I don't want to go to the bother of writing one myself about the qualities of one of your agents that would end up on *your* personal file."

Meredith looked up from his book when Lewis hung up. "Why do you think Henderson hates us so much?"

Lewis put his hands behind his head and laced his fingers. "It's nothing personal. He thought he was going to run the show when Z or X or whatever he used to call himself retired, but they brought in Charlie Mars over his head and Charlie put up the idea of drafting us types for specialised work. We remind Henderson that he missed the glittering prize, that's all."

"You could have fooled me," Meredith said ruefully. "He always gives me the distinct impression of hating us as individuals. There was a prefect in my house at school with exactly the same attitude. They're probably related."

Meredith went back to his book and Lewis studied him for a few minutes. Meredith had picked up the toasting fork that they kept in the grate for making tea on winter afternoons and began slapping his leg with it.

"You used to hold a cricket bat when you did your home-work, Gordon?"

"Actually, we called it prep," Meredith said without look-ing up. Lewis grinned. Of course. Prep. Another one of those subtleties that marked the difference between a public school education and his own childhood. Had Lewis's father sent him to a boarding school – as he could easily have done as a serving officer – instead of to a grammar school founded in the Middle Ages, Lewis would have acquired exactly the same speech patterns and manners as Meredith. It would have taken a lot of the fun out of life.

Meredith looked up again. "This poem is about a chap sleeping with a tart," he said in an indignant voice.

"That's very good, Gordon. In fact it's about a poor sod yearning for his lost love, who was a tart," Lewis explained.

"Well, it won't do. I can't send this along to Janet with a bunch of flowers. She would be deeply offended."

"Like the man with no legs said when they entered him for the knobbly knees competition, 'You should have given me more information.' Try Edmund Waller – 'Go Lovely Rose'."

Meredith searched the book again and found the new recommendation. The slapping recommenced for a few minutes. Then Meredith looked up. "Oh yes. Perfect. Thanks, Lewis. Do you think it would matter if I made the spelling modern?"

"I don't think Edmund Waller would object; he died about three hundred years ago," Lewis said, getting up from his chair and taking an ancient copy of a book entitled *A Life Of Cromwell* from the shelf. A moment later he had set off to visit Victor Smight.

He was always happy to visit Victor, a small active figure with fresh pink complexion and halo of white fluffy hair, who was well-known to a section of the public as V. J. Smight, the distinguished historian. To a much smaller circle of people, which unfortunately included the KGB, he was head of research at Gower Street.

Smight's department was on the second floor where the house became grander, as it had been the living quarters of the original occupants. In the corridor outside the two connecting rooms that housed the reading department secretaries were bent over Xerox machines diligently copying the cuttings that flowed from the desks of Smight's team of linguists. Inside, the technical, literary and scientific journals of all the advanced nations were read and gutted for anything that might bring joy – or discomfort – to Her Majesty's Government, then farmed out to translators who would return the documents once they had been transcribed into English.

Lewis entered and was slightly surprised, as always, by the pleasant airiness. Tall french windows, open now because of the balmy weather, brought the feel of summer into rooms that possessed the hushed calm of a library. An occasional breeze ruffled the masses of paper on each desk.

Victor Smight's corner provided an additional dimension of summer as the open windows behind his desk led on to a small balcony that was a riot of plant life. Vines, creepers, potted flowers and window-boxes blazed with colour and in the centre the historian, wearing a lightweight linen jacket and an old straw hat, did his duty with a watering-can.

Victor saw Lewis waiting by his desk and gestured for him to take the chair next to his own. Lewis did as he was bid and looked around. Through the archway that led into the next room he could see Mary Romonoff Brown taking tea with Colonel Karminsky of the Russian section. They drank from glasses held in silver-framed holders. Because of the distance Lewis waved but refrained from calling out a greeting. Colonel Karminsky bowed in acknowledgement. He was standing, despite his great age, as he still could not bring himself to sit in Mary's presence.

Once again Lewis marvelled at the bizarre qualities of Gower Street. He thought of the different rooms he had visited that morning and the disparate characters they all possessed: Charlie Mars's tutorial rooms; the military bleakness of Sergeant Hillary's domain; Meredith's public school study – and now a little bit of Kew Gardens.

Victor came in from the balcony and parked his watering-can. "Lewis, what a rare pleasure," he said and sat down carefully in his chair. "How is your book going? I did like the chapter you showed me on the Battle of Naseby."

"All right thanks, Victor. It's with the publisher. Incidentally I've brought back the book you lent me." Lewis nodded towards the balcony. "How about your garden?"

"Another battleground. Greenfly, slugs, cats and carbon monoxide fumes take their toll, while we fight on."

"It's the kind of war I'd like to fight," Lewis said.

"How are you now?" Victor asked with real concern in his voice and tapped his stomach to make his meaning clear.

"All better, thank you. I've come about this," Lewis said and passed him the cutting from *New Society*.

Victor produced a pair of gold-wire spectacles and gave it his undivided attention for a few moments. "Ah, yes."

Lewis took the cutting back. "What's it all about?"

"A mystery that I thought you might help to solve."

"I don't follow."

Victor leaned back in his chair and drummed his fingers on the desktop twice. "Are you familiar with the dog that didn't bark in the night?"

Lewis nodded. "Sherlock Holmes. *The Silver Blaze*. The dog didn't bark when it should have done."

Victor drummed again and smiled. "Good. Yes, well, that's what we have here. A dog that didn't bark and that dog was me."

Lewis waited for him to continue.

"How much do you know about the Third Reich?" Victor asked finally.

"Some. Not that much. I was born in 1954."

"1954. Ah well, bear with me for a few minutes. The Third Reich is probably the best-documented period in any country's history. Among other things, the Germans had a mania for keeping records. Records of everything. After the war it took us years to classify it all. Everything was there. Every crime, invention, piece of research, troop movement and political decision was in a filing cabinet. It's the only monument a police state ever really leaves. You see, if they threaten to shoot you for your mistakes you tend to keep a piece of paper somewhere that proves that anything you have done was by instruction. It's dreadfully inefficient and tends to stifle initiative . . . but I digress. The split went three ways between us, the Americans and the Russians. But the Germans had everything cross-referenced so we all knew pretty much what the others had. Are you with me so far?"

Lewis nodded.

Victor reached under his desk and produced a battered black briefcase which he unlocked and took out a plastic file. From it he extracted a single sheet of paper that was brittle and yellowed with age and passed it to Lewis.

Headed MOST SECRET and dated September 10th 1945, it was a Cabinet memo from Clement Attlee, Prime Minister, to the Right Honourable Winston Churchill, Leader of the Opposition.

The single sentence read: 'What about Carl Raeder and Operation Hermann? Are we sure the Russians know nothing?' Underneath, written in a bold hand, was the reply: 'Eisenhower has taken care of this matter. Truman knows everything. WSC.'

"Where did you get this?" Lewis asked as he handed the sheet of paper back.

Victor locked it away again before he replied. "A friend of mine came across it about ten years ago when he was writing a book on the post-war Labour Government. He asked me then if I knew what Operation Hermann was, and I had to confess I was baffled. What I didn't tell him was that it must have been very important. So he let me keep the document. I have puzzled over it ever since."

"How can you be so sure of its significance?" Lewis asked.

"Well, Reichsmarshal Hermann Goering was not the buffoon-like figure that our propaganda machine held him to be. He was tough, intelligent, ruthless and immensely powerful. He stood second only to Hitler and was tremendously popular with the German people. To call a plan 'Operation Hermann' would have been unthinkable unless it had the personal approval of Adolf Hitler, and that would automatically mean it originated at top-level and would be given the highest of priorities."

Lewis nodded again. "So what was Operation Hermann?"

"That's the heart of the mystery. No one knows. I have made the most exhaustive checks and come up with nothing. There is no reference to it in any of the documents we captured, but Churchill, Attlee, Eisenhower and Truman knew what it was – and presumably so did Hitler. We seem to have encountered one of the best-kept secrets of the war and now we discover that Professor Carl Raeder, who was also in on the secret, is not dead as the records show but living in New York and talking to young ladies." He tapped the *New Society* cutting. "That is unless Dr Hanna Pearce is imagining things. Find out what you can, Lewis, but be careful. They were vile people in the Third Reich and their nastiness has a way of lingering on."

Lewis whistled 'A Foggy Day' as he strolled past the British Museum. It was, however, a dirge-like rendition: his hangover had gone and the summer sunshine was working its customary rejuvenation on London, but the thought of Dr Hanna Pearce did not entice him. He watched a tour bus disgorge a load of Swedes laden with cameras – cultural Vikings eager for plunder. What the hell can be so dangerous about this job if it's all about research into food? he thought as he crossed the junction of New Oxford Street and Shaftesbury Avenue.

And now the Nazis were involved. They were so nutty with their comic-opera uniforms and bloodlust they'd probably invented an exploding sausage to drop on London. 'Mein Führer, ze plan has verked. In precisely ten seconds Vinston Churchill vill be detonated. Even now our glorious scientists are verking on exploding Vodka for ze Russian Front and exploding vomen zat vill vipe out ze Americans.' His fantasy cheered him all the way down to Covent Garden.

Regardless of the call of the outdoors, Snapper's winebar was crowded with customers fighting to spend their money in the gloom. Photographic blow-ups of the famous covered the walls illuminated by candles that stood in winebottles on the cast-iron Victorian tables. A long bar served those that only wanted to drink and there were enough of them to stand four-deep in the sawdust. The clientele was the usual mixture – office workers and tourists. Mostly, the groups at the bar were men in business suits with the occasional pretty secretary. Lewis made his way to the picture of Raquel Welch, and sure enough the table beneath it held a reserved sign made out in his name.

The owner of the establishment had been a Fleet Street photographer who had taken redundancy and invested wisely. Now he stood behind the bar with a clear space in front of him drinking the day's first bottle of champagne as he watched the team of waitresses scurrying between the tables. Brian Weston was a heavy man with tousled hair and a face that was starting to look like an Ordnance Survey map as motorways of tiny, burst capillaries ran across his cheeks and nose. His expression of extreme boredom did not change when he saw Lewis before him.

"Hello, Lew," he said in a soft West Country accent. "I saw you were down for lunch."

"That depends," Lewis said. "What's the food like today?"

"How the hell should I know? I never eat here," Weston said as he poured Lewis a glass from his personal bottle.

Lewis picked up his drink and let the wine trickle down his throat. It was a pleasant sensation.

"Is this a good wine?" he asked.

Weston held the bottle up. "Magnificent. Too good for this lot." He waved in the general direction of his customers.

"Well, it seems okay to me," Lewis said without emotion.

"You don't know wine from the water in a window cleaner's bucket, do you?" Weston said amiably.

"I can usually tell red from white, though." Lewis sipped again. "And this is definitely white."

Weston was about to make another comment but instead pointed a stubby finger over his shoulder. "I think your number's arrived, old son."

One of the waitresses obscured the figure that she had shown to his table but when she stepped aside the two at the bar could see Dr Hanna Pearce. Lewis had to revise the picture he had formed of a stiff-lipped raw-boned academic matron.

Her hair was the colour of jet and hung heavily to her shoulders in deep contrast with her creamy complexion. The bones of her face were good and would hold the fine quality of her features for the rest of her life. Her height created an illusion of slightness but as she removed the jacket of the charcoal suit that she wore her full breasts showed for a moment against the pale grey, silk blouse.

Lewis could see no jewellery except for a single gold chain around her throat but he knew money when he saw it: he was trained to. The simple almost severe clothes that she wore so easily must have cost a fortune. Certainly more than a young doctor who relied on a National Health salary could ever afford.

Leaving his glass on the counter, he made his way to his table and stood before her. "Dr Pearce?" She looked up at him.

"Yes." Her voice struck like the note on a tuning fork. He held out his hand and the touch of hers sent a slight shock-wave along his arm. As they shook hands he managed to knock over the candle.

"Sorry. I'm Lewis Horne. It's very good of you to spare the time to see me. Would you like a drink?"

"Yes, thank you," Hanna Pearce said with a detectable amount of feeling. The voice had a slight American burr.

"White or red?" Lewis said. She looked puzzled. "Wine," he explained. "White or red wine. That's all they sell."

"Oh, white please. Dry."

Lewis walked back to the bar and spoke urgently to Weston. "Give me a bottle of your champagne."

"Piss off. I don't sell that to the customers."

"I don't want to burn your place down, Brian, but you might just force my hand," Lewis said with conviction.

"All right, then. But you'll have to have it on the house. I won't compromise my principles."

"Thanks."

Lewis rejoined Dr Pearce just in time to light the cigarette she had produced. He also relit the candle he had knocked over. A waitress appeared with a bottle in an ice-bucket and poured two glasses. Before he touched his glass Hanna Pearce had raised hers to her lips and drained it. Lewis leaned across the table.

"Are you going to demonstrate any of your other vices, Doctor?" he asked.

"I'm sorry? I don't understand."

He gestured to the glass and cigarette. "Smoking, drinking. I thought doctors were supposed to set the rest of us an example?"

Her head came up and he noticed how firm her jawline became. He braced himself for the onslaught and she hit him below the belt. She *grinned* at him. Then she held up the cigarette. "Three a day, taken with meals."

Lewis studied her face again. "Have you had a bad morning?"

She nodded. "They're thinking of closing down my unit because of the cuts. It's rather hard to come to terms with."

"I'm sorry, I didn't know."

She looked at him rather sharply. "There was a piece about us in *The Guardian* this morning. I thought you journalists read all the newspapers?"

Lewis scratched his nose as he sat down. This one is smart, he thought. I'm going to have to be light on my feet.

"Look," he said, "to tell you the truth, this is not my usual field. I'm not a scientific writer. I do interviews: pop-singers, rock groups, showbusiness people – that sort of stuff. The features editor in the agency saw your article in *New Society* and someone told him you were good-looking. We thought you could make a good piece for the pop papers."

Dr Pearce leaned forward and stubbed out the cigarette. "I see. Well, thank you for being candid, Mr Horne."

Lewis could see she was preparing to leave. He held up a hand. "If you're fighting to stop them closing you down that's a neat angle. The publicity could do you some good."

She sat back in her chair. "Do you really think so?" the question was in such an open voice that Lewis felt a stab of remorse at his deceit.

44

"Definitely," he said and nodded his head for emphasis. "Bureaucrats hate to be attacked in the popular press. Government Ministers don't like to think they're going to lose the votes of millions of outraged readers."

She thought for a moment then shrugged. "Okay. Ask me what you like if you think it could help us."

Lewis uncrossed the fingers of the hand he held below the table. "Why are they closing down your unit?" he said.

"I suppose it's understandable," she went on in a resigned voice. "A shortage of food isn't a major problem in this country."

A clatter of noise came from another table and she turned her head for a moment. Her profile would look good on a gold coin, Lewis decided.

"I thought Britain still had to import a lot of food," he said.

"We do, but we don't *have* to," she said, turning back quickly to him so that her hair brushed her shoulders. "We grow enough here to be self-sufficient: British agriculture is about the most efficient in the world."

"Would it bother you if I took notes?" Lewis said and produced a notebook and pen.

"Not in the least. I'm in the note-taking business as well." She repeated the same shattering smile. Lewis bit hard on the end of his plastic pen.

"Do you mind if I ask you some personal stuff? It's just that there were not many cuttings on you and we like it for the colour and background."

"Go ahead. I'll scream if you touch a nerve."

Lewis had to turn away from her face so that he could concentrate. This won't do, he thought, as he looked up at the roof of the bar.

He was aware that she was waiting for him.

"When did you come to Britain?"

"I was born here. Don't let the accent fool you. My father came over during the last war. For about two weeks he was the youngest pilot in the Eighth Air Force. He met my mother here and decided to stay. I have dual nationality."

Lewis nodded. "So you went to school in England?"

"No, Switzerland."

"When were you born?"

"If that's a polite way of asking my age, I'm twenty-five."

"That's a bit young to be doing research, isn't it?"

"I took my degree early."

"Where was that?"

"Harvard Medical School. I got my accent there as well."

"At what age did you go to Harvard?"

Hanna paused just for a moment. "I was sixteen."

"You entered Harvard Medical School at sixteen?"

"Yes."

He was impressed. "It's a wonder they didn't keep you there in a bottle." He made a note in his book. "Are you married?" He held his breath at this one.

"No," Hanna said. Lewis exhaled slowly – and silently.

"Any hobbies?"

"Yes, I collect paintings."

"Any by famous artists?"

"Some. I've been lucky. My grandfather collected. I suppose I got it from him."

"What about your work? Can you explain that to me?"

Hanna Pearce sat back in her chair and for a moment Lewis was reminded of Victor Smight. He got the feeling she was trying to gauge his intelligence.

"Do you have *any* scientific training?" she asked.

Lewis shook his head.

She paused, just as Smight had earlier, and then began.

"Did you know that if you took all the people in the bar and fed them exactly the same amount of food and gave them exactly the same amount of exercise for three months some of them would gain weight, some would lose weight and some would stay more or less the same?"

"Are you sure?" Lewis spoke with a degree of doubt in his voice.

"Absolutely. The experiment has been done several times. We're trying to understand why some of these people have the kind of metabolism that would cause them to gain weight and then synthesise the process."

"In other words, make a pill."

"That's it."

46

"Who would benefit from it?"

Hanna smiled. "Thin people like you. Who don't get fat easily."

"I don't follow; surely people get fat because they eat too much?"

"Up to a point." Hanna reached across the table and squeezed Lewis's upper arm. She was obviously surprised by the hardness.

"You're very fit. Do you take a lot of exercise?"

"A fair bit," Lewis said.

"You have the kind of physique that has become accepted as the present-day ideal – lean, wiry, well-muscled. Do you worry a lot about your diet?"

"I never think about it."

"Exactly. You eat and drink what you like and never have to worry about getting fat. Well, there is a theory that our chubby friends are the best survivors."

"I thought fat people were prone to heart attacks?"

"Obese people are, but I'm not talking about them. I'm talking about people who are plump. Look, we didn't always live in cities. Our distant ancestors used to roam around looking for a square meal. Sometimes they would find a place where the pickings were good. Then they could eat huge amounts of food and they would put on a heavy layer of fat that they could live off until the good times came around again. Someone like you who didn't put on enough fat would start burning muscle and when the first sabre-tooth tiger chased you – snap! You wouldn't have enough energy to run away."

"Sometimes it's not a good idea to run away from tigers."

"That's a philosopher's remark, Mr Horne. I'm just trying to do a job of work. Millions of people are getting just a little less than they need to eat. If we could then boost the value of what they *do* get we would be getting somewhere."

"How is it going?" Lewis asked.

She sighed. "Truthfully, not so good. We keep thinking we've got the answer and then it goes haywire. It really is frustrating. However we approach the problem we end up with the same result: weight gain for about three weeks, stability for a week, then rapid weight loss."

A waitress appeared with a pad and he looked to Hanna. "Nothing for me, thanks," she said. "I usually skip lunch."

"I'll have a beef sandwich," Lewis said. "Why did you decide on your line of work?" he asked as he took another sip of wine.

Hanna thought for a moment. "UNICEF state in their World's Children Report that the deaths of forty thousand children every day are caused by hunger."

"A day!" Lewis thought for a moment. "That's something like . . ."

"Fifteen million a year, yes. Of course, that's only children. When you include adults, the figure doubles."

"You're saying thirty million people starve to death each year?"

"No. They die of a variety of diseases, but the root cause is malnutrition. At this moment something like eighteen African countries are facing famine. The list is endless. The statistics eventually numb you. There is a permanent world war being fought against hunger, Mr Horne, and the other side is winning. I'm not saying my work will solve the problem but it could help. Just a bit."

Lewis looked around the restaurant. It seemed as if there was food everywhere. The counter was loaded with sides of beef, great hams, wheels of cheese, piles of french bread and huge bowls of salad. At each table people chewed their way through heaped plates.

The waitress returned with his sandwich but Lewis just pushed it aside.

Hanna Pearce looked at him. "Don't you want it anymore?"

He shook his head.

"A common reaction. But there's nothing you can do by not eating, you know. It won't change a thing."

"I appreciate that. It's just that my stomach doesn't at the moment. Maybe you should try the same treatment on her." Lewis nodded in the direction of a heavy blonde who sat at one of the adjoining tables.

"She's already on a diet," Hanna said.

"How can you tell?"

"Look at what she's eating. Lean beef and a green salad, cheese, biscuits and a bottle of Perrier water to wash it down. High protein, high cholesterol. It won't last."

"How can you be sure?"

"It's my work, Mr Horne. And I work hard at it. Did you know that last year general practitioners wrote out 218,000 prescriptions for slimming pills alone? It cost the National Health Service more than a million pounds. The trouble is most of them can be dangerous. The World Health Organisation has placed six habit-forming drugs under international control: benzphetamine, mazindol, phendimetrazine, phentermine, amfepramone and phenmetrazine. Sixty-five per cent of British women are trying to lose weight at any given time. And, coincidentally, a quarter of a million young people worldwide are affected by anorexia nervosa."

Lewis passed over his notebook. "Would you mind writing down the names of those drugs?" he said.

She did so and he watched her hands. They were slim but capable. Unlike that of most doctors, the handwriting was clear and well-formed in the style taught in French schools.

When she had finished she closed the notebook and handed it back to him.

Lewis shifted in his chair. He glanced across the bar and a portrait of Mick Jagger winked down at him. "Your article in *New Society* mentioned someone called Professor Carl Raeder who was doing the same kind of work during the war. Can you tell me anything about him?"

She shrugged. "There's not much to tell. I was in New York last year to deliver a paper at Columbia on the work of the unit. Not many people attended, about thirty. Afterwards one of the audience approached me. He introduced himself as Professor Raeder. He was very old – even his clothes were old-fashioned. I remember he wore a stiff collar. Can you imagine? In summertime, in New York City. He spoke with a heavy German accent so I answered him in German. He seemed quite overcome and asked me if I would have coffee with him. I thought, why not? So we went to the cafeteria and we talked about my work. He told me he had become a professor at Columbia after the war and had retired in 1968. We talked about my lecture and he told me that he had been working on exactly the same lines in Germany during the war."

"Did he tell you what the project was called?" Lewis asked casually.

"Yes. He said they called it Operation Hermann."

Lewis felt a ripple race across his new scar.

"Did he say anything else about it?"

"Not really. I asked him some more questions but he started to ramble as if he'd forgotten where we were. Then suddenly he became very clear. He said the Black Dwarf had ruined all their lives."

Lewis leaned forward slightly. "The Black Dwarf? Who was that?"

"I don't know. I asked him but he wouldn't answer. Then he asked me if I remembered the night we spent in Königsstuhl."

"Königsstuhl?"

"It's a town near Heidelberg. It was only then I realised he thought he was speaking to somebody else."

"To whom?"

Hanna reflected a moment before she answered. "I think it must have been my grandfather's sister. She was called Hanna – I was named after her. She was at Heidelberg University in 1926."

"That must have been very strange for you."

"It was eerie. I made my excuses and left him sitting there in the cafeteria. Afterwards I felt sorry, but I had to come home the following day."

"Did you ever hear from him again?"

Hanna opened her handbag and searched through a wallet. "This came to the hospital about a month later." She produced a card and handed it to Lewis. It bore the name of Professor Hans Molkin with an address in Brooklyn Heights. Lewis studied the card for a moment.

"So you think Professor Hans Molkin was really Carl Raeder?"

She nodded. "Turn the card over."

Lewis did so. On the back was a single word written in German – *immer* – and the name: Carl.

"What does this word mean?" Lewis said.

"Always," Hanna said. She leaned forward, took the card and returned it to her wallet. "I like to keep it. I think it's a love letter to my ancestor." Lewis looked into the calm, beautiful face and could think of nothing to say. He took the bottle of champagne from the ice-bucket but she covered her glass with her hand.

"Come on," he said in a sorrowful voice. "I'm a freelance journalist, unmarried, with no appetite, and yesterday I missed my own birthday party."

She reached out and took his hand. He felt the same tiny shockwaves once again.

"And you're thirty," she said confidently.

Lewis raised his eyebrows. "You read palms?"

She laughed. "No, the backs of people's hands. Didn't you know they're a good guide to their age? But I was guessing as well. I'll take a raincheck on the drink. Remember, I don't eat lunch and I've got to work this afternoon."

She leaned forward with her handbag in her lap.

"One thing more, Dr Pearce," Lewis said.

"Yes," she said in an expectant voice.

He hesitated and then said, "If you can't get the answer to your problem why don't you develop your work along the lines of finding a safe slimming pill? From what you've told me it would be worth an absolute fortune."

"I've already got a fortune, Mr Horne," she said without emotion. "I don't need another one."

Hanna stood up, took the pen that was still in his hand and wrote in his notebook again.

"This is my home telephone number. I'll be there after eight. I'll tell you how I got my fortune over dinner. That's if you're free for dinner."

"Are you buying?"

"Yes. Why?"

Lewis poured himself some more champagne.

"I must warn you, Dr Pearce. I don't come cheap."

3

"A dreadful picture you present to me of life, Elshie; but I am not daunted by it," returned Earnscliff. "We are sent here, in one sense, to bear and to suffer; but, in another, to do and to enjoy. The active day has its evening of repose; even patient sufferance has its alleviations, where there is a consolatory sense of duty discharged."

The Black Dwarf
SIR WALTER SCOTT

Charlie Mars and Victor Smight sat side by side on Charlie's leather Chesterfield reading Lewis's report. The only sound in the room was the distant rumble of traffic from Gower Street and the snatches of a tune Lewis was whistling through his teeth as he browsed through the books stacked on the mantelpiece. Charlie Mars looked up from the second page he was reading.

"What's that you keep whistling?" he asked.

"I can't remember," Lewis said. "I can't get it out of my head."

"Well, stop it, please. I don't want it in mine."

"Sorry," Lewis said and drew a book from the pile that Charlie Mars had written and opened it at random. He read for a few minutes, then glanced up. Charlie had finished reading but Victor was still on the last page.

"I wouldn't have said that Cromwell was reluctant to form the New Model Army," Lewis said, holding the book up so that Charlie could see to what he was referring.

"Why not?" Charlie said, spreading his arms along the back of the Chesterfield.

"All the evidence points to the fact that he enjoyed soldiering. After all, he was pretty good at it."

"That's not the point I'm making. Michelangelo didn't *enjoy* painting the ceiling of the Sistine Chapel, but he was extremely pleased when it was finished."

Lewis was about to continue but he stopped as Victor Smight cleared his throat.

"You have our attention, Victor," Charlie said.

"This is very good, Lewis. Dr Pearce sounds like an extraordinary young woman." Lewis nodded. "She said nothing else?"

"That's everything," Lewis said.

"Ring any bells, Victor?" Charlie said and gazed up at the ceiling.

"A distant tinkling. What time is it in Virginia?"

Charlie looked at his wristwatch. "If you mean Virginia USA it's about 12.50 a.m. Why?"

Victor slowly got to his feet and removed his spectacles which he carefully placed in his top pocket. "I think I'll give one of my American chums a ring. Thank you, Lewis. And thank you, Charles. It's very good of you to indulge an old man's fancy."

"As ever, we are at your service," Charlie said. "Would you like a glass of sherry before you go?"

"At four fifty?" Victor paused. "Why not? It does one good to flaunt the conventions at my age."

"Lewis?" Charlie asked. "How are your conventions?"

"I'll have a whisky, please."

Charlie opened a cupboard beneath one of the bookshelves to reveal a well-stocked bar. He poured the drinks and the three men stood by the fireplace sipping appreciatively.

"You know, I've always thought Cromwell rather smug," Victor said after a while. "What's the point in having your portrait painted if you can't have the warts left out?"

There was a knock on the door and Sergeant Hillary entered holding a brown manila folder.

"I've got these papers for you to sign, sir," he said.

"Just leave them on the sofa," Charlie said and watched Hillary until he had closed the door.

"Is it my imagination or does that young man radiate the

most remarkable degree of hostility?" Victor said as he drained his glass.

"It's because he missed the boat by three hundred years." As Lewis spoke he could feel the effects of Charlie's whisky on top of the champagne.

"I don't follow," Victor said.

"I think Lewis means that Sergeant Hillary would have been at least a general in the New Model Army," Charlie said as he reached for the bottle of Glenfiddich and poured another drink. When Victor was topped up as well he turned to Lewis. "Oh, would you mind giving our American friends a ring on this business?"

"Anyone in particular?" Lewis said in the same easy tone.

"There's a pleasant young chap at their Embassy who is interested. I met him at one of their parties the other evening. It might be a good idea if you got to know him. His name is Lowell, Curtis Lowell. He's called a commercial attaché."

"Okay." Lewis looked into his whisky. "I'll give him a ring and take him out for a drink."

"Splendid." Charlie took another swallow of Glenfiddich and Lewis waited for him to say more. A few silent seconds ticked by.

"You two aren't telling me everything," Lewis said flatly.

Charlie and Victor exchanged glances of slight embarrassment. When Charlie spoke there was a note of apology in his voice.

"We are under instruction not to say anything that our masters consider unnecessary."

Lewis moved to the door to stand there with his arms folded. He nodded. "I see. Well, you had better make something clear to your masters, Charlie. I'll only go so far on this 'need to know' nonsense. If anything happens that gets me into trouble because someone has decided I shouldn't have a piece of information they'll be sorry. My crowd doesn't go in for Charge of the Light Brigade tactics. There aren't enough of us so we look after each other. Tell them to be gentle with me or one day they'll pull on their underpants and find them full of razor-blades."

"I'll see your message is delivered," Charlie said with a grim smile.

When Lewis got back to his own office he found Meredith fiddling with one of his fishing rods.

"Fancy a swim at the Oasis?" Meredith asked as Lewis reached for the telephone.

Lewis contemplated the five-minute walk to the pool near Tottenham Court Road.

"Yes, I wouldn't mind," he said; he could feel the effects of his recent drinking. "Just one phone call to make first. I won't be long."

The American Embassy switchboard put him through to the department he requested and in a few moments a deep, clipped voice spoke.

"Lowell here."

"Mr Lowell, my name is Lewis Horne. You met my boss, Charlie Mars, at a party the other day. He asked me to give you a ring. He thinks we might want to do some business together."

"When can we meet?" Lowell said simply.

"I'm having a drink at my sister's flat this evening at seven o'clock. Would you care to join us?"

"Sure."

Lewis gave the address and rang off.

"Ready?" Meredith said with a hint of impatience.

"Just give me a couple more minutes." Lewis rang the advertising agency where Janet worked but she was in a meeting so he left a message that he would definitely be home with a friend at seven.

"Ready now?" Meredith said half in and out of the room with his foot propping the door open.

"One more thing to do," Lewis said. "I want to check something with Mary."

Lewis and Meredith made their way to the basement and into the air-conditioned brightness of Mary Romonoff Brown's domain. The girls on the afternoon shift looked up, but Mary continued to read her copy of the *Morning Star*.

It was Mary's pleasure to inform everyone at Gower Street that she was a card-carrying Communist and longed for the liberation that would come when Russian divisions swept across Europe, although everyone knew that her actual name was Romanoff and her real desire was to see the restoration of the Tsar. When Lewis had been an undergraduate she was still remembered at Oxford, although she had gone down five years before – with a double first in Greats and the more dubious title of 'Deb of the Year'. Everything about her had seemed long, slim, elegant and pale. Lewis knew she would look good in silk pyjamas.

He approached her desk and coughed respectfully. Mary snapped down the paper and looked at him with exactly the same expression her great-grandfather, the Grand Duke, had once used when he urged his troops into battle on the Eastern Front.

"Comrade?" she purred.

"I have come to beg an indulgence, Your Imperial Highness."

"Where's your chit?"

"Come on, Mary, it'll only take you a minute. I don't want a printout, just a read from the screen."

Mary folded her paper decisively and looked at Lewis with a smile. "I will do this for you, Captain Horne, not because of your oleaginous charm. I will do it because it is expressly against the orders of that insect, Claude Henderson."

She swung round in her chair to her display terminal and her elegant hands touched the keyboard.

"Name?"

"Lowell. Curtis Lowell." Mary tapped lightly on her display terminal.

"Nationality?"

"American."

"Any other cross-reference?"

"Government official."

Mary tapped the keys for a few moments more and the computer brought forth the desired information. Lewis leaned forward to scan the screen.

Curtis Lowell. Born March 7th 1951. Boston, Mass., USA. Father: Frederick H. Lowell. Mother: Elizabeth

Lowell née Armstrong. Educated St Paul's Preparatory School, Harvard Law School, West Point Military Academy. US Special Forces Vietnam. Resigned commission (Capt) 1978. Entered USA Diplomatic Service 1978. Berlin: 1979–81. Peking '81–83. London '83–

"There," said Mary. "He sounds exactly suitable as a playmate for you, dear."

"*Spasiba*," Lewis said in reply.

"Last length under water," Meredith said as Lewis caught up with him at the shallow end of the Oasis swimming pool. Lewis turned and struck out beneath the surface of the heavily chlorinated water. He just made it and hauled himself out on to the side, his chest heaving from the effort of keeping up with his hydromanic companion.

"Had enough?" Meredith shouted out as Lewis made for the showers.

"If the good Lord had wanted me to be a duck he would have given me a shape like yours," Lewis called back as he turned his body so the stinging water could play on the back of his head. For the last half an hour he had pounded up and down the length of the baths in a valiant effort to drive the demon drink from his brain. "Are you seeing Janet tonight?" he asked later as he towelled his hair dry in the changing rooms.

"No, damn it," Meredith answered. "The God of War says he wants me on duty this evening. I was hoping the flowers would soften her up."

"Who gave you the idea of sending a love poem and flowers?" Lewis asked.

Meredith smiled in a superior fashion. "Clever, wasn't it?" he said. "My Aunt Lucy. You know, the one who lives in St John's Wood. She put me on to it; she said no woman could resist the combination."

Lewis nodded. "There's only one slight flaw in what you say."

"What's that?" Meredith asked anxiously.

"Your Aunt Lucy is a maiden aunt."

Meredith looked so crestfallen that Lewis slapped him on the back. "Don't worry. I happen to know 'Go Lovely Rose' is one of her favourite poems."

He looked at his watch: ten minutes to six. "I'm going home. Sign me out, will you?"

"Okay." Meredith grunted as he struggled with his collar-stud.

"You know, I met a doctor today who thought it was crazy to wear one of those on a summer's day," Lewis said.

"He doesn't know what he's talking about. They're much cooler in hot weather than a soft-collared shirt."

"It wasn't a he. It was a she."

"There you are then. How could a woman understand the sensual pleasure of a nice cold collar-stud sticking into your Adam's apple?"

"See you later," Lewis called out as he dumped the towel he had hired into the return basket and squeezed his bathing trunks into a ball.

His head felt distinctly clearer as he walked along High Holborn. No danger of passing out in front of Charlie's friend. When he got to Lamb's Conduit Street he saw Roland Perth pulling up the blind on the door of the Old Times Antique Shop. For a time, in the Fifties, Roland had worked steadily in the theatre where his boyish good looks had filled a variety of juvenile parts. But, like Peter Pan, Roland did not appear to grow old, unless you looked closely and could see the deep laughter lines and the streaks of grey in the fair hair. Eventually the french windows of drawing-room comedy closed gently upon him.

He opened the door with a smile, as always immaculately dressed. He stood with one hand on his hip to reveal the light blue silk lining of his jacket. "Happy Birthday for yesterday, dear," he said. "How devastatingly chic of you to avoid your own party."

"I am not to blame for once," Lewis said as he eased his way through the bric-à-brac to the back of the shop where Roland kept a chaise-longue and a sewing-chair for his own use.

"Personally I loathe surprise parties," Roland said. "Some friends gave me one in 1956 and the police came too. Mind you, they were very sweet at Savile Row once Binkie had given them a lot of theatre tickets."

Lewis sat down on the chair and put his damp swimming costume on a side table.

"I've just made a cup of tea. Would you like one, or something stronger?" Roland said.

"Tea would be fine. I'm trying to sober up."

Lewis watched as Roland carefully bent forward to pour the tea through a silver strainer. The delicate scent of Lapsang Souchong came to him and he noticed that Roland had lost a few pounds. The slight bulge of stomach was gone and the waistcoat fitted without straining the buttons.

Roland was in his early fifties but could, and frequently did, pass for thirty-five. Although he still got the odd acting part in television and occasional advertising work, his main income came from the Old Times Antique Shop that had been left to him by a friend who had died a few years before. A steady stream of ladies and showbusiness acquaintances saw that there was a regular turnover among the clutter of china and silver objects crowding every surface of the tiny shop.

Roland passed him a cup and saucer made of bone china. "Careful with that. I've just sold the set to a pop-singer for a ridiculous amount of money. How did you like your rifleman? Janet almost drove me mad to find it."

"Smashing. It was good of you both to go to so much trouble."

"Don't say smashing when you're holding that cup, dear. You'd better give it back to me." He took it from Lewis's hand and put it down gently. "No, my present is here." He slapped a large, oblong object that was shrouded with a dust-cover.

Lewis looked at it, mystified.

"Go on, you can unwrap it."

Lewis pulled aside the sheet to reveal a battered old upright piano. "Hideous, isn't it?" Roland said. "It should fit into your flat perfectly."

Lewis lifted the lid and played a few chords.

"Not a bad tone," said Roland. "It's only done ten thousand numbers – a bit like me. Now we can gather round on winter evenings and sing sea shanties."

Lewis thought of something. "Roland, do you remember this?" He played the opening bars of the tune he had been whistling in Charlie Mars's office.

"Of course I do. Play it again."

Lewis did as he was told, and Roland began to sing:

> The man who bought New York
> Says he wants to talk
> To me at a quarter to three.
> He knows I don't come cheap
> But I promised that I'd keep
> My word, am I being absurd?

I don't come cheap, Lewis thought, remembering his parting words to Hanna Pearce. The wonders of the subconscious mind. Of course – Harold Forrest Pearce! The man who bought New York.

"I was at a party once where Mary Martin sang that to Jack Buchanan," Roland said wistfully. Lewis hammered out the opening bars of 'There's No Business Like Show Business' and Roland switched his mood to suit the music. For the next twenty minutes he kept Lewis busy with a string of requests. They were halfway through 'The Very Thought Of You' when there was an urgent knock on the shop door. Roland opened it to find Janet in a flustered state.

"Lewis," she cried, "I've had a disaster."

"What's up?" he said easily, knowing that if it was anything serious she would have said she 'had a bit of a problem'. Unlike Lewis, Janet had been sent by their parents to a public school.

"I forgot to get any drink at lunchtime and your guest is due any minute," she wailed. "The off-licence doesn't open until seven. What am I to do?"

"Relax, darling," Roland said. "I've got masses of everything."

"I shall need everything," Janet said. "I've no idea what he'll want to drink."

"Who is this person that he can cause such panic?"

"An American business contact," Lewis said.

"Give him dry Martinis," Roland said decisively.

"Oh, come and make them for me, Roland, please," Janet pleaded.

"Thank God for that," Roland said with mock relief. "I would have been mortified if I hadn't been invited. Give me a hand to get the bottles upstairs. Lewis, where are you going?"

"I've just remembered a call I've got to make," Lewis said as he left them.

When he got to his living room Lewis took the telephone and walked across the room and sat on the sill of the open window where he dialled a number.

"News desk," a brisk voice said.

"Max? It's Lew Horne."

"Captain Horne? Or is it Major by now? Christ, the last time I saw you you were up to your arse in sniper fire in the Armagh."

"I gave that up years ago, Max. I'm in civvie street now. Import and export business."

"Yeah, and I've been to Tangiers for a sex-change operation, so you can call me Maxine. What can I do for you?"

"Can you get me some information on the late Harold Forrest Pearce? He was an American billionaire. Sometimes known as Cargo Pearce."

"Spelt P-e-a-r-c-e?"

"Yes."

"When do you want it by?"

"As soon as possible."

"I've got an idle little sod doing a freelance shift at the moment. He can get on with it. If we've got anything you'll have it in half an hour."

"Thanks, Max."

"What's your number?"

61

Lewis told him and rang off. He placed the telephone on the window-sill. From below he could hear Janet's doorbell ringing. He sprinted down the stairs and opened the front door.

Curtis Lowell looked like the young Henry Fonda. They shook hands and Lewis examined his guest's clothes as he entered the hallway. Grey lightweight herring-bone suit. Blue cotton shirt with plain gold cufflinks, dark blue silk tie with red polka dots, handmade English shoes. Lots of white teeth, athlete's tan, short light brown hair. An American aristocrat.

"Mr Lowell, this is my sister, Janet Horne," Lewis said when they reached the flat. "Janet, Curtis Lowell." They shook hands. "Oh, and this is a friend of ours – Roland Perth."

"Dry Martinis?" Roland said after he had been introduced.

"I think I'll have a whisky," said Lowell.

"I'm afraid we haven't got any," Roland and Janet said together. Lewis went to the window-sill and produced the bottle that Charlie Mars had left there the night before.

"I had a room-mate in college that could do a trick like that," Lowell said. "But he used to keep it up his sleeve." His Boston accent rang with money. Lewis liked him. It was the second rich person he had liked that day.

"Where did you go to college, Mr Lowell?" Lewis asked as he handed the bottle to Roland.

"Curtis, please. Harvard."

"That's a coincidence. I had lunch with someone today who studied medicine at Harvard."

"That's a tough course. I was just fooling around there until I went into the family business." Lewis knew about Harvard Law School; they let you fool around for about three minutes, then they bounced you out.

"What business is that?" Roland asked as he held out a pitcher to refill the glasses.

"Politics, I guess. Although I'm on the books at the Embassy as a diplomat."

"Don't you have to be rich to go into politics in America?" Janet asked.

Lowell smiled at her but Lewis noted that his eyes remained cool. He noticed that his sister wasn't captivated by his easy charm, realising that much of it was a professional pose.

"My great, great-grandfather, Ephraim, took care of that," Lowell said. "During the Civil War he and his brother flipped a coin for which one was going into the army and which one was going to stay and run the family business. Ephraim lost. He stayed in Boston and canned beans. His brother became a general. He was with Grant when Lee surrendered at Appomattox."

"You said Ephraim lost, but he made the money," Lewis said.

"I think I would have preferred to be in at the surrender," Curtis said with good humour.

"Well, I would have preferred the bean business," Roland said in a firm voice. "I had quite enough of the other in Korea, thank you."

"I didn't know you were in Korea, Roland," Janet said in a surprised voice.

"I know you didn't, dear. Just look on me as a big ball of wool. There are plenty of surprises to be unwound yet."

"What were you in?" Lewis asked, his professional curiosity aroused.

"The Gloucesters. Why do you think they called us Glorious?"

"You were at the Imjin River?" Curtis asked.

"I was, and the Chinese were extremely tiresome. Who would have thought you Americans would ever be so chummy with them?" Roland said, looking straight at Curtis.

"Well, we want to get chummy with the Russians, now."

"Really?" Janet said. "You think the peace talks stand a chance?"

"Yes, if it's up to us. Most Americans are like old Ephraim; they just want to make money. We'd rather trade than fight."

"What about the Russians?" Janet asked.

"They've got a lot of problems. Poland, Afghanistan" – he nodded to Roland – "and our Chinese friends. Russia

63

may be a dictatorship but that doesn't mean to say that the powers that be all agree with one another. There are big divisions in the leadership. At the moment we think the peacemongers have just got the edge, but it's damned close."

"What exactly do you do at the Embassy?" Roland asked. Lewis noticed it was his party technique to cover the pouring of huge Martinis with a question.

"I'm a commercial attaché. At the moment Lewis's company is doing a big deal with America. That's how I came to know Charles Austen Mars. Is that really his name, incidentally?" he asked with a smile.

Just then Lewis heard his telephone ringing upstairs.

"Excuse me, I'm expecting that call," he said and made swiftly for his own flat. He lifted the receiver on the tenth ring.

"My name is Tony Spender, Mr Horne," a young voice said. "Max Buller asked me to give you a call."

"Yes," said Lewis, "go ahead." The voice dictated for some minutes with Lewis making an occasional note. Finally he thanked the caller and replaced the receiver. The telephone rang again moments later.

"Horne?" The voice was Claude Henderson's. "I've been trying to get you for ages."

"Yes, Claude," Lewis said in a mellow tone.

"Have you got someone called Curtis Lowell with you?"

"Fairly close, yes."

"Well, stand by. There's a car coming to pick you both up."

"To take us where, Claude?" Lewis said, fighting to keep his voice even.

"I don't have time to go into details. Just get a move on," said Henderson and rang off.

Lewis walked slowly downstairs and rejoined the party.

They looked up as he entered.

"That was the office," he said. "There seems to be some problem with the contract. They've asked if you'd mind very much popping along for a little while to give us a hand to sort things out?"

64

Curtis looked keenly at him. "Do you think it will take long?"

Lewis shrugged. "Oh, I shouldn't think so. Just some details to go over. They're sending a car for us."

"Don't worry," Roland said. "I shall look after Janet until you're free."

Just then the door that Lewis had left ajar swung open and Meredith entered. "Hello," he said. "Driver reporting for duty."

"Young Lochinvar," Lewis replied. "It's nice to see you in this flat with your clothes on."

"Ignore my brother's tasteless remarks. He lacks a poetic soul."

Lewis glanced at Janet and could see that she was blushing. Aunt Lucy must have got something after all, he thought.

"Mr Lowell, my name is Meredith," Gordon said, holding out his hand. Lowell shook it and Meredith turned to Lewis.

"All ready then? Good show."

"Thank you for the flowers, Gordon." Janet called out as the three of them left the flat and walked to the top of Lamb's Conduit Street. Meredith beamed all the way to the car he had parked there.

When they had settled in the back Lewis turned to Lowell. "How much of this business do you know?"

Curtis shrugged his shoulders. "The head of my section didn't say much. Although there's been a hell of a lot of traffic between CIA Langley and your crowd. I've got a friend in signals and he says the lines have never been hotter."

"What did your section head tell you exactly?"

"I quote verbatim," Lowell said drily: "'There's something in the air that could really piss-off the Russians. It concerns a dead Kraut that ain't dead anymore who used to make food pills for Hitler and a limey-woman doctor who knows the Kraut.'"

Lewis nodded. "That's about as much as I've got," he said.

"You two are Special Air Service, aren't you?" Lowell said. "I looked you up."

Lewis nodded again.

"You fellows have done some neat jobs."

"We read your mail as well," Lewis said with a grin.

After a few minutes' silence Lowell spoke again. "Who Dares Wins, huh?"

"The lads have changed it about a bit," Meredith said. "It's Who Cares Wins in the Regiment."

"Just exactly where are we going, Gordon?" Lewis asked.

"Henderson gave me an address in Lord North Street and told me to drop you off there right away. I don't think he knew what it was about because he was extremely peevish."

"Where is Lord North Street?" Curtis Lowell asked.

"Not far; Westminster," Lewis said. "I do hope it's not an omen."

"What kind of omen?" Meredith asked.

"Lord North was the Prime Minister who lost the American colonies," Lewis said.

"With a little help from George the Third," Lowell added.

As he spoke Lewis noticed they were passing the statue of Cromwell outside the House of Commons; a couple of minutes later they pulled up beside an elegant little house in a narrow street. As Meredith drove away they stood together awkwardly on the pavement until the Georgian door swung open and a figure stood in silhouette against the light that flooded from the hallway.

"Horne. How good to see you after all this time," the figure said in a genial voice.

Lewis studied the figure. "Bellingford?" he said after a moment.

"The very same." He turned to Lewis's companion. "And you must be Curtis Lowell." He held out his hand. "I'm Jeremy Bellingford. How do you do? Sorry to bring you out on a lovely evening like this. We're upstairs. Let me lead the way."

As he walked behind him Lewis sought memories of his host: rich family from the North Midlands, manufacturers of industrial tiles – a fact that he did his best to conceal. An Old Etonian spiv of the nastiest sort. Strange how that school produces so many different types, Lewis mused. It must be the greenhouse effect, turning out cacti, orchids, hot-house grapes and, in Bellingford's case, forced rhubarb.

"You haven't been here before, have you, Lewis?" Bellingford said as they followed him up the narrow staircase.

"We haven't seen each other since Oxford," Lewis said.

"Of course. How silly of me. You joined the army, didn't you?"

"That's right."

"I went into Parliament."

"Yes, I noticed."

Lewis was noticing other things as well. Bellingford had lost the gawkiness of youth. He had put on a few pounds in weight but he was far from being fat. 'Plush' was now the way that Lewis would describe him. The fair hair that had once flopped over his forehead was perfectly barbered and when he turned around Lewis looked for the red indentations he had always had on each side of his nose when he was not wearing his spectacles. They were gone, but the eyes seemed a shade bluer than Lewis remembered. Tinted contact lenses, he thought.

"You took a first, didn't you?" Bellingford said, making it sound like a piece of shoplifting.

"That's right," Lewis said.

"I went for a third," he said with a laugh. "The British tend to despise intellectuals in public life, Mr Lowell. It doesn't do to be *too* clever."

Lewis couldn't be bothered to reply. He just waited until they had reached the top of the stairs when he managed to kick Bellingford sharply in the left ankle.

"Terribly sorry, Jeremy. These stairs *are* steep," he said as they entered a small sitting room, while Bellingford's snarl of "forget it" rang with insincerity as he limped ahead.

Charlie Mars was standing in front of a blazing log fire. It puzzled Lewis that they weren't all overcome by the heat until he realised that the house was air-conditioned. Charlie Mars stepped forward.

"Shall we all sit down? I'm sorry to be so mystifying, but

we're expecting somebody else and we might as well wait so that Bellingford only has to go over it once."

They sat down on a variety of furniture that had been carefully selected to fit into the scale of the house and Bellingford began to massage the ankle that Lewis had kicked. There was nothing personal about the room. Clearly an interior decorator had been handed a pile of money and told to get on with it.

Bellingford cleared his throat. "How are you enjoying England, Mr Lowell? Warm enough for you?"

"Very pleasant. A welcome change after the heat of Washington."

"Yes." Bellingford gazed at the floor for a moment. "Are you any relation to Senator Lowell?"

"He's my uncle. He asked me to give you his kind regards if we were to meet."

"Jack Lowell," Bellingford said with sudden warmth. "Does he still have that boat?"

"The *Daisy*? Yes, he does."

"I used to call it the *Busted Flush*. Good heavens, I haven't been on it since, oh, 1979."

During these opening skirmishes Lewis had been watching Bellingford's face. It wore a curious yearning expression, like a poor child with its nose pressed against a toyshop window. He noticed Lewis looking at him and got to his feet.

"How's your drink, Lewis?" He turned back to Lowell. "We're old friends, you know, from Oxford."

Lewis tried in vain to recollect their friendship until the doorbell rang again and Bellingford went to answer it. When he returned with his latest arrival they all stood up. It was Hanna Pearce. She refused Bellingford's offer of a drink and sat down in one of the tiny chairs.

"Thank you for coming, Dr Pearce," Jeremy Bellingford said. "Let me introduce everyone. I think you met Captain Horne earlier today."

"I met *Mr* Horne earlier today. Perhaps I should be re-introduced?" Hanna Pearce said coolly.

Lewis noticed that her eyes were very dark blue. It had been hard to tell in the winebar. He smiled, but was

68

confronted with a withering stare. Obviously their lunch-time friendliness had been on a limited run.

However, on being introduced to Curtis she smiled sweetly and said, "Do you have a relation called Clara Lowell?"

Lewis felt a slight stab of jealousy.

Lowell returned the smile. "Why, yes. She lives on the park in New York City."

"We've been friends for a long time," Hanna said.

Once the introductions were over a silence fell upon the room. Charlie Mars stood up. "I think it would be better if Mr Bellingford were to explain the circumstances bringing us all together, as he will be in overall charge of the proceedings. He has been specially appointed by the Prime Minister to co-ordinate action in this matter and report directly to the Cabinet. Jeremy?"

Bellingford stood up. "Thank you, Charles. First of all I would like to emphasise that what I have to say is of vital national importance to both Great Britain and to the United States. I feel sure that we can rely on your absolute discretion not to discuss what is said here with any other person. As you may know, the forthcoming talks between the Soviet Union and the Western powers are at a most delicate stage. And we have hard information that powerful sections within the Praesidium would like an excuse to stop any rapprochement. They are not alone. There are also those in the West who have motives, be they patriotic or venal, and would equally like to see the cold war continue at its present subzero temperature. Greed and fear produce strange bedfellows."

Don't overdo it, Jeremy, Lewis thought.

"In the last twenty-four hours our attention has been focused on a project that took place in the Second World War called Operation Hermann. We think it could have a grave effect on the peace talks if details of it became known to the Soviet Union. The head of Mr Mars's reading section, Victor Smight, first saw a reference in an article about Dr Pearce and because of his diligence we received the following cable from CIA Headquarters late this afternoon. I will read the whole text.

" 'Attention Victor Smight. With reference to your inquiry

re Operation Hermann/Black Dwarf. We have secured only one document, the full text of personal letter from General George Marshall to President Dwight D. Eisenhower. Text follows:

My dear Ike,

I am glad that all continues to go well with you. Are you now satisfied with the outcome of the Operation Hermann business? It sounds like an extremely thorough job of work. I'm glad it wasn't left to Hoover – he would have kept a copy, sure as hell. We both know how catastrophic the consequences would be if the Russians had ever got to know about the Black Dwarf and the appalling damage it would do to the reputations of Roosevelt and Churchill, both here and in Britain. Maybe Henry Ford was right when he said history was bunk.

My love to Mame and my very best wishes to you,

George.

Ends text 1800 hours.'"

There was a long silence in the room.

"So there we have it," Charlie Mars said. "The only person alive who seems to know what Operation Hermann was all about is Professor Raeder."

"Does it matter?" Hanna said. "It's all so obscure. It was only spotted by chance in your department. Who else is going to notice it?"

"I'm afraid we can't go on that assumption, Dr Pearce," Bellingford said. "Explain to her, Charles."

"If we picked it up, Dr Pearce, it's a safe assumption that the Russians have as well. Certainly the Americans did. That's why Mr Lowell is here." He nodded towards Curtis.

"But how do you know?" Hanna asked.

"We know the Russians have got a dozen people as good as Victor Smight."

"But what do you want of me?" Hanna said.

"We want you to go to New York tomorrow morning with Mr Lowell and Captain Horne to ask Professor Raeder exactly what the hell Operation Hermann was. And discover the identity of the Black Dwarf."

4

A single servant, selected perhaps for his stupidity, was the only person who attended them.

The Black Dwarf
SIR WALTER SCOTT

Something happens to a pub near to closing time. Drinks are ordered hastily, voices grow more insistent, cigarette smoke thickens, laughter becomes louder, tempers shorten. Like children who have been too long at a party some customers grow weary, others too excitable. The man with the beer belly and tattooes on his forearms never knew how lucky he was. He turned from the bar holding two pints of lager by the rims of the glasses and stumbled slightly, spilling some of the beer over the jacket of a slim, hollow-cheeked man who was standing behind him.

"Watch it, John," the tattooed man said in a threatening voice and flexed his massive shoulder muscles for emphasis.

"Sorry." Lewis stepped back and smiled. "My fault." The man with the lager wasn't satisfied. He thrust his tee-shirted front towards Lewis and half-drew back the right-hand glass.

"Come on, Bernie," a voice shouted out and after a moment's hesitation the man turned and shuffled to safety. Lewis bought two drinks and carried them back to a spot near the door where Roland Perth was waiting. He handed him a glass of white wine. Roland looked at the Edwardian elegance of mahogany and engraved glass and sighed.

"I do hope your ugly friend doesn't become a regular," he said.

"Which friend?" Lewis said and looked around the bar innocently.

"The one you were about to dance with," Roland said. "Now tell me more about Dr Pearce."

"There's really nothing else to tell," Lewis said, sipping his whisky. "I just made a cock-up of everything." He looked across to where the tattooed man was standing with his friends. They were pouring beer over the smallest member of the group who was trying to laugh but Lewis could see that he was frightened. It depressed him further. "Now she's gone off to have dinner with that bloody American."

Roland leaned against the wall of the pub and lit a cigarette. "I suppose you could look upon it as retribution, in a way."

"Retribution for what?" Lewis asked with surprise.

"Well, you do tend to treat women in a cavalier fashion, dear boy," Roland said with just a hint of disapproval in his voice.

"That's hardly fair," Lewis said with a faint slur in his voice. The whisky that he had drunk since his return from Bellingford's house was starting to take its toll. "Women know what they're getting into with me. I never make false promises."

"Exactly. Take it from your old auntie: friendly indifference can be heartbreakingly attractive. Tell me, have you ever been hopelessly in love?"

Lewis looked into the packed heartiness of the pub and considered the question.

"Yes," he said after a long pause.

"Who with?"

"A girl I knew at Oxford. At least, we were pretty miserable most of the time. That's what people generally mean when they talk about being in love, don't they?"

Roland sighed. The activity around them was beginning to reach some kind of crescendo. "This place is like Palma Nova tonight," he said as he turned back to Lewis. "What happened to her? The girl you were in love with?"

"She got tired of being miserable with me and married a friend of mine. They live in Silicon Valley now, probably with two houses, two children, two cars and an American Express card. Maybe they've got two of those as well. That's if he hasn't died of indigestion. She was a lousy cook."

"And you've never been in love since?" Roland persisted.

"I've never been miserable with a woman since," Lewis answered and drained his glass.

"Same again?"

Lewis nodded. Roland placed his almost-full glass of wine on a nearby table and squeezed his way to the bar. While he waited Lewis watched a seated couple across the room. They were so involved with each other they could have been listening to nightingales in Berkeley Square. The girl turned her head suddenly and her dark hair moved in a way that reminded him of Hanna Pearce.

"Not only has she succeeded in making you miserable, she also seems to have driven you to drink," Roland said cheerfully, returning with Lewis's whisky. "When are you going to see her again?"

"Tomorrow. In fact, we're going on a business trip together."

"Well, there you are," Roland went on in a consoling voice. "You'll have all the time in the world to establish a brand-new relationship. I expect you'll take every opportunity to impress her with your more sterling qualities."

Lewis nodded but he felt even more oppressed by the atmosphere. It was beginning to dawn on him that he was rather drunk. He spoke with extra care so that his words would not slur. "It's not easy, Roland. I keep thinking of her as if she's the fairy on top of a Christmas tree – except the tree is made of money. Then I wonder: is she really so great or is it the money she's perched on?"

"Dear me," Roland said. "She does seem to have got you in a state. Putting aside your reservations, how would you describe her – purely on face value?"

Lewis thought for a moment. "Purely on face value I would say she is: beautiful, compassionate, talented and rich."

Roland nodded. "I can see why you're worried. Somebody that perfect could easily break your heart."

"You're not much help," Lewis said. "I think I'll call it a day. I hate being in a pub at closing time: reminds me of an ocean-liner sinking."

"Were you ever on an ocean-liner when it sank?" Roland asked.

"No, but I was in an air crash once."

"Were you?" Roland said, raising his eyebrows. "Where was that?"

Lewis waved an arm. "Oh, in the desert. Only a little one, not many dead. Well, goodnight."

He stepped into the peaceful contrast of Lamb's Conduit Street and with great deliberation walked the few yards to his front door. When he got to his flat he turned the light on in the hallway but didn't bother with the lamp in the living room.

A shaft of light illuminated the shelf where he kept his records. He selected a 78 which he placed on the record player, carefully poured himself a very large nightcap from a bottle of Teacher's and lowered the arm of the record player before easing himself into the only comfortable chair in the flat. The melancholy sound of Bunny Berigan's trumpet filled the room for a few moments. Then Roland's comments about the way he treated women came back to him. He took the cutting from his pocket and studied Susan's face again. Had he been in love with her? When she left him for Armitage he had felt all sorts of emotion: despair, then for a while a kind of numbness. No one had caused the same turmoil since. He lay the cutting aside and thought of the women he had known in the last two years. At least, the ones who had lasted beyond the first furlong.

There had been the girl who sold advertising time for a television company, the Swedish academic on a post-graduate course at London University, and Tracy, the model whose full-time boyfriend was doing seven years for armed robbery. She had been the smartest of them all. Tracy had almost got his job right.

"Look," she had said on their first date, "I don't give a monkey's what you do but don't give me that load of moody about being a salesman, right?" He had enjoyed the six weeks they had spent together but eventually she gave him up. "I know you're a villain," she said as they parted, "but you ain't getting paid much for it. There's something funny about you, an' I've got enough trouble in my life without gettin' into anythin' new. So good luck, goodbye an' no 'ard feelings, right?"

Right.

He looked around the bleak room and thought how pleasant it would have been to be having dinner with the lovely doctor. The record player's arm clicked and started to play again. This time Lewis rested his head on the back of the chair and listened to the lyrics.

> On the golf course, I'm under par,
> Metro-Goldwyn have asked me to star,
> I've got a house, a showplace,
> Still I can't get no place with you.

He put down the glass and switched off the record player. We'll see, Hanna Pearce, he thought, and with a sigh made for the bedroom.

At six forty-five the following morning the only sound of traffic in Theobald's Road was the electric hum of a milk-float cruising in the direction of Southampton Row. Lewis turned into Gray's Inn Road and stepped up the pace for the final leg of his run. The lights changed at Chancery Lane and a lorry and two motorcars roared past him as he approached the Elizabethan façade of Old Holborn. The sweat poured from his body and coursed in rivulets down his chest and back as he forced the pace even harder. Three waddling pigeons in his path flew reluctantly into the air as he swung into Warwick Court and hammered towards home. Two office cleaners stepped out of his way. "Go on, son," one said as he passed them and the other laughed, and began a hacking cough.

His final steps brought him to a halt outside the Old Times Antique Shop. Panting, he looked at his watch. Twenty-nine minutes: not bad, he thought, as he peered through the window and saw Roland rearranging reproduction silver frames on a small side table. Roland was wearing his work clothes; designer jeans and a powder-blue, roll-neck cashmere sweater.

When he saw Lewis he came to the doorway and stood blinking at the bright morning sunlight. Then he studied the panting figure of Lewis and his sweat-soaked training top. From it a slight haze of steam drifted upwards.

"And how are we this morning?" he said as Lewis clasped his knees and took gulps of breath.

"Last night you saw the old Horne," Lewis gasped. "Drunk, maudlin and full of self-pity. Today a new man arises from the ashes. Fresh, vigorous and filled with a terrible resolution. Just let me rest here for three or four hours then watch me bound up those stairs."

"Well, before you do let me give you something," Roland said, popping back into the shop. He re-emerged with a thick manila envelope and handed it to Lewis. "This arrived for you yesterday by registered post. I forgot to give it to you last night."

Lewis looked at the label on the back. It was from his publishers. "Thanks," he said, turning into his own front door.

As he climbed the stairs Lewis opened the envelope and pulled out a wad of galley proofs. Inside the flat he walked slowly into the bedroom, reading the first page of text. Reluctantly he put down the proofs and switched on the radio, then carried it into the bathroom so that he could listen to the seven o'clock news while he showered.

The first item dealt with speculation about the summit talks. The American Secretary of State denied that the latest communiqué from the Kremlin was hostile, despite the interpretation the French had decided to put on it. And he was confident that the Chairman of the Supreme Soviet would be in London on Sunday – as would the President of the United States.

Lewis came out of the bathroom. He began to pack quickly, and with careful neatness. As he selected his clothes for the trip he mentally adjusted to his destination. New York – summer, very hot: lightweight suit, three cotton shirts, toilet bag and a black dressing-gown bought as a memento of Japan when he had once changed planes at Tokyo Airport.

Then he checked the time again. There was an hour and a

quarter to go before he met Curtis Lowell at Gower Street. He picked up the proofs of his book and went into the living room where he sat down at the plain metal desk in the corner by the window.

Sixty minutes later he flexed the muscles in his back where they had become cramped by concentration, collected the proofs together and put them into the document case, wrote a brief note to Janet saying he was going away for a few days, posted it through her letter-box and set off for Gower Street.

Curtis Lowell stood in Hillary's office with Lewis and opened the envelope that he had just been handed by the sergeant.

"British Airways Jumbo to JFK?" he said as he leaned against one of the filing cabinets.

"Yes, sir," Sergeant Hillary replied. "I've made reservations at the Algonquin Hotel as Captain Horne requested. Your tickets are waiting for collection at the British Airways desk at Heathrow."

"How about transport to the airport?" Curtis said as he tapped the envelope on his teeth.

"We can get the tube," Lewis said as he stuffed his envelope into a coat pocket.

"Tube?" Curtis said.

"Underground, subway. It's the fastest way to Heathrow."

Curtis still wasn't satisfied. "This hundred and fifty bucks, what's it for? Cab fares?"

"That's two days' allowance, sir."

Curtis paused and looked at the envelope again. "These tickets. They're tourist?"

"Of course, sir."

"Why did you bother with a hotel? We could always have slept in the air-vents around Grand Central with the rest of the bums," Curtis said with cheerful disgust.

"There's a premium to pay on the hotel, sir," Hillary said in a stiff voice. "Captain Horne insisted on the Algonquin and it exceeds our budget." Curtis looked aghast at Sergeant Hillary who stood expressionless before him.

"You guys are wonderful, you know that? What are you doing here, saving up to buy back India?"

"Come on," Lewis said. "You don't want to keep Dr Pearce waiting."

"Lead me to the subway," said Curtis in a resigned voice. "That is, unless you've changed your mind and decided we're going to walk."

An hour later they disembarked at Heathrow and made their way with the rest of the crowd to Terminal Three. Curtis turned to Lewis. "That was kind of nice. I thought it was going to be like New York."

"When were you last on the subway, Curtis?" Lewis said with a smile as he studied Lowell's beautifully cut suit and the gold Rolex on his tanned wrist.

"When I was in college. I had a room-mate that liked to go down and pick on muggers. I used to hold his coat. Jesus! Will you look at this place? It's like a convention for the confused in mind and spirit."

Terminal Three was in its usual state of pandemonium as people of all known nationalities seemed to mill aimlessly about the great concourse. "This way," Lewis said, leading Curtis expertly by the arm.

"Over here," he added, and a minute later they stood before the British Airways desk. They announced their names to a lady who smiled at them with the automatic brightness Lewis had encountered in airline ground-staff all over the world.

"Here are your tickets, gentlemen, and I have a message for you from a Dr Pearce who says will you meet her at the Concorde desk?" The two men exchanged a glance of surprise and headed in the direction indicated by their smiling lady.

After weaving their way through a party of Indians with a pile of luggage to rival the size of the Taj Mahal they entered the peaceful oasis of the Concorde area. Hanna Pearce was sitting on one of the sofas, wearing a pink cotton jump-suit. To Lewis she looked as fresh as a rose tipped with dew.

"Good morning," he said with a cheerful smile.

"Good morning. Look, I've rebooked us on Concorde," she said briskly as she rummaged in her handbag.

78

"That's great," Curtis said. "Have you told the British Government? They'll probably have to hock Gibraltar to pay the difference."

Hanna spoke in a low voice to them. "Please let me settle that. I can afford it. Really. Besides, if we go by Concorde we can see Professor Raeder this afternoon and get the early morning flight back." Her voice changed to one of gentle pleading. "I really am busy at work. I can't spare much time."

Curtis smiled. "Speaking for myself, Dr Pearce, I graciously accept your kind offer on behalf of the Government and people of the United States of America. However, I cannot speak for my companion. He is British and they are a proud, incorruptible nation."

Lewis shrugged. "I always knew my price was pretty low," he said. "Lead on."

Their bags were taken from them and bound with white tape by a uniformed man.

"What the hell's that?" Curtis asked.

"It's a special deal they have with the baggage handlers. Don't ask me what it means – it just speeds things up," Hanna explained.

They passed through passport control and made their way to the Concorde waiting-room, where Lewis got himself in front so he could commandeer the boarding-passes.

"Two together and one four rows behind," the girl on the desk said brightly.

"Excellent," Lewis said, taking the boarding-passes and thereby consigning Curtis to a lonely flight.

Through the window they could see the familiar dart-like shape of the aircraft.

"She certainly is a lovely lady," Curtis said as they gazed out of the window.

"I get the same thrill every time I fly in her," Hanna said.

"Do you do that very often?" Lewis asked.

"Every couple of months. It comes from having a family split by the Atlantic. But I still like to sit by the window."

Although Lewis nearly always flew tourist there were occasions when necessity demanded that he travel first-class. He recognised the types who waited with them. Nearby was a group of casually dressed young men who lolled to excess in their seats. They were almost certainly in the music business. A couple of seasoned businessmen in shirt-sleeves and loosened ties worked, their papers spread on the document cases on their laps. A slim, stylishly dressed woman with a shade too much jewellery and the make-up and hairstyle of a soap-opera starlet sat next to a restless child who was beating a toy on the edge of his seat. The woman's eyes flickered around the room past Lewis – but paused for a few seconds longer when they lighted on Curtis and Hanna. It was clear she possessed a sixth sense where money was concerned.

Hanna went to make a telephone call and Lewis got himself and Curtis a cup of coffee. They had hardly begun to drink it when a voice announced that boarding would now commence. Hanna came back and joined them in the shuffling queue. Lewis casually handed Curtis his boarding-pass, after making sure he was sitting next to Hanna.

"I made sure you got a window seat," he said as he handed her the ticket.

Once they had boarded, Lewis relaxed for a moment in his seat next to Hanna. Curtis was several rows behind them. As he strapped himself in he felt the familiar tightening in his chest. To take his mind off the pounding of his heart he gazed around the aircraft, memorising the details. It seemed disappointingly conventional. The body was narrow so that the two seats each side of the gangway seemed cramped. He had expected the interior to be fitted out in stainless steel and leather but the decor was a familiar blend of plastic and fabric. As they lined up ready for take-off Lewis reached into the pouch in the back of the seat in front of him and took out a menu. The descriptions of Cordon Bleu food swam before his eyes as he felt the aircraft hurtling away from the earth. When they levelled out he relaxed his shoulders and replaced the menu knowing that he would not eat a thing. After take-off a steward approached them to take their order for coffee.

"How are you, Dr Pearce?"

"Just fine, Eddie. And you?"

"My legs are still killing me," he said cheerfully.

"You should go back to Jumbos."

"And give up showbusiness?" Eddie said with a smile, and moved on.

"What's wrong with his legs?" Lewis asked as soon as Eddie was out of earshot.

"Nothing medical. It's just that Concorde flies at an angle when it's subsonic. Other aircraft fly level, so the cabin staff of Concorde are always pushing those trolleys uphill – or stopping them from running away from them. It's very tiring; especially on the legs."

After a time the captain's voice came on the intercom and told them they were now flying faster than a rifle-bullet.

Lewis thought about rifle-bullets. He recalled what it was like to have them fired at him, the different ways they sounded whether it was in a city street or whether they bounced off a rock in the desert or thudded into a rain-sodden field. From now on, he decided, he would always imagine them as tiny Concordes packed with minuscule passengers delicately eating caviare and drinking champagne.

He had spent a lot of his life in airports and knew the grinding boredom of waiting for delayed flights and the endless dreariness of baggage carousels. Crossing the Atlantic in three hours and fifty-nine minutes with no waiting was real luxury. It was a pity he couldn't enjoy it more.

Hanna Pearce had taken a bound report from her leather travelling-case and had started to read it the moment they sat down. Lewis studied her profile for a moment and decided to test her concentration.

"I put us in the non-smoking section. I hope you don't mind," he said.

"I'm glad that you should be so concerned about my health but there's really no need to go to any trouble on my behalf," she said in a frosty voice and without looking up from her report.

Lewis noted the cool draught of her indifference: no chance of a rift-healing conversation at the moment, he thought. He took the book proofs from his case and settled down to read. After a while he pulled out a felt-tipped pen and made a mark in the margin.

So they sat for nearly two hours in silence. Both refused the meal when it was offered. Lewis settled for a stiff whisky. Hanna finished her report and put it back in her travelling-case. She sat watching Lewis marking the proofs until curiosity overcame her.

"What's the book about?" she asked.

"The Civil War," Lewis answered without raising his head.

"The American Civil War?" she said with a certain amount of interest.

This time he turned to her when he answered and looked into her eyes. "No; ours, actually. It's about the New Model Army." He glanced away and made another small correction.

"That was Cromwell's army, wasn't it?" Hanna asked. Lewis could hear the interest in her voice. She had turned slightly in her seat and was studying him.

"Yes, he created it," he said looking back at her.

"What exactly do you do, Captain? Yesterday, at lunchtime, you were a reporter, then by dinnertime you seemed to be some kind of secret agent. Today you turn out to be a writer."

"I'm just a soldier, Dr Pearce."

"And a writer?"

"Lots of soldiers write books."

"Why did you become a soldier in the first place? Obviously you could have done other things." She gestured at the galley proofs.

"I suppose it's the family business. My father was a soldier, and my grandfather and his father." Lewis folded up the proofs and stowed them back in his case. "How about you? Why didn't you go to work for the Pearce Corporation?"

"What do you know about my family and the Pearce Corporation?" Hanna asked in a slightly defensive voice.

Lewis thought for a moment. "Your grandfather was Cargo Pearce – 'The Man Who Bought New York'. He was believed to take a percentage of every ship's load that came into the New York waterfront."

Hanna folded her arms as Lewis began to speak. "Go on," she said in a non-committal voice. "Impress me."

So Lewis did. Cargo was the black sheep of a wealthy family, he told her, and had founded his own fortune during Prohibition rum-running out of Cuba and the West Indies.

"This he achieved with the co-operation of some of Britain's most distinguished distilleries. He anticipated the crash of 1929 and sold short, held his fortune and went into aircraft production and shipbuilding. When the Depression was finally over he owned vast tracts of Manhattan."

Hanna nodded slightly as he spoke. Lewis plunged on.

"His best friend was probably President Roosevelt who gave him immense power during World War Two. After the war his health was broken by overwork. Your father took over European operations and your Uncle Henry ran the American end. In the post-war boom the Corporation went into plastics, chemicals and electronics and latterly the entertainments industry. Your brother Jack was killed in Vietnam. He was a Marine Corps pilot. You have three cousins in Los Angeles – all boys – and between the four of you you will inherit one of the largest fortunes in the world."

"You've done your research well," she said drily.

"Thank you, Hanna." It was the first time either had called the other by their first name. For a moment she said nothing.

"Lewis – that is your real name, isn't it?"

"You heard Bellingford call me Lewis. He's known me since university days."

"I can't say that I cared for him that much," Hanna said. "What was he like then?"

"What, at Oxford?" Lewis answered carefully. "I didn't see much of him. He worked very hard at his social connections."

"That's an English way of saying he was a creep, isn't it?"

"I suppose it is."

"No wonder Americans think you people are so crazy. You use language like a secret code. Why can't you just say what you really mean?"

Lewis smiled. "We live in a tiny, overcrowded island with the most intricate class-system in the world. Constant

83

plain-speaking leads to confrontation. Real English is the polite, evasive speech that most people use in everyday life."

"That's probably why there's been no real confrontation in Britain," Hanna said.

"We've had our share," Lewis said. "Our strikes and our riots."

Hanna shrugged. "Not like the French. When they have a riot there's a lot of blood on the streets."

Lewis tapped his case with the proofs in it. "We cut off a king's head once. That was hardly an act of reconciliation."

"Who's having an act of reconciliation?" Curtis said as he leaned over their seats.

"We are," Lewis said. "Hanna has forgiven me for my deception yesterday. How's your flight been?"

"Excellent, I've made a new friend. We've drunk champagne and told each other our life stories."

Lewis raised himself in his seat so that he could look to the back of the aircraft. The stylish woman he had noticed in the airport lounge raised a glass of champagne to him. He smiled and nodded back to her, then lowered himself into the seat again. "She looks as if she has a life story to tell."

"She's a fine woman, Lewis, and she's had a very difficult time."

"Have you offered to adopt the child?"

"I saw the child as a problem and was prepared to treat it as my own; send it to the finest schools and give it every opportunity in life, but it turns out the little bastard belongs to her sister, so I've been torturing it every time Auntie went to the can."

Hanna and Lewis laughed.

"I don't think that's funny. I'm distressed by the pace of modern life. Do you realise that fifty years ago we would have been crossing on an ocean-liner and I could have had time to explore my relationship with Hanna instead of three hours flirting with a triple divorcee?"

"You could have got the captain to marry us as well," Hanna said lightly.

"No." Curtis shook his head. "Beauty like yours deserves

a cathedral. Well, happy landings." And with that he made off in the direction of the other lady.

The request went out that everyone should return to their seats in preparation for arrival at JFK. Lewis tightened his belt and sat rigid in his seat as the muscles tightened in his chest once more.

"Flying is a real ordeal for you, isn't it?" Hanna said in a low voice.

Lewis looked at her and tried to think of something flippant to say but he could see real sympathy in her face. "I had a bad flight once."

"Really bad?"

He nodded and she reached out and took his hand in hers. It was like an act of faith-healing. He could feel the security flow from her and his jangling nerves returned to their normal tempo.

As the aircraft taxied across the apron after touchdown, she turned to him. "Do you fly very much in your job?"

"Yes, a fair amount," he said.

"And is it always like that for you?"

"Yes," he said shortly.

"You must possess a remarkable degree of will power," she said in a cool voice, but she still hadn't let go of his hand. Lewis wanted to hold it aloft in a victory salute that Curtis could see. But he didn't bother. Somehow, he sensed that it wasn't necessary.

As they walked out of the exit a warm wet sheet of humidity hit them. It was like breathing the steam from a kettle. Every pore in Lewis's body opened at the same moment and in seconds he felt as though he had just got out of a bath and dressed without towelling himself dry. Hanna turned to him and he noticed she had fine beads of perspiration on her upper lip. "It's days like this when I really feel British."

"What are we waiting for?" Curtis said. "An English summer day?"

Lewis noticed that Curtis had loosened his tie. It was the first time he had seen him less than immaculate.

A small man appeared beside Hanna. He was dressed in a

black suit and had a face like a walnut. His thick white hair was cropped close to his skull and the china-blue eyes that peered out at them suspiciously were as cold as December.

"Da car's over here, Miss Hanna," he said.

Lewis recognised an authentic Bowery accent.

"Thank you, Vincent," said Hanna. "These gentlemen are coming with me."

"This guy is an old family retainer," Curtis whispered as they picked up their bags.

"How do you know?" Lewis muttered back.

"Well, he sure as hell isn't a *young* family retainer."

"Dis way," said Vincent in a tone that was used to being obeyed and led them to a great black car that must have been made when Lindbergh flew the Atlantic.

Lewis had never seen a private motorcar of such proportions. There appeared to be enough room to park a London taxi in the boot.

"My God, a Hispano Suiza!" Lowell exclaimed. "I've only ever seen them in photographs before."

"Six Presidents of the United States have ridden in dis car," Vincent said proudly. Lewis noticed the alteration in the tone of his voice: there almost seemed to be a note of tenderness. He opened the door for Hanna then got into the driver's seat, leaving Lewis and Curtis to climb in after her unaided.

"God, I hate characters," Curtis said in a low voice.

When the door was closed the air-conditioning returned their body temperatures to normal, and they sat back in the deep leather upholstery. The car was built to carry four in a great deal of comfort. Lewis sat facing Hanna with his back to the driver; between Curtis and Hanna, who sat side by side, was a dark wood cabinet. Lewis looked through the tinted windows at the people outside who were coping with the heat and wondered which was the real world.

Curtis rebuttoned his collar and once again reverted to being the Boston gentleman.

"Sorry the air-conditioning is a bit fierce," Hanna said as she made some adjustments on a panel built into her door. "We only had it installed a couple of years ago."

"A cool breeze never bothered me," Curtis said lightly.

"Shall we drop your stuff off at the Algonquin?" Hanna said. "We can go on from the hotel to my apartment and make arrangements for meeting Professor Raeder from there."

Lewis and Curtis shrugged. "Sounds fine," Lewis said and settled back and dug his heels into the deep pile of the white carpet.

"Algonquin Hotel first, Vincent. Then we're going on to the apartment." Vincent held up his hand to acknowledge the instructions and the car glided away from the airport terminal and on to the freeway heading towards Manhattan Island.

They had travelled for a couple of miles when Vincent's voice came through a concealed broadcasting system: "It's well past noon London time, Miss Hanna. Maybe these gentlemen would like a drink?"

Hanna looked at them. "I'm so sorry. Would either of you like anything?" She pulled down a section of the cabinet beside her and revealed a bar. Eight cut-glass goblets rested in holders, and there was a selection of crystal decanters.

"I wouldn't say no to a beer," said Curtis.

"Same for me," Lewis said.

"Is there any?" said Hanna.

"Under the ice-tray," Vincent growled back.

Hanna passed a glass and a can of ice-cold Budweiser to Lewis. The can hissed as Lewis pulled the tab and when he looked up from pouring his drink he caught a glimpse of the New York skyline. The great towers formed a pale silhouette against the grey-blue sky. As always the spectacle thrilled him.

Silently he raised his glass towards the shining city in the distance. Forty minutes later he was cursing the traffic, as Vincent edged his way towards West 44th Street. Even the majestic springs of the Hispano Suiza could not cope with the ruts and potholes in the roadway. The cars around them lurched and swayed like punch-drunk boxers.

The heat was getting to New York. Lewis could see it in the crowds that surged along the sidewalks. There was a

87

desperation about the people. The city throbbed like an overloaded circuit.

Eventually the great car turned into West 44th Street from Sixth Avenue and came to a gentle halt in the deep shadow outside the entrance of the Algonquin Hotel. The doorman, clad in a Victorian livery of pale and chocolate brown, came forward and opened the door.

Vincent opened the boot and the doorman seized Lewis's and Curtis's bags and in six swift strides they had passed through the muggy air and into the coolness of the lobby. A desk clerk was scribbling with a ball-point pen on some concealed document as they stood before the tiny reception desk.

"Yes, gentlemen?" he said and raised a slightly disapproving eyebrow.

"Curtis Lowell and Lewis Horne. We have reservations," Curtis said. The desk clerk flicked through a collection of cards.

"Yes, gentlemen, I have your reservations," he said, slightly surprised, as if he had first believed that they were trying to present false credentials. He handed them their registration cards then punched out a code on an obscure piece of equipment before giving each of them a further plastic card with a series of holes made in it.

"What the hell is this?" Curtis asked.

"It's the key to your room," Lewis explained. "You stick it in a slot in the door."

Curtis stared at the piece of plastic and shook his head. "I should have stayed at the Plaza," he said.

"Can you take our bags up to our rooms?" Lewis called out to the desk clerk as he led Curtis in the direction of the Hispano Suiza.

"Wait a minute," Curtis said. "I just want to take a look at the place."

They stepped around the partition that faced the reception area and looked into the sedate lounge. "So this is where Harpo Marx used to chase Dorothy Parker," Curtis said.

The walls were panelled in dark polished wood. Scattered around the room were groups of sofas and old upright armchairs, covered in a variety of light materials. The room was discreetly lit by large lamps with cloth-covered shades. In the corner to the left of the entrance was an old-fashioned book and newspaper stand. In front of the groups of chairs and sofas were coffee tables with brass bells set on them.

"Let's go," Curtis said. "If we stay here any longer I might turn into one of Thurber's dogs and start talking like you."

They made their way back to the car. Vincent cast off and headed towards Madison Avenue. Lewis glanced out of the window and noticed that the drivers of other vehicles had to look up quite a way to see them. "This car is wonderful," he said. "I feel like I'm travelling in the Graf Zeppelin."

"Mr Pearce didn't like airships," Vincent said over the intercom. "He never put any dough in them."

"Vincent went to work for my grandfather when he was sixteen," Hanna explained.

"I would have thought the Pearce Corporation could have afforded a decent pension scheme," said Curtis.

"Listen, Mister, I retired the day I walked outa Hell's Kitchen in 1923. Since then, I've been on holiday," Vincent growled, as he turned the car into Fifth Avenue.

On the other side of the road the dark green of Central Park looked invitingly cool as they pulled up at the entrance to an apartment block. Vincent left the car and came with them. The heavy glass doors opened automatically as they approached. Inside the marbled entrance hall a uniformed portly security guard saluted. Despite the magnum strapped to his side he looked every inch the genial grandfather as he beamed at them. "Welcome home, Miss Hanna."

"Hi, Max. How are they running for you?" Hanna replied.

"They've all got three legs, Miss Hanna. If I didn't have Vincent to play poker with, I'd be on Skid Row."

"He cheats! The cops never change in New York," Vincent said in a warm voice. Lewis could see the pair were very old friends.

They walked to a separate elevator from the regular bank while Hanna produced a key. The doors slid open and they entered a huge compartment panelled in cedar wood with rows of seats upholstered in the same white leather as the interior of the Hispano Suiza. On one of the great panels was a cubist mural of a circus scene. Lewis studied it for a moment. "Good God, a Picasso!" he exclaimed.

"Yeah, Miss Hanna's grandmother had it done as a birthday present for da boss. Ya should've seen his face when he opened the door an' Picasso was standin' there in a cowboy hat wid his arms out like dis." Vincent gestured towards the painting.

As the doors of the elevator opened, they stepped into the most dazzling room Lewis had ever entered.

They stood at the head of a great staircase and looked into an art deco dreamland of glass, chrome and polished wood. The massive room was divided into areas by banks of angular white sofas. One wall was plate-glass which led to a balcony, scattered with trees and climbing plants. A pure white grand piano stood in the well of the staircase. The other walls blazed with paintings: Miró, Léger, Braque, Gauguin, Modigliani, Cézanne. The work of some of the twentieth century's greatest painters glowed down on them.

"Fantastic, isn't it?" said Hanna. "Hardly anything has been changed since my grandfather's day."

"Including me," said a voice that at first Lewis took to be Vincent's growl.

He looked away from a Derain landscape and saw a short dark woman standing on the far side of the room. Despite the Saks silk dress she was wearing the woman was pure peasant stock. Lewis had seen her a hundred different times, squeezing melons in the cities of southern Europe.

"Connie," cried Hanna. "I want you to meet some people. This is Curtis Lowell and Lewis Horne, and this is Connie Costello, Vincent's wife."

"Hi," said Curtis, who was standing by the window.

Lewis had crossed the room. "How do you do?" he said, and held out his hand.

Connie shook it but looked at him suspiciously. "You English?"

"Yes."

"I thought so. Ya sound like Noël Coward. He used to come here, ya know. In fact, he did dat painting." She indicated a rather amateurish landscape. "He said all de others were lousy. Wadda you think?"

"I think he did everything superbly; except paint." Lewis smiled. He was still enjoying her verdict on his voice.

Then Connie did a strange, almost eerie thing. She looked at Lowell and slowly turned to study Lewis. She spoke rapidly to Hanna in French with a heavy Marseille accent. "These men are dangerous."

"Not to me," Hanna replied in the same language.

"Dangerous men are dangerous to everybody," continued Connie. "It's like having loaded guns lying about the house. Everything is fine and then suddenly – poof!"

Hanna switched back to English. "Could we please have coffee?"

As Connie left the room Lewis noticed that Vincent too had disappeared. Hanna picked up the telephone, punched a button and spoke: "Dr Pearce here. Will you please inform all services?" She replaced the receiver and it buzzed almost instantly. "Hello, Wendy . . . Yes, a good flight. How are you? . . . Good. Will you get me the following number? It's a Professor Hans Molkin in Brooklyn."

She read the number out and replaced the receiver. After a few minutes the telephone buzzed again. "Hello? Can I speak to Professor Molkin please . . . I see . . . Well, would you tell him Dr Pearce called . . . Yes, and I would like to come and see him at one thirty this afternoon . . . Good, thank you, goodbye." She hung up. "That was his housekeeper. He goes to hospital for some treatment today but he will be home at one o'clock."

They consulted their watches. "That gives us time to have some lunch," Curtis said. "Good! I know a great restaurant in Brooklyn but I'd better call my office first. Can I use your telephone?"

Hanna gestured her permission and Curtis got his number. When he began to speak Lewis noticed that he ceased to be the Boston sophisticate and lapsed into the easy tones of his college days. Lewis wondered how many other personalities he could assume.

"Hello, it's me . . . Curtis Lowell . . . Goddammit, Buzz,

of course it's me," he said impatiently. "What do you mean, prove it? Listen, the last time I was here in New York we had lunch at the Harvard Club. You had four Martinis and told Walter Holden they hadn't yet devised an obscenity that was adequate enough to describe him. Okay, if you still don't believe me we both dated Judy Adams in our freshman year. She told me you have a strawberry birthmark on the inside of . . . yeah, it's me . . . How did I get here so early? The British have got this time machine that gets you to New York before you leave London. It's called Concorde, Buzz . . . Work it out with the time difference. Look, I'm coming in and I need transport . . . Something discreet. Yes, fully equipped. Okay, see you in about ten minutes."

He hung up and turned to Lewis and Hanna. "I'll book the restaurant and pick you up at eleven forty-five on the side-walk. I think the Hispano Suiza might be a shade ostentatious to go calling in." He waved towards the door of the elevator. "Is it easy to get out of here?"

"Oh yes," replied Hanna. "It's getting in that's the hard part."

As Curtis left the apartment Connie returned with the coffee. "I see one of the gangsters has gone," she said to Hanna, again in Marseille French.

Lewis stood at the window with his hands behind his back, looking out over the skyline. Without turning he spoke in exactly the same accent as Connie: "*Café crème avec sucre, s'il vous plaît, madame.*"

Connie banged the tray down and spoke in English again: "Ya see, da guy's a spy as well. Listenin' ta what ya say and not lettin' on he unnerstans."

Hanna started to laugh. "Just pour the coffee."

Connie did as she was asked and stomped back to the kitchen.

"What do you think of the apartment?" Hanna asked.

Lewis grinned. "It's magnificent. You say it's exactly as he left it?"

"As far as you would notice. There's a movie somewhere, shot in very early Technicolor. It was to record a party my grandparents held sometime in the Thirties. Everyone who was famous in America was there. Politicians, movie actors, sports stars. Nothing is different. Sometimes I feel it's haunted by that party."

"Where's the library?"

"What's makes you think there's a library?" Hanna said.

"I know he collected rare books."

Hanna gave Lewis an old-fashioned look, then got up and walked across the massive room to the giant glass and chrome bar. She pressed a switch and the whole great edifice swung away from the wall, revealing rows of bookcases.

Lewis looked on in admiration. "He really had an original mind. Most people hide drink behind books. It doesn't surprise me that he made money during the Depression."

Hanna nodded. "He always used to say to my father, 'Never do the obvious except when it's the obvious thing to do.'"

Lewis raised his eyebrows. "Really? What did your father say?"

Hanna turned to him with a grave expression on her face. "My father used to say that it was the most meaningless damned expression he had ever heard."

Lewis nodded. "I go with your father."

They both laughed. "Where are they now . . . your parents?" asked Lewis.

"My mother will probably be gardening and my father will either be at the laboratories in Cambridge or on the fourth floor of the Pearce Corporation European Headquarters on Cheapside."

Suddenly there was one of those moments of shyness that fall upon people who are deeply attracted to one another. There was a strand of hair loose across Hanna's forehead. Lewis reached out and gently brushed it away. "Will you have dinner with me tonight?" he asked quietly.

Hanna smiled. "You really don't care that people will think you're after my money?"

Lewis looked at her perplexed. "After your money? I'm after your medical experience. I thought you knew I was a hypochondriac."

"A hypochondriac who has a fear of flying. You don't sound like a soldier to me." Hanna ran an index-finger along the spine of a Thackeray first edition.

"Oh, it takes all sorts to be soldiers. I know one who wears a cloth cap and an old raincoat when he goes into battle."

"Is he a good soldier?"

"One of the best."

Hanna suddenly looked sad. "My brother was a soldier, you know. He was killed. It's a pity the world needs soldiers."

"It's a pity the world needs doctors, Hanna," Lewis said gently.

5

They danced and sung for an hour after supper as if there were
no such things as goblins in the world.

The Black Dwarf
SIR WALTER SCOTT

A battered pale blue Ford with New Jersey number-plates
crossed the Brooklyn Bridge coming from Manhattan Island,
its tyres making a curious drumming noise as they came into
contact with the studded surface of the roadway.

Lewis looked out of the window on to the landscape of
Brooklyn. There was a run-down feel to the place that reminded him of somewhere: the juxtaposition of once-grand
buildings that had lost their purpose. The majestic Supreme
Court and Borough Hall, a dignified post-colonial building,
looked like aristocrats that had been stranded in a seedy
neighbourhood. Liverpool! Lewis thought.

Curtis jammed on the brakes and reversed into a parking
space by a shop that sold gentlemen's hats. Lewis and Hanna
stood on the sidewalk as Curtis fiddled with something on
the dashboard of the Ford. The people on the streets seemed
more relaxed than their counterparts over the bridge. But
Hanna seemed to be having a certain effect on the men.

A black youth wearing a green silk running-vest and
matching shorts glided past on roller-skates and turned to
stare at her as he effortlessly skated backwards, ignoring the
surrounding traffic. A very old man carrying a walking stick
and wearing a black alpaca jacket came out of the hat shop
and stopped to look hard. Finally he raised the straw boater
he was wearing.

And that's before they know she's got as much money as

the Chase Manhattan, Lewis thought as Curtis finally joined them, and the three of them crossed the road.

Next to a garish bargain emporium that spilt its wares on to the sidewalk stood a porticoed doorway supported by twin Grecian pillars. They passed through and found themselves in a piece of New York unchanged since the days of Diamond Jim Brady. Stately white-aproned Negro waiters, their black jackets emblazoned with gold service braid, served with easy dignity. "Some place, isn't it?" Curtis said, as they were shown to their table on the centre row of three long banks that appeared to run to the horizon because of the huge mirrors at the far end of the room.

"Welcome to Gage and Tollner. Can I get you people a drink?" said a tall waiter with iron-grey hair.

"A glass of dry white wine," Hanna said.

"Gin and ice," Curtis ordered and Lewis settled for a scotch and soda.

The waiter nodded as he made a note on his pad. Lewis pronounced him a professional: he hadn't once tried to look down the front of Hanna's dress – an ambition that seemed foremost in the minds of the men at the tables either side of them.

"Why is he wearing an eagle on his jacket?" Hanna whispered to Curtis.

"That means he's worked here for more than twenty-five years," Lowell explained. "They all have service decorations. A gold bar for every year, a star for five years and so on."

They studied the menu for a while until Curtis said, "I can recommend everything."

They all ordered New England clam chowder. Hanna asked for a grilled dover sole, Curtis a steak and Lewis an English mutton chop, something he never would have requested at home. Hanna just wanted vinegar on her salad but Curtis and Lewis went for the blue cheese dressing.

"How did you find this place?" Hanna said after they had ordered. "I've never heard of it."

"That's because you live over on the Island," replied Curtis, nodding in what he imagined was the direction of Manhattan. "One of my uncles is a Supreme Court judge.

He brought me here a couple of times." He gestured around the restaurant. "A lot of these people are lawyers."

When the clam chowder had been served Curtis leaned forward. "By the way, the fellows in the office told me that the Library of Congress, the *Washington Post*, the *New York Times* and *Time Magazine* have all received requests for information about Operation Hermann. Each request got a negative."

"How about the letter to Eisenhower?" Lewis asked.

Curtis swallowed some soup. "That was incredible. You know your man Smight?"

Lewis nodded.

"Well, he rang some wartime buddy of his who was in the OSS. The man's been retired seventeen years, for God's sake. He remembered the letter in a private collection. The man who originally owned it was a personal friend of Eisenhower, and he left the collection to his grandson.

"It was in the kid's bedroom in Georgetown when we called. Luckily the boy's father works at the Treasury, so he was happy to co-operate. The document isn't registered in the National Archives so there's no public access problem. Unless the Russians have been hanging around the kid's bedroom it should be secure."

"What does all this mean?" Hanna asked.

"It means that somebody else wants to know about the operation but just at present we seem to be ahead in the game," Lewis explained.

Hanna shrugged. "'Game' is the word. It still sounds juvenile to me."

"Let's hope it stays that way," said Curtis a little sharply.

"Amen to that," Lewis added as their salads were placed in front of them.

A feeling of well-being flooded through Lewis as he swallowed the last mouthful of English mutton chop. He took a long pull from his glass of iced water and watched Curtis and Hanna, who continued to work at their lunches. Both ate in the American manner, cutting their food into tiny portions then transferring the fork to their right hand and placing the knife at the side of their plate.

He reached for the scotch and soda he still had by his plate and noticed that Curtis also had hardly touched his drink. The waiter arrived with coffee and Curtis asked for the check. They paid the bill and strolled in a contented fashion to the car. Hanna took the card from her wallet and checked the address once more.

Within a few minutes they were in the tree-lined neighbourhood of Brooklyn Heights, still a solid prosperous suburb. There was a brooding block-house quality in the streets. The dark red brick of most of the houses was occasionally interspaced with a façade of granite or stone. Although the roadway was badly repaired and the paving stones of the sidewalk cracked, the houses were clearly maintained by people with money.

Curtis parked the car near the end of the cul-de-sac at the beginning of a paved promenade that branched away to the right at the top of Raeder's street. They walked to the promenade which commanded a superb view of Buttermilk Channel where it became the East River. Across the water, downtown New York rose from the waterfront in all its glory. What always pleased Lewis about New York was the way you could see the place. In the great cities of Europe one only had a collection of views: it was like opening a book on a series of pictures. Manhattan rose up from the water that surrounded it as European cities had in the Middle Ages, before they sprawled beyond their walls and engulfed the countryside that gave them definition. New York came in one big bite. 'Big Apple' was about it.

They stood for a while gazing at the view until Lewis glanced at his watch: one twenty-five. "Time to go," he said.

The easy relaxed attitudes both men had adopted throughout lunch had now disappeared and there was a feeling of purpose as they turned and started to walk. When they drew level with their car there was about fifty yards to a group of children playing on the pavement in front of Raeder's house. As he watched them, Lewis saw a green Volkswagen van cruise slowly up the avenue. At first glance he knew it meant danger. Logic played no part in his reaction: it was some deeper, more primitive warning system that made him call to the others, "Get back in the car!"

Without stopping Curtis took Hanna's shoulder and pushed her into the back seat of the Ford. Lewis slid into the front. Moments before Hanna had been gazing at the serene waters of Buttermilk Channel; now she could feel the tension, and was aware that her pulse rate had risen. The car made her feel claustrophobic, and she sensed the raw edge of danger that emanated from her two companions.

"What's the matter?" she asked anxiously.

"That Volkswagen," replied Curtis softly, nodding at the green van that had pulled into the curb where the children were playing.

"What's wrong with it?" Hanna looked from Curtis to Lewis in bewilderment.

"The people in the front don't look right," Lewis said curtly.

As he spoke two men got out of the van and walked swiftly through the playing children and up the steps in front of Raeder's house. Both men carried coats over their arms. The driver looked forward and Lewis caught a glimpse of a woman's face, an olive complexion framed by jet-black hair.

"What do you think? A snatch?" Curtis asked.

"Looks like it," Lewis said. "If it was a hit they'd be in a car. Go to the end of the street, turn around and park out of sight."

Curtis did as he was told, bringing the Ford to a stop around the corner, out of sight of the Volkswagen's rear-view mirror.

"Amateurs," said Curtis.

"How do you know?" asked Hanna.

"They're facing the wrong way. The driver should have turned the van around. This is the only way out of the street."

"What have you got?" asked Lewis.

"What do you want?" Curtis answered, leaning over the seat and pulling down the section of the rear seat next to Hanna.

Lewis looked at the rack of weapons, leaned over and

took a Colt .45 automatic and an extra clip of ammunition. "How about you?" Curtis held his coat open so that Lewis could see the quick-draw holster under his armpit. Lewis checked the automatic and slipped it into the waistband of his trousers.

"How shall we play it?" asked Curtis.

"No time for anything subtle. Ram her up the back and I'll take the driver as she gets out. Then go straight in for the other two." Lewis turned to Hanna. "Stay on the corner," he said. She nodded and got out of the car. Lewis got out with her and then moved into the seat behind Curtis.

"Ready?" Curtis called out.

"Ready."

Curtis engaged gears and the car shot forward and squealed around the corner. As they hurtled towards the van it became apparent that the driver realised she was parked in the wrong direction; she was in the process of turning the Volkswagen round.

The children stopped playing and watched open-mouthed as the blue Ford smashed into the van's left offside wing. The two vehicles swung together at the impact.

Lewis rolled out of the rear left-hand door. As he came to his feet he could see the slim figure of the woman driver running towards the promenade. Automatically he raised the Colt which he had drawn from his waistband before the impact but didn't shoot. The street was full of running children. As they scampered out of sight, their softball game abandoned, his eyes took in a bat clattering on the street and the ball rolling towards the gutter.

He turned and ran towards Raeder's house, where he could see the door was ajar. He hit it hard with his left shoulder and bounced into the hallway where he landed next to the body of a woman whose head was lying in a pool of dark blood. She looked like the housekeeper. Still moving, he put his full weight on the ball of his left foot and leaped to the right. As he did so he heard the soft puttering sound of a machine-pistol fitted with a silencer and saw the heavy calibre bullets chew their way across the wooden floor of the hallway.

He brought the Colt up with both hands and fired two shots at the figure on the staircase who was trying to retrain his weapon on him. Although only seconds had passed Lewis had a clear impression of the man – heavy-set, with black curly hair and thick fleshy features. As soon as he had fired Lewis threw himself to the left. The black-haired man tumbled down the curved staircase like a rag doll and landed next to the body of the woman, the blood from both their bodies mingling into a larger pool.

Where's the other one? he thought. The puttering sound started again and the stained-glass window that covered the full drop of the hallway collapsed behind him as bullets sliced across a beautiful Victorian image of entwined flowers. Lewis raised the Colt again as he saw the other gunman. He was staring at him over the balcony at the top of the stairs. The man's left arm was round the chest of a frail-looking old man and with his right hand he was trying to control the fire from an Uzi machine-pistol. Lewis could see a blossom of blood on the old man's white shirt: it seemed to form a giant rose.

Lewis raised the Colt again. It was a clear head-shot from about thirty-five feet. His first round hit the gunman in the bridge of the nose and snapped back his head. The second entered the underside of his chin. The dead man's grip loosened and the old man slumped forward against the balcony. Eight seconds had passed since Lewis first came through the door.

"Jesus, this place is in a mess!" Curtis Lowell was standing in the hallway.

Lewis had to agree. His ears still rang from the sound of the .45 being fired in a confined space. There was a stink of cordite and the floor and walls were covered in blood. Curtis crunched through the broken glass.

"Up the stairs," Lewis said. "The old boy doesn't look so good."

Curtis ran to the frail figure slumped against the banister rail and lifted him gently into his arms. There was a door open across the corridor: the American carried him into the room beyond.

"Lewis . . . Lewis!" It was Hanna calling from outside.

"It's all right. You can come in," Lewis shouted back and she entered the hallway.

"Are you . . . dear God!" she exclaimed when she saw the battlefield.

Lewis put the safety catch on the Colt and stuck it back into his waistband. Adrenalin still coursed through his body but now that the action was over he felt shaky and slightly sick.

"Are you all right?" asked Hanna in a professional voice.

"I'm okay. Professor Raeder looks pretty bad, though. He's upstairs."

She made at once for the bedroom. Lewis followed her. They entered a small room overcrowded with dark rosewood furniture. Raeder lay on a bed with Curtis leaning over him.

"Out of the way," Hanna said sharply and began to examine him. Raeder's breath was erratic.

"Shall I call for an ambulance?" Curtis asked as Hanna ripped open the old man's shirt. There was a moment's silence as she bent her head on to Raeder's chest. Slowly she shook her head.

"Is there no hope?" Lewis asked.

"None," Hanna said flatly.

Raeder's eyes fluttered open and he focused on the face before him.

"Hanna?" he said in a voice that seemed to come from a great distance.

She spoke to him gently in German.

"Ask him who the Black Dwarf was – and about Operation Hermann," Lewis said urgently.

Hanna turned and looked at him sharply.

"I know he's dying," Lewis said. "But ask him."

Hanna still hesitated, and it was Curtis now who spoke rapidly in German. Raeder tried to focus on him, then his eyes flickered back to Hanna. He spoke again and in the sentence there was an English name. She leaned forward and kissed him lightly on the forehead. He smiled as the life went out of him.

102

"He said Lord Brockwood knew the Black Dwarf," Curtis said quietly.

Hanna closed Raeder's eyes and folded his hands across his chest. Lewis glanced down at the table by the bedside: there was a framed photograph of a young woman in her twenties. The face in the picture could have been Hanna's.

"You two had better get out of here. I've got some work to do," Curtis said, as he handed the keys of the car to Lewis. "I'll call you later at Hanna's apartment."

Lewis hesitated for a moment, then took Hanna by the shoulders. "Come on," he said and gently pushed her towards the door. On the street a crowd had started to gather. "Has anyone called the cops?" Lewis spoke in a commanding voice with a strong American accent. The crowd drew back with the reluctance of those who wish to see all without getting involved. Lewis and Hanna got into the Ford and Lewis turned the car, blowing the horn to move the gaping crowd out of their way. As they reached the end of the street a police car, its siren howling, raced past them.

Hanna and Lewis did not speak until they were across Brooklyn Bridge and in the downtown traffic of Manhattan. At the lights Lewis glanced down and saw that she was holding something in her lap. It was the photograph from the bedside table. He looked up and he could see the tears on her face. "He thought I was her," she said, choking suddenly.

Lewis looked ahead into the traffic. "It's not a bad way to go," he replied, "looking into the face of someone you love." He eased the car forward. "This is a bad business. I thought it was going to be easy. But there are too many mysteries. I must know more. Tell me about her." He nodded at the photograph. "Everything you know."

"Where shall I start?"

"As far back as you can."

Hanna looked out of the car window, then began talking quietly. "My great-grandfather came from one of the most socially prominent families in New York. In those days they wore their respectability like steel corsets. You English think Victorian times were strait-laced; it was ten times worse here in America. He married an actress. It caused a fantastic scandal at the time. Not only was she in the theatre; she was foreign – a Hungarian – and was also suspected of having gypsy blood. That was about as low as you could get, as far as New York society was concerned. Anyway, they did it, and they had two children: Cargo Pearce, my grandfather, and Hanna.

"When the children were small both parents were killed in bizarre circumstances. It was one of the first automobile accidents in America. Of course it brought the whole scandal up again and the family were mortified. The children were separated. Grandfather was kept in New York and Hanna sent to relatives in Boston. The family was determined to make them respectable – with predictable results. Cargo became an adventurer, and Hanna ran away to Germany.

"She wanted to study medicine, which was unthinkable for a woman in those days. The family eventually lost touch with her. When Cargo was old enough he traced her, although they were not close. He discovered that she was happily married so they never saw each other again. It seems she became Hanna Raeder."

"How do you know she was married to Raeder? They could have been lovers," Lewis said.

Hanna held up the photograph. "There's an inscription here. It reads: 'To my darling husband Carl. With all my love, Hanna.' That's how I know."

The lights on Sixth Avenue stopped them again and Lewis banged on the steering wheel with the palm of his hand: "How the hell did they know we were coming for him? Who is Brockwood? Why should an Englishman know the Black Dwarf . . . ?"

Lewis turned the pieces over in his mind. "Concorde!" he exclaimed. "They thought we'd be on a later flight. We got to the house too early." Then the implication hit him. "There must be a leak." Lewis drove on for a while, the chips of information whirling in his mind. "Does the Pearce Corporation have a good research department?" he asked finally.

"What kind of research?"

"Could they find someone for me?"

"Yes. Easily."

"Are they secure?"

"They have to be."

"All right. Now: is there a car park in your apartment building?"

"Yes."

"We'll leave the Ford there."

Hanna directed him to the entrance. When they had parked she turned to him.

"You'd better give me the gun you're carrying. The security system will pick up a non-resident with a concealed weapon."

Lewis handed her the Colt as they walked to the lift that took them to the entrance lobby. He could see the remote TV cameras and the metal detector devices as they passed through. Once they were in the lift the disembodied voice of Max, the security guard, came from a metal grill: "You carrying a gun, Miss Hanna?"

"Yes, Max," she said, opening her handbag and showing the pistol to the TV camera.

The vigilance made Lewis relax slightly. They took the grand elevator up to Hanna's apartment and Lewis made a quick tour of the whole layout. Vincent and Connie followed him as he explored the floor below, where there were two self-contained suites – Vincent and Connie's quarters – and two storerooms. "Is this the service entrance?" he asked Connie, indicating a door with a chain and a dead-bolt.

"Yeah," she replied. "Everyone comes here we don't want coming through the main entrance."

"Don't let anyone in without my permission," Lewis said firmly.

Vincent and Connie looked at Hanna for confirmation and she nodded. After the tour Lewis and Hanna went back to the main apartment and Lewis sat her down at the telephone.

"See if the Pearce research department can find out who Lord Brockwood is, and get them to cross-check for anyone with the pseudonym 'the Black Dwarf'."

"What are you going to do?" she asked.

"I'm going to play for a while. It stops me thinking." And with that he headed for the white grand piano by the window at the far end of the room.

It was nearly two hours later and Vincent had taught Lewis and Hanna to sing 'East Side, West Side' when Connie appeared with an envelope addressed to Hanna.

> Boys and girls together,
> Me and Molly O'Rourke,
> Trip the light fantastic,
> On the sidewalks of New York.

They harmonised as Connie passed over the message. Without opening it Hanna gave the envelope to Lewis. He got up from the piano and started to read.

The telephone purred and Hanna answered. "It's Curtis — he's on his way up," she said.

They looked expectantly towards the lift doors until they parted with a gentle hiss.

"What's going on? It looks like a leak," Curtis said as he walked across the massive room.

Lewis nodded. "Could it be your end?"

Curtis thought and shook his head. "I don't see how. They didn't know we were here until I called in this morning. And they've never heard of Raeder. It's got to be Gower Street."

Lewis walked slowly to the window, his hands thrust deeply into his pockets. "It certainly looks like it," he said.

"Hell, I've got to get out of here," Curtis said. "Langley will be blowing their top. They really hate getting involved with the cops. I suppose I'll be writing a ten-million-word report for the rest of the night."

"Have you mentioned Brockwood or the Black Dwarf to your people yet?" Lewis asked.

"Not yet."

"Can you leave it out?"

"Are you crazy?"

"It's the only way we'll plug the leak."

Curtis studied him for a moment. "Okay, I suppose it's time America had a new Benedict Arnold. When are we going back to England?"

"We'll catch the early Concorde," Lewis said.

After Curtis left Lewis continued to stare out of the window. Hanna came and stood beside him with her arms folded.

"You killed two men today," she said. "How do you feel?"

Lewis looked at her. "I'm glad to be alive," he answered bleakly.

"But you said you were a soldier. That wasn't warfare today. You fought like criminals."

Lewis folded his arms and leaned against the window. He was silent for a while, then he started to talk in a quiet voice. "I told you that the last four generations of my family served in the same regiment. Oddly enough it was originally called the Royal American. It has a glorious past, but my wars won't appear on its battle honours. Where soldiers like Lowell and I fight there are no medals to be won.

"But I still believe it's worthwhile. I still believe we are the good side. I know we live in an imperfect society, but a lot of people keep trying to improve things. There are still barbarians in the world, Hanna, ready to kill, mutilate and maim for a variety of crazy causes. Someone has got to hold the line against them. It's still a war although there is no Field of Gold anymore. Gunpowder blew away chivalry. The machinegun ended the cavalry charge. Nuclear weapons made great armies obsolete. This is the age of secret armies and, I suppose, that's what I am. A secret soldier."

Hanna thought about what he had just said and Lewis could see that she accepted his argument. "Forgive me. I'm used to injury and death but I'm not used to violence." She turned and smiled at him. "You have such sad eyes," she said. "Sometimes you don't look like a soldier at all."

Charlie Mars sat beneath the portrait of one of his wife's ancestors and drank a weak whisky while Jeremy Bellingford kept up an incessant stream of bright small-talk. In one way

107

Charlie was fascinated by Bellingford's attitude towards him, both obsequious and patronising. The prospect of lunch stretched before him like a featureless prairie, bereft of interest or colour. It was Bellingford's faultlessness that irritated him. His precise voice, the perfect cut of his suits, the impeccable knot in his Jermyn Street tie. It was as if someone had produced a do-it-yourself kit for assembling the perfect English gentleman. Charlie began to wish that he would burp or fart or drop an aitch. Moodily he watched a redcoated steward walking towards him across the mosaic marble floor.

The steward leaned towards him. "There is a telephone call for you, sir. Are you in the Club?"

"Who is it?"

"An American gentleman, sir. Mr Bill Holiday. He says he is an old friend from Oxford."

"Bill Holiday? Good heavens!" Charlie exclaimed. "I haven't seen him in years. Don't you remember him, Bellingford? Or was he before your time? He was with us for a sabbatical from UCLA."

Bellingford smiled, eager to please. "Yes, I think I do."

Charlie crossed the great hall and went into one of the telephone booths in the entrance. "Duke Ellington here," he said as he picked up the telephone.

"Charlie – Lewis. I'm glad I caught you. Things are bad."

"How bad?"

"It's turned out to be a very wet job. I think we've sprung a leak at Gower Street."

"When will you be coming back?"

"Tomorrow morning. On Concorde. For God's sake don't speak to anybody. Tell Meredith I need him, Sandy Patch from Lambeth, a large-scale map of Oxfordshire and a magic van. I want a pick up at Heathrow. And a safe house for tomorrow night."

"Use our house," Charlie said without hesitation.

"There are some nasty people involved," Lewis warned.

"That's all right. Sybil could do with the excitement. I await your arrival with interest."

"Who are you lunching with?" asked Lewis.

"That pompous young prick, Bellingford. God, he's appalling."

"Well, if you will mix with people from your old school . . ."

"He was in quite a different house to me," Charlie replied in a hurt voice, and rang off.

Lewis hung up and took Hanna by the arms. "I'm afraid you won't be able to go back to work for a few days," he said.

"Why not?" asked Hanna.

"You're in great danger. The people who tried to kidnap Professor Raeder knew who we were. Now they're certain you are involved. I would prefer it if we didn't leave the apartment until tomorrow morning, when we go to the airport. How about dinner in front of the television?"

"I think we might do better than that," she said with a wry smile.

"If you're in a fixing mood," replied Lewis, "I could do with a change of clothes. Mine are still at the hotel."

Hanna buzzed the telephone. "Connie, bring me in a tape measure. Oh, and we'll be staying in for dinner tonight. Two of us. If it cools down we'll eat on the terrace."

Connie brought in the tape measure and, with Hanna giving directions, Lewis allowed himself to be measured. When Connie had finished Hanna buzzed the telephone again. "Wendy, I want some men's clothes sent up. Enough for two days and a piece of luggage for them." She read out the measurements. "Shoe size?"

"Eight," Lewis said.

"Eight," Hanna repeated. "Good, right away." She studied him. "No, not the Warren Beatty type. More like Al Pacino. Yes, a touch conservative." She hung up. "Why are you smiling?" she said.

"The last time I was measured for a suit was in Hong Kong," Lewis said. "The tailor didn't have quite the same touch."

"I hope you enjoyed it," Hanna said with a slight smile.

Lewis nodded. "I could take to the life of a gigolo."

Hanna shook her head. "Sorry, no vacancies. I was brought up to believe people who do nothing are nothing."

"I could manage a few light duties."

Hanna decided to change the course of the conversation. "I'll have Vincent show you your room. If you feel like working, polish the furniture. Shall we meet at the bar at seven thirty?"

"I look forward to it," replied Lewis with a slight bow.

The suite of rooms Vincent led Lewis to was on the floor below the main apartment. They descended by an open lift that was at the end of a corridor. "That's a bit extravagant for one floor, isn't it?" said Lewis after the very short journey.

"Da boss had it put in for President Roosevelt," replied Vincent.

Lewis looked around the sitting room. It was generously furnished with American antiques: solid, elegant pieces made by eighteenth-century craftsmen.

"Dat was President Grant's desk," Vincent said, pointing at a great black monstrosity which stood in stark contrast to the earlier furniture.

"Thank you, Vincent," Lewis said.

"Anything ya want, just call out."

After Vincent left Lewis explored the suite. There was a bedroom furnished with Edwardian comfort in mind. The bed was huge, with a massively carved headboard. The bathroom was on the grand scale too; a masculine room of marble, brass and mahogany. Lewis examined a shelf stacked with toiletries and took a bottle of Johnson's baby oil and a box of Kleenex tissues back to President Grant's desk where he pulled out the Colt he had retrieved from Hanna.

He stripped the weapon and cleaned it as best as he could. Then he put it to one side and got out the galley proofs of his book. After some time there was a knock on the door and he went to open it. Vincent stood outside, loaded with boxes.

"Here's ya clothes," he announced. Lewis helped him into the room with them. Together they piled up the boxes on the bed.

"Brooks Brothers," said Vincent, in a slightly disparaging voice.

"Don't you approve?" asked Lewis as he unwrapped a box of cotton boxer shorts.

"It's okay for college boys," replied Vincent. "But if ya want real clothes ya gotta go to Savile Row. Da boss us'ta go over once a year to buy his clothes: Gieves and Hawkes. Say, how's da Connaught Hotel these days?"

"It's still there. I haven't been in recently."

"Dat's a great place. We always stayed dere."

Vincent began to unpack the clothes while Lewis ran a bath thick with suds and got in.

Five minutes later Vincent came to the door and held up two suits: one charcoal grey, the other dark blue with a fine stripe. "Which one ya fancy?"

"The grey," Lewis answered.

"White shirt and a paisley tie?"

Lewis nodded his agreement.

"Dat should look okay for college-boy stuff," Vincent said. "I'll see ya at da bar."

Lewis dressed slowly, the unfamiliar textures cool and crisp on his skin. He slipped on the black tassled shoes and set off to the bar with a certain jauntiness in his step. Vincent was there as promised.

"What'll ya have?"

"What do you recommend?"

"I mix a great champagne cocktail."

"That's for me," Lewis said with enthusiasm.

"Da barman at Eden Roc taught me how ta makes dese," said Vincent, as he carefully poured out measures of brandy and Cointreau. "Da boss had a villa at da Cap. Dat's where I met Connie. She was da cook at da place next door. I hadda teach her English, ya know!"

Lewis nodded, savouring the first taste of the drink. "Vincent, you are a man of surprising qualities. This is the finest champagne cocktail I have ever experienced."

"In that case, I'll join you," Hanna said.

Lewis looked round and took a long swallow from his drink. Hanna had taken up her jet-coloured hair and covered it with a delicate cap made of fine gold thread and tiny pearls. She wore slightly more make-up than usual, so that her eyes

111

seemed enormous, the colour of malachite. The cream silk dress matched her complexion and was cut with deceptive simplicity to emphasise the slimness of her body and the fullness of her breasts. She wore gold high-heeled strapless shoes and her tanned legs were bare.

Lewis was glad they were staying in the apartment.

"Have you ever heard of Zuleika Dobson?" he asked when he got his breath back.

"Why?" replied Hanna.

"She was supposed to have caused every single Oxford undergraduate to throw himself in the river for love of her."

"So?"

"So don't go near Oxford."

"How many drinks has he had, Vincent?"

"One," Vincent said evenly.

Hanna raised her glass and took a sip. "Give him another."

Two hours later Lewis and Hanna sat facing one another across a tiny table on the terrace. The air had cooled to a perfect summer evening and was so still the candle between them burned without a flicker. The cocktails and the wine they had drunk with dinner had combined with the time difference between London and New York so that it was hard for either of them to keep awake. It was will power that kept them at the table; that and the pleasure of each other's company.

The next record dropped on to the turntable and the velvet tones of Nat King Cole blended with the starry darkness above them.

"Would you like to dance?" Lewis asked.

Hanna smiled lazily. "Mmm."

Lewis took her hand and they swayed gently together on the terrace above the glittering city.

"I like your hairnet," Lewis said as he looked at the delicate web of gold and pearls that was level with his eyes.

"A girl does her best," Hanna replied and started to hum the tune they danced to. "I wonder who wrote this."

Lewis listened for a moment. "Hoagy Carmichael."

"How do you know? This was one of my grandfather's records."

Lewis could feel the muscles move in the small of her back as they danced; it distracted him for a moment.

"Oh, the man who taught me at Oxford is a jazz fanatic. He's one of the world's greatest authorities on Duke Ellington – and the sixteenth century."

"He sounds a well-rounded man."

"He is. You'll meet him tomorrow. We're going to stay at his house."

Lewis could feel her cheek brushing his. "Wouldn't it be nice if we could just stay here?" she said.

Lewis nodded; wherever he touched her a current of pleasure seemed to pass between them. "And you could give up your job at the hospital."

She stopped swaying to the music. "I couldn't do that," she said simply, then she looked into his eyes. "Neither could you. Give up your work, I mean."

He smiled and shook his head.

And with that the moment passed. The current still flowed between them but it wasn't going to blow any fuses.

"Am I really in that much danger?" she said.

"Yes," Lewis said. "You more than me or Curtis."

"Why?"

"Because it's our stock-in-trade. We're used to it; that's what we're paid for. You earn your corn looking after other people. We're used to looking after ourselves."

"Surely I would be safe enough at the hospital?"

"No, Hanna. You look on a hospital as a place to make people well, a sanctuary. To them it would just be an easy target. You've got to realise these people have crossed a line the rest of the human race still try their hardest to respect. They would murder anyone to get at you."

"What do you intend to do, then?"

"Get you to a safe and secret place. Identify them, isolate them and then destroy them."

"You make it sound simple enough. What about them trying to kill you?"

Lewis smiled again. "At times like that I remember

Frederick the Great's words of encouragement to his troops."

"What did he say?"

"Dogs, would you live for ever?"

But it didn't make Hanna laugh.

The music ended and they returned to the table.

Connie had served them dark, powerful coffees; Lewis drained his cup.

"Tell me about your gypsy blood," he said. "How does it manifest itself?"

"Rages. Passions," Hanna said lazily. "I'm a terrific dancer and occasionally I steal the odd child from its parents, just to keep my hand in."

"How about fortune-telling? Can you read my palm?"

Hanna reached out. "I'll read your coffee grounds. Give me the cup."

Lewis handed it over and she took it with a smile. Then her expression became serious.

"What do you foretell?" Lewis said lightly.

Without speaking Hanna turned the cup around and tilted it so that Lewis could see. The black grounds formed the unmistakable shape of a small man, like a woodcut from an old book of children's fairy tales.

As they looked into the cup a sudden breeze extinguished the candle and Hanna shivered in the sudden gloom.

6

"Had all my master's benefits been conferred like the present,
what a different return would they have produced! But the
indiscriminate profusion that would glut avarice, or supply
prodigality, neither does good, nor is rewarded by gratitude.
It is sowing the wind to reap the whirlwind."

The Black Dwarf
SIR WALTER SCOTT

Accompanied by the thunderous roar of an outward-bound
Tri-star, his nostrils flared to the pungent sharpness of
burning aircraft fuel, the young policeman walked with
slow deliberation towards the man who peered beneath the
bonnet of a Bedford van. There were a set of aluminium
ladders lashed to the roof and the sign 'Bamford and Son,
Decorators' painted on the side.

It was a warm evening, so the policeman was in shirt-
sleeves and conscious of his rather frail frame. He stopped
beside a 'No Waiting' sign and watched the short stocky
figure in white painter's overalls who was savagely poking at
the engine with a large screwdriver.

Taxis and cars flowed around the van as people left the
international terminal at Heathrow.

"What's up?" the policeman asked the sweating figure,
whose head was under the bonnet.

"Tha poxy thing's busted, that's what's the matter," the
man said in an angry Glaswegian accent, as he looked up
from the engine and scratched his thinning ginger hair with
oil-stained fingers.

"Well, you can't wait here," the policeman said, a trifle
apprehensively, as he had not been prepared for the mechanic's
aggressive tone.

"Do you think I wanna be here?" the man said. "Ma tea's in the oven an' here I am at this scum-hole waitin' ta pick up tha boss's missus. She can go off screwin' in Florida while we hafta drive this heap a crap around." He banged his fist down on the side of the cowling to emphasise his point then, gripping his screwdriver like a dagger, he turned and fixed the young policeman with a stare. "Do you know why she went to Florida?"

The policeman took half a step back. "No," he said weakly.

"Because she'd had everyone in Hounslow under the age of sixty-five! See him?" He indicated the passenger in the van, who was also wearing white overalls and who was busily engaged in rolling a cigarette. The policeman looked and nodded.

"She's even had him, and he canna count beyond his third finger."

As if to confirm this judgement the passenger gave a thumbs-up sign and grinned half-wittedly at them.

"What do you think is wrong with it?" the policeman said, returning his attention to the engine.

"It's broken down, friend," the man said in a soft tone one would use to a young child.

"Well, if you don't fix it soon I'll have to have it towed away," said the officer of the law and walked off before the man with the screwdriver took any more liberties with his dignity.

"Come on, Lewis, *come on*," Gordon Meredith intoned from his seat in the van, and as he muttered the incantation he saw Lewis, Hanna and Curtis come out of the exit a few yards from where they were parked. He hit the horn twice, at which Sandy Patch slammed down the bonnet and swiftly returned to the driver's seat.

The next moment the engine roared into life and as it did so Meredith threw the switch on the radio-signal detonator he held on his lap.

There were three bangs that sounded like large fireworks exploding around the exit from which Lewis and the others had hurried and thick white smoke began to pour from a

116

duty-free plastic bag left by one of the doorways, a cheap suitcase in a baggage trolley and from a litter-bin. In seconds the entire area was engulfed by a dense white cloud.

Hanna and Curtis, with Lewis bringing up the rear, had meanwhile scrambled into the back of the van. Sandy edged forward a few feet to where the smoke was thin and roared away. As soon as they were through the lights and into the tunnel that led from the airport Lewis called out, "Have we picked up anything?"

Meredith, who was checking the mirrors, said tersely, "Dark green Capri."

"Are you sure?" asked Lewis peering through the rear window.

"Positive," Meredith replied. "They were three behind us outside the terminal. The police were trying to move them on as well. He must be a good driver."

Once clear of the tunnel Sandy accelerated into the round-about and made for the motorway.

"Head east, towards London," Lewis called out.

Sandy held up a hand in acknowledgement. "There's a lot of traffic around at this time of night. He's going to have to stick close."

Once on the motorway he pushed the van up to seventy and switched to the fast lane. The Capri kept with them. Sandy switched to the centre lane and still it stuck to their tail.

"How soon do you want me to lose 'em?" Sandy called back.

"The sooner the better."

Sandy waved again and took the van up to eighty. Signs appeared for the Hillingdon slipway and he shouted, "Brace yourselves!" He weaved through the traffic on to the slipway and braked violently, so that the Capri almost ran into the back of them. Lewis could see the faces in the front of the following car clearly. Both were young, fair and wearing sunglasses. They seemed to be enjoying the chase. Immediately Sandy changed down and gunned the supercharged engine, easing his foot from the clutch so that the van shot forward. As he did so, he reached up and pulled a release toggle that dangled above his head. As the Capri jumped after them the ladders on the roof of the van slid back and crashed into the windscreen of the pursuing vehicle.

Lewis saw the expressions on its occupants' faces turn from eagerness to panic in the moments before the windscreen crazed into a million tiny cracks with the initial impact and the ladders punched a jagged hole in the glass.

Sandy crossed the slipway and came back on to the motorway. A Volvo hurtled past them blowing its horn in righteous anger. Sandy settled down to a steady sixty-five, a contented smile on his face.

"Come off at Brentford," Lewis said. "Then head north through Ealing until we get to the A40, and the road to Oxford."

Fifty minutes later they were passing the Uxbridge roundabout heading west. Now Lewis was driving, with Hanna in the seat beside him. Gordon and Sandy had stripped off their overalls in a side-street in Brentford. They had also removed from the side of the van the contact paper with the builder's name on it, to reveal a new panel with the legend 'Harris Brothers – Family Butchers' in Old English lettering.

"Where are we going?" Curtis asked from his cramped seat in the back.

"I thought I'd take you all for a drink in a typical English pub," replied Lewis cheerfully.

When they reached the Oxford ring road Lewis headed towards Godston, and the surrounding suburbs gradually became more rural. They turned off the main road into a narrow lane. Eventually they reached a small bridge and pulled into a car park. He stopped beneath some trees and they all got out and stretched. "This way," Lewis said and led them across the road into the garden of a stone-built public house. There was a rustic bridge over the babbling stream and trees that fringed the bank: Hanna and Curtis were immediately enchanted.

"Welcome to The Trout," Lewis said proprietorially. "What will you have?"

"Beer," Curtis said enthusiastically. "Some real English beer."

"A small one for me," Hanna added as they sat down at one of the logs that served as tables by the stream.

Lewis returned with a loaded tray and handed out the drinks.

"Real English ale," Curtis said contentedly, holding up his pint with a smile of approval like a squire in a sporting print. He took a long pull and his expression changed. "Jesus Christ!" he exclaimed. "Is there something wrong with this stuff?"

"Mine's fine," Sandy said. Lewis nodded his agreement.

"No wonder my ancestors emigrated," Curtis said with some feeling. "If you sold this in a bar in the States they'd report you to the Health and Sanitation Department. Now I know where you get your stiff upper lips from." He went to the bar and bought a gin.

There was some change on the tray and Sandy started to show Curtis and Meredith a complicated game involving the movement of coins. Lewis and Hanna took their drinks and strolled along the embankment. When they got to the bridge they walked to the middle and leaned against the rough handrail.

They stood for a while looking down into the clear stream until Hanna said, "What was her name?"

Lewis raised his eyes from the rushing water and smiled ruefully.

"Susan – how did you know I was thinking of her?"

Hanna reached up and pulled some leaves from a tree branch. "Oh, elementary deduction. You were an undergraduate at Oxford. You must have had a girlfriend. It's a potent time in anyone's life. You probably brought her here. It's a very romantic spot. Then, when you come here years later with another woman, she's bound to cross your mind."

"That's very good."

"Don't forget that Sherlock Holmes's creator was a doctor."

"Go on, tell me more."

Hanna dropped the leaves into the stream, and they watched them whirl away. "It was a hot summer evening like this. You rode here on bicycles. She looked like one of those girls who wait for fighter pilots in old British movies. When you

119

realised how you felt about one another you stopped on the way back to Oxford and made love in a meadow full of buttercups."

"That's pretty clever; now tell me about your first love," Lewis said.

Hanna threw some more leaves in the stream. "He was at medical school with me. I thought he wanted to be a great doctor but medicine was just a way of getting enough money to buy all the condominiums in Florida." She looked at him again. "Was I right about you?"

"You were right about the way she looked. Wrong about everything else. We came here in her sports car. It was February and snowing. It didn't happen in a field of buttercups, but in front of a gas fire in a house in North Oxford and I kicked over her cup of cocoa. Anything else you'd like to know?"

Hanna looked into his face with a grave expression. "What's cocoa?"

"It's a British beverage used to inflame sexual passion. I think Americans have something similar only they call it drinking chocolate."

Hanna took the empty glass from his hand and placed it alongside hers at their feet. "Do you realise we can't be seen from here?" she said.

Lewis glanced around and saw that the low foliage from the trees gave them their privacy.

Hanna stepped into his arms and they kissed for a long time. It was a tender romantic kiss, she thought, the kind that stayed in the memory when other urgent, more passionate encounters had been forgotten. Hanna would have liked to press it into an old book along with a flower to dry and keep for ever.

When they had stopped Lewis held her for a moment and she whispered, "What are you thinking of now?"

"I was wishing we had the time to look for a meadow full of buttercups," he said.

"But duty calls."

"And another pint of bitter." They walked slowly back to the others.

Meredith appeared to be lounging about near the car park as he kept watch for any intruders. Sandy and Curtis sat around one of the tables and continued their game with the coins, despite the fading light.

"This sergeant of yours has taken me for about three dollars," Curtis complained as they sat down.

"I'll spend it on another round of drinks," Sandy said generously.

And they sat quietly chatting until dusk fell.

At last Lewis drained the last drops from his glass and got up. "Okay; we'd better make a move for Charlie's house now."

They made their way back to the van and Lewis drove them through the country roads until it was dark. The head-lights made a tunnel of light as they passed along the high-banked lanes. Finally he turned into a driveway that wound through a wooded thicket. Occasionally they would catch glimpses of a house. The driveway led into a gravel-covered forecourt. The lights from the downstairs windows and from the headlights of the van revealed a Georgian building with a pillared entrance. The front was heavily clad with wistaria so that only small portions of the rose-coloured brick could be seen. Great trees rose behind the house, silhouetting it against the night sky. Laurels flanked the sides. Lewis cut the engine of the van and dogs could be heard barking in the still countryside.

As the five of them crunched their way across the gravel the door opened and the tall slim figure of a woman with a cardigan draped across her shoulders stood in the doorway.

"Hello, Sybil," Lewis said stepping into the pool of light from the hallway.

"Lewis?" she called into the darkness. "Hello, my dear." She leaned forward to be kissed. "Charlie told me you were coming. How lovely to see you."

A golden retriever with a grizzled muzzle waddled up to Lewis and rubbed itself against his leg, while a much younger red setter leaped playfully close by. Once inside the hallway Lewis made the introductions while the dogs circled, sniffing the strangers, until Sybil ordered them away.

Lewis watched Hanna as she glanced around. He knew she liked what she saw. No interior decorator could achieve the effect brought about by generations with similar taste. Persian rugs lay on the dark polished wood of the floor. From their places on the walls the faces of Charles Austen Mars's ancestors gazed down with haughty disinterest. Hanna ran her hand over the silk-like surface of a table on which the Mars family had kept their letters for the past one hundred and eighty years. The grandfather clock and the barometer that flanked the table were of the same period. Antique dealers would have swapped their children for them.

"Let me show you to your room, Dr Pearce," Sybil said. "I'm afraid the servants are away today. Lewis, will you give the gentlemen a drink in the living room? We shan't be long."

Sybil took Hanna up the stairs while Lewis ushered the others into a large squarish room, where a white marble Adam fireplace was flanked with bookcases.

Like the house, the furniture in the room had long lost the bloom of youth but would still look good for a couple of hundred years yet. Lewis dispensed drinks from a table near the open window. The scent of honeysuckle hung heavy in the air. The room was filled with the sound of Vivaldi coming from a concealed hi-fi system. It was not long before Sybil reappeared.

"Does everyone have a drink?" she asked as she entered. "In that case I'll have a gin and tonic, Lewis, darling."

She sat down on a large sofa near the fireplace, the dogs collapsing at her feet. Lewis brought over her drink and noted, as he had a thousand times before, how exactly she looked what she was: a very beautiful member of the English upper-class. In the soft light of the room it was hard to believe that she had two daughters who shared a flat in Knightsbridge from whence they sallied forth to crack hearts like peanut shells. Both of them had been in love with Lewis when he was an undergraduate but they had been nine and ten years old in those days. Above the mantelpiece there was a huge portrait of them sitting each side of Sybil, with the dogs lying at their feet. It had been exhibited two years before at the Royal Academy Summer Exhibition.

"The painting looks well. This is the first time I've seen it in this room."

"Good gracious! Has it been that long since you were here? You have been neglecting us," Sybil said warmly.

As she spoke there was the sound of a car in the drive and the dogs moved towards the hallway when a door slammed. After a few moments Lewis could hear the voice of Charlie Mars greeting them in the hall. "Hello, hello," he said as he entered the room.

"Now, I know everyone except Mr Patch." He shook hands with Sandy. "Has everybody got a drink?" he asked after he had kissed Sybil.

"We're fine, Charlie. In fact, we've had a skinful," Lewis replied, and then reflected briefly on the pleasures of the afternoon. It seemed incredible that they could be in danger here in these charming surroundings. Then he relaxed. They had been as careful as possible: for the time being they were safe and he decided to enjoy it.

"In that case I've got some catching up to do. I think I'll have rather a large one. Oh, hello, Dr Pearce." Hanna had entered the room. "Can I get you a drink?"

Hanna declined. Sybil got up. "I'm going to the kitchen. Mrs Patterson left us supper in the oven – I'll see how it's coming along. It's only shepherd's pie, I'm afraid. Is that all right for everyone?"

Everyone agreed that it was, Meredith with particular enthusiasm. "Can I give you a hand, Mrs Mars?" he ventured.

"Yes, you can, Gordon. Come along."

"What the hell is shepherd's pie?" Curtis muttered to Lewis at the far side of the room.

"Ground-beef casserole under a layer of mashed potatoes," Lewis answered after a moment's hesitation.

"Why then is Meredith so pleased? I imagined it was something Escoffier concocted, the way he cheered up."

Lewis smiled. "The English upper-class send their children to boarding schools where they are systematically starved, so they spend the rest of their lives craving for working-class food."

Curtis shook his head. "This entire country is like something out of Disneyland. You pride yourselves on being the oldest democracy in the world and do everything in the name of the Queen. You say you don't have an Empire anymore but the cleaners at London Airport look like extras from Gunga Din."

Sybil popped her head around the door. "Oh, Charlie, Dad telephoned. He said there was some talk going around the House of Lords about a political murder in New York. Something to do with the peace talks. He asked if there was anything in it?"

Sybil's head disappeared and Charlie slumped down on the sofa next to Hanna. "These bloody politicians. Their idea of a secret is to tell only the people they went to school with."

Meredith returned with the news that the shepherd's pie was ready and they all trooped into the stone-flagged kitchen. Charlie produced some bottles from the cellar and poured the drinks.

Curtis took a mouthful of the wine and held the glass at eye-level. "This is fine Burgundy," he said with pleasure.

"Yes," Charlie replied. "I made a good buy that year, but I'm told that it won't last much longer, so you had better drink up."

Curtis shook his head. "Disneyland," he repeated.

They made quick work of the pie and after cheese and fruit Lewis gave Charlie a brief résumé of the events in New York. Then they cleared a space on the table and spread out the map of Oxford that Meredith had brought from the van.

"So where is Lord Brockwood now?" Charlie asked.

Lewis scanned the map for a few moments. "Here," he said, putting his finger on a spot on the map.

Charlie bent closer to the point Lewis had indicated. "Upper Farm," he said. "Do you know if he's actually there?"

"We can easily find out," Lewis replied. "Let Hanna telephone now and if he's in she can ask him if we can come and see him in the morning."

"All right, let's give it a try," Charlie answered.

Lewis took out the sheet of flimsy paper he had been given in New York and walked to the telephone extension on the wall of the kitchen. He dialled a number and held the receiver out to Hanna. She took it and listened to the ringing tone. Eventually a woman answered.

"Good evening," Hanna said. "My name is Dr Pearce. May I speak to Lord Brockwood, please?"

There was a short reply, then a pause until a second voice said, "Brockwood here."

"My name is Dr Pearce. I'm sorry to bother you so late in the evening, but I have a personal message for you from a Professor Carl Raeder. Can I come and see you with a colleague in the morning?"

"Perhaps you could give me more of an idea of what this is all about, Doctor?"

"I would rather not discuss it on the telephone."

"It has been a long time since I last saw Carl Raeder: I understood that he was dead," Lord Brockwood said. "Are you positive it was him?"

"Quite sure."

There was a long pause.

"Very well, I'll expect you in the morning."

"What time would be convenient?"

"As early as you like."

"Shall we say . . ." Lewis mouthed nine o'clock. "Nine o'clock? Thank you, sir. Until the morning."

Hanna hung up and turned to the others. "He sounded very reluctant," she said.

Charlie sat back in the chair, drank a little more wine and dabbled with his fingertips in the crumbs of Stilton on the plate before him. "How much do we know about Brockwood?" he said.

Lewis shrugged. "Not much: just that he's a retired academic who used to teach at Oxford. I can't say that I've ever heard of him. He inherited the title in 1948."

"Well, this sheds no light on the problem at all," said Charlie Mars. "We can only await the outcome of your conversation in the morning. There is one thing I can do, though." He went to the telephone and dialled. "Hello," he

said, "I'd like to talk to Lord Pickford. Yes, I'll wait . . ."
There was a pause. "Hello, Fred, Charlie here. Sybil said
you rang . . . No, nothing to do with the peace talks . . . Put
it around with your lot that it's a load of nonsense, will
you? . . . Yes, see you soon. Goodbye." He sat down again at
the table where Lewis was still studying the map.

"Sandy, Gordon," Lewis said at last, "go and check out
Upper Farm. You stay there, Gordon, and keep a radio with
you. Sandy, take a good look and then come back here."

"Shall we take the van?" Gordon asked.

"No. Charlie, can they use your car?"

"Certainly," Charlie said and passed the keys to Sandy.

The two men got up and said their thanks to Sybil. Lewis
walked with them to Charlie's Jaguar. He looked up at the
sky. It was clear, with an almost full moon. Gordon went to
the van and returned with a bundle of equipment.

"Stay sharp," Lewis said. "See you in the morning."

Gordon handed Lewis a radio set, threw a bundle of equipment into the back of the Jaguar and himself in the front, then
waved his farewell. Lewis watched the car leave the forecourt
before walking slowly back to the house. He found the
others had returned to the living room where Charlie was
plying them with port and brandy. Lewis accepted a glass of
brandy and sat down on the sofa between Hanna and Curtis.

"Well, if we're making an early start I guess I'd better get a
good night's sleep," Hanna said.

Curtis and Charlie exchanged glances.

"I don't think it would be a good idea for you to come
with us in the morning, Hanna," Lewis said.

"Don't be ridiculous," Hanna said. "You can't cut me out
now." She looked at each man in turn and her voice changed.
"You're going to do something dangerous, aren't you?" she
said with sudden conviction.

There was an awkward silence until Charlie said, "Explain
to her, Lewis. She has a right to know."

Lewis lifted his brandy glass from a side table: "Tomorrow
Charlie will inform the usual channels that we have made
contact with Brockwood. If they come for us we'll know for
certain the leak is at Gower Street."

"So you're going to set a trap, with yourselves as bait?"

They all sat still: frozen with embarrassment at the bluntness of the remark.

"Don't worry, Hanna. We all taste lousy," Lewis said gently.

"You think that's funny? I don't understand you. How can you do this? Don't you have people you can pay to undertake this kind of thing?"

"We are those people, Hanna," said Curtis.

Hanna looked at them, trying to comprehend. She could only hold out her hands. "I know. It's just that you all seem so ordinary. Normal. I just can't adjust to the idea that you are prepared to go through the same thing again."

"Remember the score," Lewis said. "At the moment it's four-nothing."

Hanna stood up and they could see she was angry. "Suppose they send an army against you. They could even the score in a flash. What will they put on your tombstone, Captain Horne? 'He was ahead at half-time?'" She walked to the door and turned. "Goodnight. If I never see you again I'll remember you in my nightmares. Forgive my lack of manners. It's just that my profession takes a dim view of suicide."

Each of them gazed at their drink.

"That young woman has a vivid turn of phrase," Charlie said, finally breaking the silence Hanna had bequeathed to the room.

Sybil rose as well. She took Lewis's hands in hers. "Be very careful tomorrow, Lewis. We don't have many friends."

She turned to Curtis. "And that goes for you as well, Mr Lowell. Now I think I'll go up." She looked at her husband. "What time are you leaving for town in the morning, darling?"

"About eight, if the car gets back in one piece."

"Don't forget we're having dinner with Dad tomorrow night. Mrs Patterson can look after Dr Pearce. I'll be at your office by six."

"All right, Syb. I think I'll hang on with these fellows until Mr Patch gets back."

The dogs tried to leave the room with her but she ordered them back. They reluctantly joined Charlie as he poured another glass of port.

When Sandy got back from Upper Farm the night was almost gone. He found Charlie and Curtis playing gin rummy. Lewis was reading one of Charlie's books and Vivaldi had been replaced by the sound of Billie Holiday singing softly to the band of Benny Goodman. As Charlie poured him a brandy Sandy spread the map before them once again.

"It's good," said Sandy, as he traced the area round Upper Farm with his finger. "There's pasture behind the house, about four square acres. Flat, almost no cover. The house itself looks down a steep incline to this stream. It's ten or twelve feet wide but quite deep. There's a bridge to the house. The stream feeds a trout farm and watercress beds to the right here. On the left there is a dense wood, a couple of hundred yards deep, thick with undergrowth: Tinkerbell couldn't get through it without making a noise. The road stops here." He pointed beyond the wood. "There's an unmade pathway from the road to the area in front of the bridge."

"Why is it good?" queried Charlie.

"Difficult to attack by surprise. Easy to defend," Lewis replied.

"Where's Meredith?" Charlie asked.

Lewis pointed to a spot on the map.

As if he could feel the weight of a giant finger pressing down on him, Meredith hunched his shoulders and raised the night-glasses to his eyes. His hiding-place was at the edge of the wood, at the brow of the hill, level with Upper Farm. From his vantage point he could sweep the ground behind the farmhouse and the frontal approaches.

He was dressed in blue-black overalls, his hands and face smeared with camouflage cream. He was practically invisible. Anyone who tried to come at him from behind ought to make a noise like an electric coffee grinder as they passed through the undergrowth of the wood. Suddenly Meredith heard a slight rustling very near to him. Slowly he lowered his glasses and curled his hand around the grip of the Browning automatic.

He thought he had been completely silent, but he must have made some slight noise. He carefully raised his pistol. The fox that stood on the edge of the wood, a few feet from him, turned and gazed into his eyes.

7

"Air, ocean, and fire," said the Dwarf, speaking to himself, "the earthquake, the tempest, the volcano, are all mild and moderate, compared to the wrath of man. And what is this fellow, but one more skilled than others in executing the end of his existence?"

The Black Dwarf
SIR WALTER SCOTT

At seven o'clock the following morning Lewis stood, fully dressed, and looked down through his bedroom window on to the garden behind the house. Practically every part of it held a happy memory for him. In the deep shadow made by the morning sun he could just see the swing on the horse chestnut tree. He remembered when he had pushed Charlie and Sybil's girls as they squealed to go higher. Light splashed on to the tennis court and he smiled when he thought how Sybil had taught him the game. He moved his gaze to the spot near the kitchen garden where they had built bonfires for November 5th and then on to the place in front of the sundial where snowmen had stood, next to the shaded part of the lawn where they had eaten teas after savage encounters over croquet.

When he had first been invited there as an undergraduate it had seemed like a foreign country after a childhood spent in grim garrison towns.

As he watched, he saw Sybil and Hanna, accompanied by the dogs, strolling down the path towards the paddock where two hunters waited patiently for their early-morning snack. He turned and left to go downstairs. In the corridor he met Curtis who nodded good morning. Sandy was already in the kitchen tackling a formidable breakfast. "Mrs Mars does a great fry-up, boss," he said as he cut into another sausage.

Lewis poured himself a cup of coffee from the pot in front of Sandy, and pinched a piece of the toast before him.

When Charlie arrived he was dressed for London but was still wearing carpet slippers. He sat down at the head of the table after a gruff "good morning" and looked over his copy of *The Times* at the remainder of the gargantuan meal Sandy Patch had consumed.

"I see the British soldier has not lost his skill for living off the land," he said drily before he buried himself in the leader page.

Sybil came into the kitchen without Hanna. "Would anyone else like some breakfast?" she asked.

Lewis and Curtis refused: Charlie said he would settle for a boiled egg.

"We'd better be off in a minute," Lewis said. The other two nodded.

"Hanna's down at the paddock with the horses, Lewis, if you want to say goodbye," Sybil said in a matter-of-fact voice, putting the saucepan on the hob.

Charlie looked at her but made no comment.

"Fine," Lewis said. "I'd like to speak to her. I'll see you two at the van."

Curtis raised a hand and Sandy muttered, "Okay, boss," through a mouthful of marmalade and toast.

Lewis left by the kitchen door that led into a conservatory heavy with grapevines and then out into the garden. The morning air was fresh and cool with all the promise of a fine summer's day. He followed the same path he had watched Sybil and Hanna take and passed beyond the tennis court to where Hanna was standing, by the three-bar gate to the paddock. She was holding a carrot out to the bay mare. As Lewis approached the horse snorted and shied away. "Hello," he said as he leaned on the gate next to her.

"Hello, Lewis," Hanna replied, "I asked Sybil to tell you I was here."

He turned and rested his back against the fence. "Well, I'm very glad you did. I wanted to see you before we left."

"I owe you an apology for what I said last night," she said in a formal voice.

Lewis looked towards the house. "That's all right. There's really nothing to apologise for."

"There is," she said. "I couldn't bear the thought of you dead – like the men in that house. I'm sorry."

Lewis reached out to touch her but knew that if he did he would not be able to let her go. "No man could ask for more than what you have just said, Hanna, believe me," he said, desperately wishing that he could think of something to say that didn't sound stilted, clichéd or silly.

She nodded but wouldn't turn to face him. Instead she looked towards the horses. "There are buttercups in the meadow," she said softly. "Take care of yourself, Lewis."

Just before the stone bridge at Upper Farm the dirt and gravel road widened out in front of a building made of Cotswold stone. It had once been a stable and ivy grew on the walls and flowers on either side. There were no doors, so that Lewis could see a Land-Rover and a Morris Minor parked inside. It was the prettiest garage he had ever seen. In fact, the whole of Upper Farm was idyllically beautiful. From the opposite side of the rush-fringed stream a steep lawn rose to a garden that was a riot of colour. Yellow roses climbed up the outside wall of the stone farmhouse. To the right, where the land fell away to the watercress beds, fruit trees grew on the slopes.

"It looks the sort of place where Rupert Bear would spend a holiday," Lewis said softly as they stood gazing up towards the house. But they did not see it as a piece of countryside. Instead they looked upon it as a battlefield. As their eyes swept the landscape they sought areas of cover and fields of fire, safe places and killing ground. When they had committed the detail to memory Lewis walked back behind the barn where he couldn't be seen from the house and switched on the radio he was carrying.

"Gordon, do you receive me?" he said.

Through a crackle of static came the reply. "I receive you."

"Any sign of life?"

"They've been up and about since seven o'clock. I've only seen two people, a man and a woman."

"Okay, stay there until I call you in."

"Right."

Lewis handed the radio to Sandy and walked across the hump-backed bridge. He started to climb the steep stone pathway towards the house. When he was halfway up the hill the front door opened and a man wearing an open-necked shirt with the ends of his trousers tucked into Wellington boots stood gazing down at him. Although the figure looked youthful Lewis could see that his shock of hair was iron-grey. When Lewis reached the top of the path he spoke. "Lord Brockwood?"

"Yes," the man said.

"My name is Lewis Horne. I'm afraid Dr Pearce couldn't make the appointment. I've come in her place."

Brockwood studied him for a moment. "You must be pretty fit, Mr Horne. Most people are puffed by the time they get up here."

Lewis looked into the open doorway behind Lord Brockwood: despite the dark shadow he could see the figure of a woman. She was holding a shotgun in a competent fashion.

"That's my wife," Brockwood said in an easy tone. "She's a farmer's daughter and a much better shot than me."

"I can assure you, sir, we mean you no harm," Lewis said.

Brockwood nodded. "I'm glad to hear it, but I'm sure you can understand our precautions. Last night I received a mysterious telephone call from a woman I do not know and today three strangers appear at my door."

Lewis could see Brockwood looking over his shoulder down the hill towards Curtis and Sandy. He waved towards them. "Is it all right if my companions join us?"

"As you wish," the older man said in a pleasant non-committal voice.

Lewis motioned to Sandy and Curtis and they started up the hill. When they reached the top Brockwood raised his eyebrows quizzically. "*Three* fit men. An unusual coincidence. Are you all members of the same sports club?"

"More or less, sir," Curtis replied.

Brockwood noticed his American accent. "An international sports club. Are there any more of you lurking about?"

Lewis coughed. "As a matter of fact, there are." He made a hand signal in Gordon's direction and Gordon broke from cover and started to walk towards them. Within a couple of minutes he had joined them looking rather sheepish.

"How long have you been there, young man?" Brockwood asked in a sharp voice.

Gordon looked at Lewis who nodded for him to answer. "All night, sir."

"You have been spying on my house *all night*?" Brockwood's voice was edged with anger.

"Guarding your house, sir, not spying on it," Lewis said.

Brockwood looked at them in turn. "You had better come in," he said and led them into a hall cluttered with walking sticks and Wellington boots. "Through here." He indicated a passage that led into the farm's kitchen.

It was a large room, with a big open-range fireplace. There was a heavily laden Welsh dresser and a long scrubbed pine table with several wooden chairs. The floor was of polished stone. Children's paintings were pinned to one of the walls bearing the inscriptions, 'For Grandpa and Grandma'.

At one end of the long room the woman stood, still cradling the twelve-bore shotgun. Her hair was almost the same iron-grey shade as Brockwood's and she held herself with the poise of an athlete. Lewis thought of the climb to the house. "Now can you tell me one good reason why I shouldn't call the police?" Brockwood said.

"We have come to see you in connection with Professor Carl Raeder and the Black Dwarf, sir. Please hear us out," Lewis replied.

Brockwood thought for a moment, then gestured to his wife to lower the shotgun.

"My dear, this young man has been sitting in the wood all night. Perhaps he wants to wash his face," he said, waving at Meredith.

"Have you really been up all night?" said his wife as she

walked over to the sink and produced a towel and a bar of soap.

Meredith nodded.

"I expect you would like a cup of tea, then," she said, not at all put out by his curious appearance.

Lewis noticed the beautiful scale model of a Victorian town house that was under construction on the table. Brockwood followed his glance. "A certain amount of role-reversal goes on in this household," he said, picking up a pipe from the collection of tools on the table. "Now: what is this all about?"

Lewis took a deep breath and began. "What I am about to say may seem melodramatic, Lord Brockwood, but I can assure you it is quite true. We believe that you and your wife are in grave danger."

Brockwood began to rake out his pipe with a small screw-driver and without looking up said, "Not from you people, I hope?"

"No, sir," Lewis said with some emphasis.

"But your presence is a contributing factor?"

Lewis hesitated. "I'm afraid that's true."

Brockwood took out a tobacco pouch and began to pack the bowl. "Go on," he said. "You still have my attention."

Lewis watched Gordon as he stripped off his overalls, revealing civilian shirt and trousers. He realised how extraordinary what he was about to say would sound in these surroundings, but there was no way of blunting the message. "We work for the British Government. That is, with the exception of Mr Lowell, who is an American, but our Governments are co-operating in this – "

"Escapade?" Brockwood said, smiling for the first time.

"I think you'll see it's rather more than that, sir. We have reason to believe the proposed summit talks between the Soviet Union and the West could be endangered by certain revelations. We also believe you have some knowledge that could help us to stop those revelations taking place."

"Go on," Brockwood said, holding a match to his pipe.

"The day before yesterday, Professor Carl Raeder was murdered in New York. Before he died, he told us that you knew about Operation Hermann and the identity of the Black Dwarf. It is possible his killers know you are connected with him. If so, you could be in terrible danger."

Brockwood picked up a piece from the doll's house. It was a tiny chaise-longue, which he gazed at for a moment before putting it down with great care. "I'm sorry, Mr Horne, I haven't seen Carl Raeder since 1938. I know nothing of an Operation Hermann or any Black Dwarf. Are you sure I'm the man you want?"

"Yes, sir," Lewis said quietly. "Quite sure." He looked across at Curtis, who shrugged.

Brockwood got up and stood behind his wife, his right hand resting on her shoulder. "You said Carl Raeder told you about this operation. You were actually with him just before he died?"

"Yes, sir. Mr Lowell and I were there. Two men tried to kidnap Professor Raeder. There was a gun battle and the men were killed. Professor Raeder died of a gunshot wound." Lewis could see the hand tighten its grip on Lady Brockwood's shoulder. Instinctively she reached up and covered his hand. "Even if you can't tell us anything I must repeat that you are in danger. I urge you to take your wife away somewhere safe."

There was a silence, broken by the snap of the flap opening in the door that led outside. A marmalade-coloured cat stalked into the room, crossed the kitchen and leaped on to the Welsh dresser, to curl up with its back turned on the company.

"Is there anyone I can ring to check your credentials, Mr Horne?" Brockwood said.

Lewis slowly shook his head. "I'm afraid not."

"But you still insist that we are in danger if we stay here?"

"Very grave danger, sir."

Brockwood looked down at his wife. "I think it might be for the best if you went into Oxford and stayed with the boys, dear," he said gently.

"Won't you be coming with me?" she asked, her voice edged with anxiety.

"I'll drive you in but then I'll come back. Come on," he said, "I'll give you a hand to pack. Excuse us, gentlemen." Together they left the room.

The cat uncurled itself and looked at the four dejected figures who sat in various poses around the long table. Tired of their depressing presence, it stood up and made its exit through the flap.

"So where do we go from here?" Curtis asked.

Lewis threw his head back and stared at the ceiling. "If he rings anyone he blows our cover. If he can't verify us he's not going to talk. I think this is a case of being hoist by one's own petard." He got up and began to stroll aimlessly around the room, his hands thrust deep into his pockets. He studied the children's paintings on the wall for a moment, then rapped his knuckles on the Welsh dresser. His eyes fell on an open copy of the *Radio Times* and he scanned the programmes without any real interest. It is a well-known phenomenon that the eye will pick a familiar name out of a page of print: it happened to Lewis just then. He turned as Brockwood came down the stairs with his wife. "Can I drive you into Oxford, sir? I think we could speak to someone there who could help you to make up your mind."

The Provost stood in his garden, staring at the great stone head that lay resting against a wall surrounded by clumps of daisies. The features that stared back were worn and blunted by time. Lichen grew over the pitted cheeks. Once it had represented the head of a Roman emperor but now it could have been the pagan god of a south-seas tribe.

It's the material, he thought. Always the material. Carve in marble or cast in bronze and the image will stay sharp for ever. But if the stone is soft the work won't last. A bit like undergraduates, he mused as he continued his walk. He loved the garden and tried to spend a couple of minutes walking there each day whenever he was at Oxford.

"Darling . . . visitors!" his wife called from the downstairs window of their house.

How does she manage to shout in a soft voice? he wondered as he walked back towards the house. "Who is it?" he asked as he joined his wife in the reception room, where she sat at a large table.

"I don't know, dear. The maid said they wanted to see you on important business. I'm up to my eyes in these invitations." She held up a handful of envelopes. "I really don't have a moment."

"Very well," he said. "I do hope they aren't going to be tiresome."

As he was about to leave he looked down at the table where his wife was working and saw the *Radio Times* folded open at the same page that Lewis had scanned in the Brockwoods' kitchen. He read the notes on the programme he had recorded the day before.

"Is that young man as grisly as he seems to be?" his wife said as she started slipping the invitations into envelopes.

"I'm afraid he is," the Provost said. "Show business has removed all the rough edges that Oxford gave him." He walked to the door and stopped. "Do you know he actually asked me what I thought about something 'history-wise'?" he said with gentle amazement.

"Well, that's what you are, darling," his wife replied as she continued to work on the envelopes.

"Am I? Yes, I suppose so," the Provost said vaguely as he entered the hallway. He blinked in the contrasting darkness and gradually his eyesight adjusted to the gloom. Both the figures before him were familiar but he could not make a connection between them. "My dear Brockwood," he said as he approached them along the hallway. "And Lewis. Did you come together?" He shook them both warmly by the hand and ushered them into his study. "Now, to what do I owe the honour?" he enquired as he sat behind a desk piled high with books.

Lewis was surprised that his new host should have known Brockwood but on reflection it was typical of the man. He seemed to know everyone important. If anyone could be said to know what was happening in Britain it was him. An envious colleague had once said that he didn't just have his finger on the pulse of the country: if he felt inclined he could grasp it by the throat. "How are you enjoying retirement, Brocky?" he now said, smiling broadly.

"Enjoying myself more than I could ever have imagined," Brockwood replied.

"And you, Lewis? How are you and Charlie getting on?"

"As well as ever, Provost," Lewis answered. "It is in connection with my work that we have come to see you."

The Provost glanced rapidly at each of them.

"Will you tell Lord Brockwood what I do for a living?" said Lewis.

The Provost sat back in his chair and clasped his hands across his stomach. "Aren't you still working at Gower Street? Import and export, isn't it?"

"No, sir," Lewis said. "Will you tell him what I – what Charlie *really* does?"

"Is this important, Lewis?"

Lewis nodded and the Provost turned his thick glasses on to Brockwood so the reflection totally obscured his eyes.

"Charles Austen Mars is in charge of a branch of British Intelligence," he said at last. "He tells me that Lewis is one of his ablest assistants."

Once they were clear of the town and on their way back to Upper Farm, Brockwood got his pipe going and sat back. The whole journey was conducted in silence as Lewis nursed the car expertly through the lanes.

He parked the Morris Minor alongside the Land-Rover and walked behind Brockwood as the older man strode ahead up the pathway to the house. When he reached the doorway he stopped and turned to look over the Oxfordshire countryside towards Gloucestershire. Finally he turned and Lewis could see that he had made up his mind. "Come for a walk with me," he said. "I want to tell you a story."

8

After my usual manner, I made farther enquiries of other
persons connected with the wild and pastoral district in which
the scene of the following narrative is placed, and I was
fortunate enough to recover many links of the story, not
generally known, and which account, at least in some degree,
for the circumstances of exaggerated marvel with which
superstition has attired it in the more vulgar traditions.

The Black Dwarf
SIR WALTER SCOTT

Lewis and Brockwood collected Curtis Lowell from the
farmhouse and the three of them set out in silence across the
pastureland behind the house. The older man strode one pace
ahead of his companions; occasionally he would slash at a
hummock of grass with the ash walking stick he carried. The
marmalade cat stalked at his feet pausing only to glance with
contempt at Lewis and Lowell.

Eventually Brockwood stopped by the remains of an elm
tree and indicated with his stick for Curtis and Lowell to be
seated on a nearby log. They settled themselves and watched
as he prepared to speak. First he placed the stick on the stump
of the tree and vigorously scratched his head, then he settled
his weight evenly on his legs which he had spread wide apart.
He folded his arms and buried his chin into his chest for a
moment, then, as he raised his head slowly, he began to talk
in the clear measured tone of a college lecturer.

"In June 1942, I was working for the Ministry of Food
as a nutritionist. My job was to prepare information on
how to produce nourishing meals from unappetising sources.
I hated the work: everyone else of my age seemed to be in
uniform. It sounds ridiculous now but I felt people looked

at my civilian clothes with contempt, almost as if I were a leper."

Brockwood continued to talk in the same easy measured tones about his time in Vosbach as Lewis and Curtis sat spellbound before him. When he reached the point of his story where he had decided to escape, he paused for a while and Lewis spoke. "So the Black Dwarf was Heinrich Himmler?" he said softly.

Brockwood looked up sharply. "Himmler?" He shook his head. "No, the Black Dwarf was the actual mountain. It was the most incredible place. From a certain angle it looked just like a crouching dwarf with the lake set into the hump on its back. The local legend was that it ate people. Of course the mountain was hollow so I suppose some wretched peasants had wandered in there in the past and perished. There is generally some grain of truth in all folk stories.

"But let me continue. I would sometimes go to Mass and when I got back to the Black Dwarf that particular day I could see that there was some great commotion taking place. Two officers were shouting instructions and directing one of the lorries to reverse close to the edge of the plateau. A group of soldiers ran to the edge and secured three ropes to the tail-gate of the lorry and began to descend to the valley below. I walked over to one of the soldiers and asked what was going on.

"'One of the officers, Captain Werner, fell over the edge,' he said simply.

"'How did it happen?' I asked.

"Another soldier answered, 'I saw it. He stood near the edge for a moment, then he seemed to double up, and just pitched forward. He didn't cry out.'

"As he spoke a stretcher was lowered and the troops below lashed the body to it.

"I went into the bunker and searched the labyrinth for Carl Raeder. Eventually I found him in front of one of the rabbit cages making soft noises to the captive animals. 'I want to escape tonight, Carl,' I told him.

"'How?' Raeder said frowning. 'The guard will not open the doors for us without permission from Colonel Mueller.'

" 'I know another way out,' I said.

" 'Where?' Raeder asked.

" 'There's a crack in the dome, just beneath the second rib of the Dwarf. Willie Keuen showed it to me: we use it as a short cut when we go swimming in the lake. Willie made me promise not to tell anyone in case they sealed it up. If we get down the cliff do you think you could get us to Switzerland on foot?'

"Carl thought for a moment, then said in a voice that seemed full of relief, 'If you can get us down the cliff, yes, I can get us to Switzerland.'

"That evening after supper we strolled out on to the perimeter. The lorry with the ropes had been reparked in the motor pool and to my alarm I saw that teams of soldiers were unreeling tangles of barbed wire all around the edge of the precipice. We walked towards the wiring party.

" 'See if you can steal a pair of wirecutters,' I whispered urgently. Carl nodded.

" 'What's all this, Sergeant?' Raeder said in a friendly voice.

" 'Colonel's order, sir,'' the sergeant said. 'I hate this bastard stuff,' he went on in an angry voice. 'I wish I had a mark for every metre I laid across France in 1917.'

" 'You fought in the last war?' Raeder asked. As he spoke, I leaned casually against the tool wagon and turned away from the group to light a cigarette.

" 'All through it, sir. Then in the freecorps against the bastard Poles; then back in the regular army again. I've been in uniform since the age of sixteen,' he said proudly.

" 'You've certainly done your duty for the Fatherland, my friend,' Raeder said. 'Well, goodnight.'

" 'I got the wirecutters,' Raeder whispered as we walked back towards the main gates. For my part I had lifted two pairs of heavy-duty gloves.

" 'One word of warning,' Raeder continued. 'Don't bring anything with you tonight. No money. No documents. If we are caught we might be able to pass ourselves off as a couple of hikers out for a walk in the mountains.'

"Back in his cubicle I examined the gloves I had stolen. They were made of canvas and reinforced with leather. I

142

wondered if they would stand up to the job. I sat on my cot for a while thinking how I could strengthen them. An idea came to me. I hid the gloves in my blankets and made my way through the passageways to the medical room.

"The orderly stood to attention when I entered. 'Can you help me, Corporal?' I said. 'I want to repair a piece of equipment. Could you let me have a couple of reels of surgical tape?'

"He handed the tape over. I thanked him and returned to my own cubicle where I further reinforced the gloves, then lay down on my bunk to rest.

"I waited until it was just before midnight and the guard was about to change on the main gate. I got up and changed into the shorts I used for bathing. I put on a grey woollen army shirt, thick socks and a pair of rock-climbing shoes I had bought in Vosbach, removed the work gloves from the cot and set out for Carl's cubicle.

"He held up the wirecutters and I handed him one of the pairs of gloves. We made our way through the maze of corridors to the domed hall and paused to look for any sign of movement: we could see the gate operator in his lighted box. In the centre of the vast hall, the coffin of Captain Werner stood draped with a flag, with four spotlights from the gantries illuminating it. Bearing in mind the way the hall amplified sound, we trod as softly as we could as we climbed one of the iron staircases that led to the gantry. It took us several minutes to be sure we were in the right place. Once we had located it, I saw how easy it was to climb the rock to the opening.

"We emerged from the tunnel into moonlight so bright I could see the pine trees on the mountainside across the valley. The tiniest sound seemed to be magnified as we crossed the perimeter and made for the barbed wire that was closest to the motor pool. Working with the wirecutters, I parted the double strands of wire and wrapped it securely around the back axle of the lorry parked nearest to the edge. Moving about thirty feet along the coiled wire, we cut through the strands then, very gently, we lowered the wire over the cliff.

"All the time we worked I expected to hear a shout of

alarm and feel the impact of a bullet in my back. But there was nothing: just the sound of our panting breath as Carl and I lowered ourselves down the precipice. After walking for several hours we crossed the border.

"Once we were in Switzerland it was easy to get a passage back to England. A week later I was outside the Cabinet Room in 10 Downing Street. This time the fireplace was radiating heat. It was a cold winter's afternoon.

"A man with an apologetic smile on his face hurried down the corridor and nodded slightly to me, tapped on the door and entered. As he did so I could hear a burst of laughter come from within.

"Almost immediately the door opened and the Prime Minister stood glowering at me. 'Dr Whitehaven? I did not know you were already here,' he said. 'Please come in.'

"The man with the smile departed and I entered, to stand facing a man with sunbleached hair and a deep tan. He was of average height and was wearing a curious mixture of uniforms: whipcord slacks and a pale olive tropical jacket over a beige roll-necked sweater.

"'Dr Whitehaven, allow me to introduce Colonel Neil Fitzpatrick. The colonel has just returned from North Africa, where he has been engaged in acts of daring sabotage against the enemy. Dr Whitehaven has, until recently, been a guest of the Third Reich.'

"We shook hands and waited for the Prime Minister's directions. 'Please sit down, Whitehaven,' the Prime Minister said. 'And feel free to speak in front of Fitzpatrick. He has my complete trust.'

"I sat in the same chair I had occupied when I had been summoned to Downing Street the first time. Churchill waited for me to speak. 'How much do you want me to tell you?' I asked eventually.

"'Everything,' Churchill replied.

"And so I told him what had happened to me. When I reached the part of my narrative where Werner showed me the film he had shot in Russia the atmosphere in the room became very still. When I had finished there was a long silence. Finally Churchill spoke.

"'These groups . . .?'

"'Einsatzgruppen,' I said.

"'Yes, their sole function is to murder people, Jewish people?'

"'That is so,' I said.

"Churchill turned. 'Dear God, Fitzpatrick. Have you ever heard of such an abomination? And what of the film you took with you?'

"'It is still there inside the mountain,' I said.

"Churchill got up and walked to one of the telephones. 'Please bring me a large-scale map of southern Germany, some Imperial sheets of cartridge paper, pencils and a ruler.' He returned to the table and sat down to face me again. 'Now, Doctor, I want you to give precise instructions to Colonel Fitzpatrick of the whereabouts of the Black Dwarf.'"

9

> "All are of a piece, one mass of wickedness, selfishness, and ingratitude – wretches, who sin even in their devotions; and of such hardness of heart, that they do not, without hypocrisy, even thank the Deity himself for his warm sun and pure air."
>
> *The Black Dwarf*
> SIR WALTER SCOTT

Lewis, Brockwood and Curtis stood amongst the great logs of a felled elm tree in the north-eastern corner of the pasture-land that lay behind Upper Farm. In the distance Lewis could see the tiny figure of Sandy raise Brockwood's shotgun to his shoulder and jerk from the recoil. Seconds later the soft bark of the gun came to him across the field.

Lewis pushed himself away from the log he had been leaning against and brushed his hands together to rid them of the dust from the bark. A few feet away was the gate that led into the road running alongside the farm. He stood and looked into the lane that was sunk below the level of the fields on either side. Brockwood picked up his walking stick and began to knock the fat semicircles of fungi that grew on the stump of the felled tree.

"What happened to Carl Raeder when you got back?" Curtis asked.

Brockwood sat down on the stump. He looked up and studied a light aircraft performing aerobatics in the clear sky above their heads. "After the war Carl went to a medical colony in the Belgian Congo. Eventually his health failed. Some strings were pulled and he was allowed to become an American citizen. His job at Columbia University was pretty much a sinecure."

146

"And this guy Fitzpatrick. What did he do?" Curtis asked.

Brockwood shook his head. "I'm afraid I don't know. I never saw him again after that first meeting in Downing Street, or heard another word about Operation Hermann. That is . . . until you came along."

"The Lost Legion," Lewis said softly.

"What was that?" Curtis asked sharply.

Lewis turned to the American. "Fitzpatrick was one of Sterling's best men in the Long Range Desert Group."

"What was that? And who was Sterling?"

"The Long Range Desert Group specialised in deep penetration behind enemy lines. David Sterling founded them in North Africa. They did an incredible job knocking out German airfields. Eventually, Sterling founded the Special Air Service."

"What about Fitzpatrick?" Curtis pressed.

"The official story was that Fitzpatrick bought it after he was dropped into France, but there were always rumours about a raid that nobody came back from. It became a joke in the Firm. Even today, if anyone goes missing some of the old hands will say he's joined the Lost Legion," Lewis said.

"So we have to assume that Fitzpatrick failed to recover the canister of film?" Curtis said.

Brockwood shrugged. "I suppose so. But I have no way of knowing. As I said earlier, I heard no more about the matter."

"If you're right," Lewis said to Curtis, "it could still be there, inside the mountain. Anyone with that letter could set the cold war back to the days of the Berlin Airlift."

Brockwood stood up and knocked the last of the fungus from the stump of the tree. "Who are these people trying to wreck the summit talks?"

"We don't know, sir," Lewis said. "We don't know what information they possess or even what their motives are. Maybe some of the other scientists who were in the Black Dwarf with you are involved. Have you ever heard of any of them again?"

Brockwood shook his head. "As you are probably aware, the scientific fraternity is a narrow one. I made a few tentative enquiries after the war, but no one had heard anything of any of them. One must assume that none of them survived."

"It could all still be there," Curtis said in a voice betraying controlled excitement.

"A bloody strange kind of Aladdin's Cave," Lewis replied. "A film with the potential to destabilise the world and a formula that could make someone a billionaire."

Above them the tiny aircraft began to fall through the sky like a leaf, until the pilot took it into a series of rolls. Lewis envied him his careless abandon.

The three of them started to walk back to the farmhouse keeping to the edge of the field as it ran parallel with the lane. Every fifty yards or so they would come upon the remains of another fallen elm tree. Brockwood struck each corpse with his walking stick. "Thank God for the horse chestnuts and the oaks," he said, waving to the remaining trees that interrupted the hedgerow until it ran into the dense wood where Meredith had concealed himself the night before.

"What do you use this field for?" Lewis asked.

"Nothing now," Brockwood replied. "I rent it to a neighbour. He uses it for his dairy herd."

Lewis nodded. "So the field to the far south is wheat and the next root crop, and then this pasture."

"That's it," Brockwood said. "Beyond that is Whitford's place."

Lewis printed the layout on his mind as they approached the rear of the farmhouse. When they entered the kitchen, there was a rich smell of cooking from the range.

Sandy sat at the large kitchen table, cleaning the shotgun. "I hope you don't mind, Lord Brockwood. I took the liberty of using your gun," Sandy said as he gave the barrel a final wipe with a rag and snapped the breech shut. He replaced it on the two hooks over the fireplace and went to the kitchen sink where he began to wash the oil from his hands.

"You're most welcome," Brockwood said. "I heard the shots. Did you have any luck?"

Sandy grinned and jerked his thumb towards the saucepan on the range. "Rabbit stew," he said. "It should be ready in about an hour."

"Is Meredith still sleeping?" Curtis asked as he sat with his head close to the surface of the table, so that he could peer into the doll's house.

"Yeah," Sandy said. "He should be done about the same time as the stew."

Lewis stood by the children's paintings looking down at the pile of equipment that Sandy and Meredith had brought from the Bedford van earlier in the day.

Brockwood joined him. "Tools of the trade?" he asked.

Lewis grinned. "I suppose they are!" He straightened up and faced his host. "Lord Brockwood, I told you this morning that you are in danger, but I'm afraid that I didn't tell you everything. My superiors don't know that I am here, and I didn't pass on the information that Carl Raeder gave me about your involvement in Operation Hermann. I think we have a security problem at our headquarters."

Brockwood gestured impatiently. "Are you sure about this?" he asked.

"I'm not sure about anything," Lewis replied. "All I have are my suspicions."

"And are your suspicions usually correct?" asked Brockwood with a slight smile.

"We're still alive," Sandy said without emotion, as he gave the stew a stir.

Lewis looked around the kitchen. The early-afternoon sun slanted through the windows, throwing shafts of light on to some surfaces and leaving others in dark shadows. Flowers blazed in the light or glowed in the darkness. The textures of the room blended perfectly. It was a peaceful place that had been created by happy people.

"What do you want of me?" Brockwood said at last.

"I want to fight a battle here," Lewis replied.

Charlie Mars climbed the last flight of stairs to his Gower Street office, carrying a two-gallon plastic container of pale green liquid. As his hand reached for the brass door-handle, he heard the braying laughter of Claude Henderson coming from within the room. Once inside he found Jeremy Bellingford standing in front of the fireplace with a glass of whisky in his hand.

Henderson also had a drink. Charlie put the container down on the floor beside the Chesterfield before he spoke. "Drinking at lunchtime, Claude?" he said in a cheerful voice. "I thought that you didn't approve of alcohol before sundown."

Claude flushed with embarrassment and was about to reply but Bellingford spoke before him. "I'm afraid I'm to blame for imposing on your hospitality, Charles. I've just had one hell of a committee meeting at Number 10 and Claude was kind enough to steer me to your bar." Supported by Bellingford's remarks, Henderson relaxed and leaned against the fireplace. Not being very tall, he struck a rather awkward pose.

Charlie couldn't help thinking that they looked like a television comedy team. He could imagine them in shiny dinner-jackets with very wide lapels, greeting second-rate entertainers as dearly loved friends. 'Smart and Lump' would be good names for them, he thought.

"Yes. I wasn't sure where you were," Claude said. "So I offered our distinguished guest a drink. Surely you don't mind, Charles?"

"Of course not, dear boy. In fact, I was downstairs with Victor Smight. He was kind enough to bring in a sample of his own concoction for dealing with greenfly and other assorted garden pests. This hot weather is bringing them out in profusion." After helping himself to a drink Charlie addressed his next remark to Bellingford. The man was a cad, Charlie decided. "I'm sorry to hear that there's trouble at Number 10," he said with concern in his voice. "Could it have anything to do with us?"

Bellingford lit a cigarette and waved the smoke away from his face as he spoke. "I'm afraid that it does, Charles. There is a certain amount of concern in other circles as to whether this department is handling things in, shall we say, a proper fashion. The recent business in America has appalled everyone and there doesn't seem to be any explanation forthcoming. Tell me, have you heard from Horne or Dr Pearce since they left the country?"

Charlie sighed and shook his head. "I'm afraid not. And I'm getting rather anxious as to their whereabouts."

Bellingford threw the half-smoked cigarette into the fireplace with a petulant gesture. It bounced out and landed on the carpet.

Charlie got up slowly, picked up the cigarette and put it out in an ashtray.

"Well, it really won't do. Are you sure you have the right man on the job, Charles? Maybe it's time for a change of bowling. A man with a more benign view of his masters, perhaps," Bellingford said.

Charlie sipped his whisky. "I can't think where you got the idea that Captain Horne was difficult to work with," he said in an innocent voice. "As for his bowling, I never was one for sporting metaphors. Are you referring to his prowess or his attitude?" He could see that Bellingford was getting angry.

"I'm talking about his loyalty, Charles. Look at his background. Why would a man with his brains go into the army? He reminds me of one of those damned Central American colonels who go 'red' and proceed to take over the country. His family hasn't got any money. What has he got in common with people like us?"

Charlie nodded his head vigorously. "I see, I see. You think Lewis Horne could be politically unsound." He turned to Henderson. "And you, Claude. Do you share these reservations?"

Claude put his glass down on the mantelpiece next to Bellingford and folded his arms. "Well, it might well be the case, Charles. You must admit that most high-risk personnel turn out to be brilliant but unstable." As Henderson spoke Charlie noticed that the full smooth flesh that hung beneath his chin shook with passion. "Anyway, we know they're back in this country, so why haven't they called in?" he said with his voice full of barely suppressed triumph.

"How do we know they're back in this country?" Charlie asked with surprise.

"I did a standard sweep of the airlines," Claude said in a smug voice. "They home-based last evening on Concorde."

"What an elegant turn of phrase," Charlie said. "But of course, you're a Cambridge man aren't you, Claude!

No unstable brilliance there . . . just good old-fashioned traitors."

He held his hands up as Henderson began to splutter a protest. "All right, I take the remark back. There's plenty of unstable brilliance at Cambridge: I only meant you couldn't be considered part of it." Henderson was still trying to work out whether he had been insulted again as Charlie rose from the Chesterfield and gently propelled him to the doorway. "Will you excuse us, Claude. I must have a private word with Jeremy."

Charlie shut the door behind Henderson and turned back to face Bellingford. "How many people are on your committee?" he said brusquely.

The younger man seemed taken aback by the tone and a flicker of fear crossed his features. He knew that Charlie was about to attack in strength, and like all born survivors Jeremy was looking for safe ground to leap upon. "About ten, I suppose," Bellingford thought for a moment. "Yes, ten. Why?" he asked in a cautious voice.

"That's too many," Charlie said. "Somebody is talking."

Bellingford shook his head in disbelief. "Impossible! The Prime Minister personally approved them all."

Charlie took a cigarette from a silver box on the table and lit it with a red-tipped match he struck on the mantelpiece. He inhaled deeply. It was the first tobacco smoke he had inhaled in eighteen months. "What was Henderson doing before I entered the room . . . giving you lessons in logic? My father-in-law rang me last night. The House of Lords' smoking room was agog with the rumour that the New York killings were somehow connected with the peace talks. I requested a Code One on this operation this morning." Charlie took a slip of paper from his pocket. "Here is my confirmation." He handed the paper to Bellingford. "Your committee has been dissolved. I'll inform you when there's something to report, and you can then report to the Prime Minister in turn."

Bellingford was shaking with anger when he took the slip of paper. He thrust it back into Charlie's hand. "How could you do this without telling me?" he said in a voice of suppressed fury. "How could you go behind my back like this? You've turned me into a mere messenger boy. It's outrageous. I shall protest immediately."

Charlie sat down on the Chesterfield and rested his feet on the pile of books on the coffee table before him. He looked at Bellingford's quivering figure in the doorway and spoke in a mild voice. "I was just behaving like one of us, Jeremy. Remember the song: Pull, pull, together."

Bellingford left in a fury as Charlie leaned forward and stubbed the cigarette out. His mouth tasted sour from the smoke. He took another pull at his whisky and felt a wave of tiredness pass through him. He put his feet up on the Chesterfield and in moments was asleep, dreaming of the Thames at Windsor and his blade on the feather.

As Charlie nodded off at Gower Street, Meredith was rousing himself at Upper Farm. He had chosen to sleep in a small boxroom on the attic floor. Most of the space was taken up with trunks and suitcases labelled for passenger-steamers and ocean-liners that were now just memories of the Empire. He lay on a hard mattress on the narrow single bed and stretched comfortably, counted to three and got up.

He found the bathroom and washed, then leapt down the stairs towards the scent of rabbit stew. The others were sitting around the table eating when he arrived in the kitchen.

"Stew's in the pot," Sandy said and waved him in the direction of the food.

Meredith helped himself to a generous portion and joined the others at the table. "The weather's got cooler," he said.

"There's a cold front coming," Lewis said. "Could be rain. It's going to be a dark night."

Meredith raised a spoonful of stew and paused before eating. "Who cooked this?" he said, suddenly suspicious.

"Mr Patch," Brockwood said. "I can recommend it."

Meredith looked at Sandy who smiled back and winked at him. "What did you put in it?" Meredith asked as he peered down at the mixture of meat and vegetables on his plate.

"Just some things I shot and trapped this morning," Sandy said as he spooned up some gravy.

153

"It really is delicious," their host proffered. "In fact, I think I shall have some more."

Meredith still wasn't satisfied. "You haven't been up to any of that survival rubbish, have you? I'm very allergic to rats."

Sandy protested his innocence. "Blimey! Would I do a thing like that in the middle of England? We're not in the jungle." Then he looked thoughtful. "Mind you, one of those rabbits did look a bit funny. I just thought all the fur had worn off his tail. Anyone had a mouthful that tasted a bit gamey?"

They all laughed and Meredith began to eat the stew. But Lewis noticed that Lord Brockwood didn't have anymore.

The green telephone on Charlie Mars's coffee table rang loudly, rousing him from a fitful sleep. He swung his feet from the Chesterfield and picked up the receiver.

"It's Lewis, Charlie. All is well here. I'm going to relay a standard message through the Edinburgh station at 1700 hours."

Charlie rubbed his face with his hand and ran his finger through his hair. "Why?" he asked.

"The message will state that we have located the target and are heading for him from Edinburgh. If you give it out to all department heads, whoever is leaking should try to get their operators to the farm before we can make it from Scotland. If they turn up, then we will have the confirmation we need. I'll send Curtis Lowell out later with Lord Brockwood to collect Hanna from your house and take them both to London. You had better find them somewhere really safe in town. Even if it's the Tower of London."

"Understood," Charlie said. "I shall stay here and await your next call. Good luck."

Lewis put down the receiver and turned to watch Meredith who was operating a piece of electronic equipment about the size of a half-pound of butter. He tapped out a code in morse on the key that was built into the piece of equipment, and as he did so Brockwood could see a tape revolving through a clear plastic window.

"Finished," Meredith said and pressed a button to rewind the tape.

Lewis picked up the telephone again and dialled a long-distance number. "Can I speak to Mr Williams please, Accounts department," he said and then: "Hello, Bob, it's Lewis Horne here. Yes . . . okay . . . It has been a long time. Look, I want you to do a favour for me . . . It's important . . . Yeah . . . The real thing. I'm putting through a signal. Will you hold it until 1700 hours, then put it through to Gower Street and tell them I delivered it personally but that I was in a hell of a hurry? . . . Good! Do it yourself, will you, Bob and don't mention this to anyone. Thanks, that's one I owe you. Ready for transmission? Starting now."

Lewis took the piece of equipment and attached the telephone receiver to it. He pressed a button and there were three pips and a zipping sound that lasted for a few seconds. He detached the telephone receiver and spoke again. "Okay . . . Fine, thanks, Bob."

He stood up and slowly walked to the window overlooking the land in front of the house. Low clouds, the colour of dirty tea-towels, were moving in fast from the north-east. As he stood looking out, a flurry of rain struck the window-pane in front of his face.

Charlie Mars had sat through the long afternoon trying to read a biography of the Duke of Wellington. He hated rainy summer afternoons in London. The city was like a cat that grew miserable and bad-tempered in the wet. He had switched on one of the bars of the electric fire in the grate, more for the comfort of its glowing light than the heat that it produced. The swan-necked card lamp threw a pool of light on to the book in his lap but his mind refused to campaign with the Great Duke in India. Every few minutes his thoughts would return to Oxfordshire.

Finally Sergeant Hillary knocked on the door and Charlie called out for him to enter. He looked up expectantly as the sergeant stood to attention before him.

"A signal has just come in from the Edinburgh station, sir, from Captain Horne. It's being decoded at the moment."

"Is it personal to me?" Charlie asked as he closed the book in his lap.

"No, sir, it's general to all heads of department."

Charlie nodded. "Good, tell all section heads I want to see them when they've read the signal and run their checks."

Hillary left the room and Charlie pulled out his half-hunter and looked at the time. 5.05 p.m. He pushed the watch back into his waistcoat pocket and listened to the rain beating on the roof. "Rain stopped play," he muttered without meaning as he thought of Bellingford's bowling remark.

Ten minutes later Sergeant Hillary returned with a single sheet of paper. Charlie thanked him and stood at the mantelpiece while he read the message. At five thirty Sergeant Hillary buzzed him to say the section heads were outside. Charlie asked him to show them in. He glanced at the sheet of paper again as they filed into his room. "Well, this seems straightforward enough," he said and proceeded to read the message aloud.

"Have traced connection between Carl Raeder and Lord Brockwood, retired scientist. Present address: Upper Farm, Nr Cherbury, North Oxford. Proceeding there with all haste accompanied by Lowell. We shall make contact again when satisfied Brockwood has useful information."

Charlie looked up at the assembled company. "When would you estimate Lewis's arrival in Oxfordshire, Claude?" he asked.

Henderson looked at his copy of the message. "We must assume he's travelling by car – if they left Edinburgh at five o'clock. I can't see them getting there much before eleven."

Charlie looked towards Peter Lloyd, who was duty officer for that night. "I want a full staff on tonight, Peter. Claude will sign the overtime dockets."

"What about this Brockwood? Is he on the computer, Mary?"

Mary Romonoff Brown sat on the arm of the Chesterfield with her customary cigarette-holder clamped in her mouth. "Nothing at all. He might come up on a cross-check but I haven't consulted the readers yet."

Charlie looked around the room and saw June Linklater,

156

Victor Smight's assistant. "Where's Victor?" he asked with slight surprise.

She answered defensively, "I thought you knew, Mr Mars!"

Charlie looked puzzled. "Why should I know?"

She looked around the room and flushed. "I saw you talking to him earlier today, when he gave you that container of liquid, and I naturally assumed he had told you he wouldn't be in this afternoon."

Charlie thought back to their brief conversation. Victor had said nothing about taking time off and he was usually meticulous about such matters. He felt a whisper of concern like a light breeze touching him. "No . . . he said nothing to me. When did you last see him?"

June held up one hand, palm outwards. "When he went to lunch at one thirty."

"Do you have any idea where he was going for lunch?" Charlie asked in a gentle voice. It was obvious that the girl was now worried, and he did not want to force her into a further defensive position.

"He's been going to the reading-room at the British Museum for the last month or so. He doesn't actually eat anything at lunchtime. He says it spoils his evening meal these days."

"Thank you, everyone," Charlie said and they left him alone in his office. When the door was shut he buzzed Sergeant Hillary and asked him to get Victor Smight or his wife at home.

After a few minutes Hillary called back. "I'm sorry, sir, there's no reply from Mr Smight's home number but your wife is here and Mr Bellingford is on the other line."

"Put him through," Charlie said and waved Sybil into his office from the doorway. "Hello, Bellingford. We have had a communication from Lowell and Horne but I am heavily involved here. Can I put you over to Claude Henderson and he'll give you the details. Tell him where you are and I'll get back to you." He buzzed Hillary and transferred the call before Bellingford had a chance to speak. "You may have to go on without me," Charlie said as he reached for an old raincoat he kept on a bentwood coatstand in the far corner of the office.

"Oh, Charlie!" Sybil said in a crestfallen voice. "I've been looking forward to tonight for ages."

Charlie buttoned up the coat and looked up at her.

"It's bad, isn't it?" she said as she saw the expression on his face.

Charlie smiled. "I don't know yet, but yes, it could be. Look, go on to the flat and I'll ring you there. I'll get Sergeant Hillary to call you a taxi now."

"Where are you going?" she asked with a hint of anxiety.

"I've got to pop round and see Victor Smight. I won't be long." Charlie walked to the duty room on the second floor and found Peter Lloyd watching a portable TV set with Paul King, another one of Charlie's operatives. "Do you have a gun in the office?" Charlie asked Lloyd.

"Yes, sir."

"Can you break into a flat if you have to?"

"Yes, sir."

"Come on, then. You stay here and keep an eye on things until we get back," Charlie said to Paul King who mentally cursed himself for lingering about the building when he was off-duty.

"Where are we going, sir?" Peter Lloyd asked, as Charlie hurried ahead of him through the rain that lashed down on Gower Street.

"Not far," Charlie replied. "Victor Smight's flat is in Montague Street. It's the other side of the British Museum."

The rush-hour traffic ground along the street beside them and they had to dodge through the pedestrians on the pavement. Lloyd cursed the fact that he had worn a pale fawn suit to work that day as the rain soaked into the material of his trousers and turned them a darker shade of brown.

When they got to the house, they climbed a short flight of steps and Charlie pushed the front door open. He climbed the stairs to the top flat, three steps at a time. There was no need for Lloyd to break in, as the door was ajar. Charlie hesitated for a moment and then took a deep breath and pushed the heavy door open. Lloyd looked at the massive piece of oak and was glad that he didn't have to break it down. The growing dread that Charlie had felt since he had left Gower Street was confirmed as soon as he entered the living room.

Marjorie lay on the sofa and Victor sat upright in a chair near the window. It had been left open so that a pool of rainwater lay on the wooden floor and soaked into the carpet at Victor's feet. Charlie looked down at Marjorie. Bile rose in his throat. She lay on her side with a towel stuffed into her mouth. The top of her body was naked and there was a length of flex wound around her throat. Victor had been similarly trussed.

"What are these marks on her?" Charlie asked Lloyd, his voice choking.

"Cigarette burns, sir. She was probably tortured while Victor was made to watch." Then he added quietly, "I think he must have told them what they wanted to know."

"Have you seen anything like this before?" Charlie asked in a low voice.

"Yes, sir," Lloyd replied without emotion. "It's not uncommon in Ireland, at least the part I've been to."

Charlie took a deep breath and folded his arms across his chest. "You said he probably told them something. What makes you think that?"

Lloyd looked at the bodies again. "Mrs Smight hasn't been tortured too much and Mr Smight doesn't have a mark on him. It's my guess he talked when they started on her and when they got what they wanted, they strangled them both."

Charlie nodded. He lifted the telephone on the sideboard. It was still working. "Get on to Special Branch. Inform them that the Firm is involved in these murders. If they want any sort of clearance, tell them to get on to Jeremy Bellingford – he'll take care of it. Stay with them. I'm going back to Gower Street."

Charlie walked back slowly, fighting the grief that he felt. He tried to think what information they could have got from Victor. He hadn't known about Brockwood, only about

Hanna and Carl Raeder. And they knew about them already. Could Victor have deduced anything and not told him? He had a mind as sharp as an open razor and he had spent a lifetime making connections. The right ones.

Charlie thought back to their last conversation, when Victor had given him the container. What did I say? Charlie thought over and over in the rain. Then it came to him. "Sybil told me last night that the roses are under severe attack." Last night!

Victor would have known I went to Oxfordshire while a job was on. He would have known instantly that the visit had something to do with the job. My God . . . Hanna and Brockwood were there now. Charlie began to run between the people who walked the pavements of Gower Street.

10

"I've parked the van out of sight," Sandy said as he entered the kitchen at Upper Farm and quickly closed the door against the cold gusts of rain that blew against the front of the building.

Lewis checked the action of the Browning automatic he held in his right hand. When he was satisfied, he snapped in a magazine, clipped on the safety catch and slid the pistol into the holster on his hip. "Okay, get changed," he said as he looped a pair of binoculars around his neck and slung the Heckler and Koch submachine-gun in a similar fashion so that it hung in front of his body. His hand automatically checked the magazines of ammunition that hung from his webbing and the knife that was clipped, handle down, in the sheath that was part of the blue-black overalls he was wearing. He stamped a couple of times to settle his feet into the heavy rubber-soled boots.

Meredith, who was dressed in identical fashion, examined a walkie-talkie radio. Satisfied with the batteries he had just changed, he looped it over his shoulder. In his hand was a black ski mask which he slipped over his head. He picked up a coil of black nylon rope and clipped it to his webbing.

"It's only me from over the sea, said Barnacle Bill the

161

sailor," Sandy sang as he dressed like the other two. "I'm all dressed up like a Christmas tree, said Barnacle Bill the sailor."

"Did you remember your clean underpants?" Meredith asked him as Sandy carried out his weapons' check.

"Certainly, my man," Sandy replied. "If a bleedin' bus knocks me down I want to be a credit to the Regiment."

They each slipped a poncho over their shoulders and walked out into the rain. Meredith and Sandy skirted the house and Lewis made for the bridge over the stream. He looked down at the rush of water. It was swollen and muddied from the rain so that it covered the reeds growing at its edges. Lewis could see them waving beneath the surface of the stream like the arms of drowning people. He crossed the bridge and entered the garage which smelt musty in the rain. Only the Range Rover remained; Curtis and Brockwood had taken the Morris Minor to go to Charlie's house.

Lewis climbed the ladder into the hayloft and looked out of the small window at the rear. Here he had a clear view of the watercress beds, the trout farm and the slopes – covered in fruit trees – that ran down to the hedges of the Brockwoods' neighbours. He pulled up an ancient bale of hay and lay his poncho on it. The inside of the window was grimy with dirt and bird lime so he took a handful of hay and cleaned the glass. When he was satisfied he propped his submachine-gun against the wall and systematically started to sweep the rain-soaked landscape before him.

Back in the farmhouse the telephone rang persistently but no one was near enough to hear.

Meredith reached the top of the great oak tree that grew at the edge of the wood by the hedgerow next to the lane. He wedged himself between two branches where he could see the surrounding countryside in all directions. The only blind spot was the ground behind the farmhouse, which Lewis now covered. Meredith could see the road for at least a mile in each direction. He looked towards the felled elm that once stood in the corner of the field and tried to spot Sandy, who was deep in the bracken of the ditch near the remains of the elm tree, fairly snug in his poncho.

162

Lewis's voice came softly through the radio. "Everyone comfortable?"

"Crow's-nest fine," Meredith said as he clipped his harness to the branches of the oak.

"Okay, boss," Sandy said.

"Settle down," Lewis said. "We might be in for a long wait."

"Car coming from the east," Meredith said. "Rover 2000, not stopping."

The car swished past the edge of Upper Farm and headed towards Stow-on-the-Wold, the occupants cocooned against the lashing rain that hurled against Meredith.

"Just to repeat, I want to take at least two alive," Lewis said as he continued to search the countryside before him with his binoculars. In a distant field he watched the lonely figure of a cowman herding cattle from the pasture.

Charlie put down the green telephone in his room and stared at the mantelpiece. The room was chilly despite the electric fire. He realised he was still wearing his wet raincoat. He took it off and switched on the other bar of the fire. Then he sat down on the Chesterfield to think. Before long the other bar glowed with its full intensity. He lifted the telephone and buzzed Sergeant Hillary. "I want a duty car and a helicopter standing by at Battersea Heliport to go to Oxford. Tell Mr Henderson I want him right away."

Claude appeared almost immediately and saw Charlie putting his damp raincoat on again. "Is it true about Victor and Marjorie?" he asked.

Charlie nodded. "Yes, I'm afraid so. Quite true. I found them, Claude."

"Oh, dear God, how terrible," Henderson said. "I told Bellingford about Horne's message. He seemed to be in a very bad temper."

Charlie looked up at the ceiling and slowly exhaled. "You're always writing memoranda about the use of firearms, Claude. Can you use one yourself?"

"Yes," Henderson replied. "In fact, I'm quite a good shot."

Charlie turned to him. "Go and get a pistol. We're going on a trip to Oxford."

Charlie rocked backwards and forwards in frustration as the car stood in a solid jam of traffic at the bottom of St Martin's Lane. "There was no reply from my home at all?" he asked. "It's very ominous."

Henderson wiped the condensation from his nearside window and looked out at the people sheltering under the portico of St Martin-in-the-Fields. "I don't think the people who killed Victor and Marjorie are agents," Claude said. "They must be terrorists of some kind. In all my years I've never known the Russians behave like this. They can be nasty – at times very nasty – but they don't go in for gratuitous killing. At least, not when they're abroad."

Charles nodded and looked unseeingly at the handful of people who leaned into the wind-filled rain as they crossed Trafalgar Square.

Gradually the car inched through the traffic towards Battersea and finally they turned into the alleyway leading to the heliport. Henderson studied his surroundings. They looked more suitable for a light-engineering works than a jumping-off point for jet-setters, he thought.

The girl on duty at the reception desk told them that their flight was delayed. "I'm sorry, sir," she said to a fuming Charlie Mars, "the weather really is very bad. I can't tell you exactly when your take-off will be."

Charlie went to the telephone and called Gower Street.

"Still no reply from those two numbers, sir," Peter Lloyd said.

"Very well," Charlie replied. "Keep trying and if you have any luck, call me here at Battersea." As he hung up there was a shattering explosion from the gentlemen's lavatory. Charlie looked around and couldn't see Henderson anywhere. He thrust open the lavatory door and found a white-faced figure holding a Smith and Wesson revolver.

"My God, Charles. I could have killed myself. No one told me it had a hair trigger. I've been carrying it in my inside pocket with the safety catch off."

Charlie looked down at the floor where the contents of the shattered lavatory bowl had cascaded over Henderson's feet. He began to laugh and it was as if all the pain he felt for Victor and Marjorie were part of it. Tragedy and farce, he thought. A day to please all the Gods.

Lewis eased each shoulder in turn and thought about Meredith in the eye of the storm. He looked at his watch. It was seven twenty-nine.

Meredith's voice came over the radio. "Three cars coming from the east – fast. A white Mercedes, a dark blue Audi and a steel-grey Ford Granada."

Two hours, Lewis thought. That's about the right length of time.

"They've all stopped at the gate near you, Sandy," Meredith said.

"Three drivers are consulting a map. The Mercedes is coming on . . . passing me now. Looks like two in it. A man and a woman."

Lewis rolled into the deep shadow of the hayloft and looked along the gravelled road to where he could see the Mercedes which had stopped at the head of the lane. Two people got out of the car. He could see that they were expensively dressed.

The woman wore a Burberry raincoat and high leather boots. She carried a large golfing umbrella, which she opened into the wind. The man was a bear-like figure, with a black beard and sharply chiselled features. He wore a large tweed cap and a cream leather trench-coat.

His companion pointed at the telephone line to the house and the man took something from inside his coat. Lewis refocused his binoculars and watched the man take the awkward-looking piece of equipment and screw on a length of what appeared to be tubing. Lewis recognised it as an Ingram submachine-gun – the bearded man had just attached a silencer. He aimed the Ingram and Lewis could not hear the popping sound as the man shot away the junction and a section of the telephone line. Bloody cowboy, Lewis thought contemptuously, he probably cuts up his food with it as well.

165

Lewis trained his glasses on their faces. The woman moved her head in a darting motion, like a bird of prey, and he noticed an eagle-like arrogance to the set of her features.

Lewis had seen her before. In Brooklyn.

"They look like Arabs," Meredith said, as he reported on the others. "Young, casually dressed. And they've got radios."

"How are they armed?" Lewis asked.

"Two machine-pistols," Sandy replied.

"Christ! One of them has a Kalashnikov. The other three have got small-arms," Meredith cut in. "Two automatics and a .38 revolver."

"How are they coming?"

"Spreading out to form a skirmish line. How do you want us to play it?"

"Come down, Gordon. Don't let them reach the farmhouse. I'll keep the two here alive. Don't take any chances with them."

Lewis lay down the submachine-gun and binoculars and removed his webbing-belt of ammunition. The man and the woman reached the bridge and turned their backs to him. Lewis drew his Browning and holding it in his left hand, placed his right on the edge of the hayloft platform and vaulted down to the ground behind them.

They both came around fast and the man reached for the Ingram. Lewis gestured with the pistol and the man held his hands out with a pushing motion. The woman seemed almost relaxed but Lewis could see the deep fury in her eyes. Despite remembering her from New York she looked familiar to him in another way, but he was too preoccupied to think about how he knew the face.

"Take off your coats," Lewis said in Arabic and he noticed a flicker of surprise from the two. "If you make a sudden movement, I will shoot."

Slowly they did as they were told. The woman let go of the umbrella and the wind caught it as it sailed away.

"Throw your coats over there," Lewis said, pointing to the stream to the right of the bridge. He could see that the man had discarded his firearm with the leather coat. But he wasn't sure about the woman. "Turn around with your hands on your head and walk to the house," he said. "If you try anything, I will kill you."

The man and woman were halfway up the slope to the house when the sound of the Kalashnikov's distinctive coughing bark came to them. The woman tried a straight karate kick at Lewis's face. She was good. But he managed to ward off the attempt with the hand that held the pistol and it clattered on to the pathway as the man lunged towards him. Lewis brought up his left hand, the fingers rigid, and poked him in the hollow of the throat beneath the Adam's apple. He made a gurgling sound as the full weight of his body hit Lewis and the momentum carried them both in a tumbling fall down the steep embankment and into the swollen river. Just before he hit the surface, Lewis heard the distant sound of a Heckler and Koch submachine-gun fire a burst as the bearded man's body bore him down into the water.

Lewis found it strangely peaceful lying on the bed of the river; the opaque water was warmer than the cold air above him. The weight of the bearded man pressed down upon him and he could feel his hands around his throat. Lewis remembered the words of his first unarmed-combat instructor: No one has any muscles in his eyes or his balls. He slid his hands along the length of the body on top of him and grasped the man between his legs.

He arched his body convulsively at the attack and Lewis squirmed from beneath his weight and broke the surface of the dun-coloured water. As he gasped air into his aching lungs, he received a clear image of his surroundings – like a television set that was suddenly tuned after the total lack of picture underwater. There he saw the woman raise an automatic and aim it at his face. It made a curious booming noise as his ears were still filled from the stream. The bearded man rose like Neptune, seized him by his collar and started to drag him underwater once again.

Lewis was glad to be there. Punching effectively was difficult underwater so the man's greater weight advantage couldn't tell too much, and if he surfaced, the woman stood

167

a good chance of blowing his brains out with his own gun. He scrabbled along the bed of the stream, feeling the tangle of weeds and slimy mud, fighting to move away from the woman with the weapon. The man caught hold of his left ankle but Lewis kicked free. He judged that he had about sixty seconds before he had to take air.

The bearded man caught him again and resumed his attempt to drown Lewis by using his mass of weight to keep him underwater. This time he had tried to encircle both of his arms and pin them to the sides of his body in a bear hug, but he had failed to trap Lewis's left arm. He reached up and racked his fingers into the man's eyes, which were tightly shut. The raking caused the bearded man to lean away from Lewis's chest so Lewis could reach up and draw the sheath knife from his shoulder. The man intensified the bear hug so Lewis stabbed him twice in the left buttock which caused him to break his grip. He clambered to the bank shouting in pain, and Lewis seized him by the front of the shirt and pulled him under the surface where he inhaled a large draught of muddy water.

Once Lewis had leapt from the hayloft, Meredith clipped his harness to the coil of rope he had thrown to the ground and abseiled down from the oak tree, keeping the great trunk between himself and the line of men crossing the field. As his feet touched the ground the cowman Lewis had seen earlier in the far field entered Brockwood's pasture where the men had left the gate open. Seeing the men in the field, the cowman shouted out to them in an angry voice to get their attention. The man with the Kalashnikov rifle crouched down and fired a burst at him. The bullets caught him full in the chest and threw him against the fence-post.

Sandy broke cover as the man with the Kalashnikov fired. "Drop it," he shouted but the man swung the rifle towards him. Sandy fired a burst that hit him in the breastbone. As he fired, he threw himself backwards into the ditch and rolled ten yards to the right as a variety of bullets hosed into the ground he had just vacated.

Meredith edged around the oak tree and could see the

others lying in the long rough grass of the meadow. One of them shouted instructions to the others but the gusting wind carried the words away. The two machine-pistols opened up covering fire while one of the men with pistols began to run towards Sandy's position. Meredith hit him before he had covered six feet. He pitched forward and the pistol fired as he fell upon it. Meredith jumped back behind the oak tree. He could hear one of the men with the machine-pistols shouting instructions again. This time he could make out quite clearly that the man was speaking Arabic. "Surrender," Meredith shouted in the same language, which obviously inflamed them. They stood up and began to charge towards him. He hit the first and fourth while Sandy knocked out the two in the centre, judging from the way they fell. As he stopped firing, Meredith started to run towards the farmhouse.

He reached the edge of the pasture and leapt over the wire fence on to the lawn behind the farmhouse. Still running, he came around the house and into the front garden without pause, stomping through Lady Brockwood's white daisies. He unslung his submachine-gun and binoculars at the run and dropped them on the lawn.

The woman was aiming at the threshing figure of Lewis in the water. Meredith launched himself over the shrubbery at the edge of the long grassy slope down to the river. Instead of firing at Lewis, the woman turned and snapped a shot at Meredith as he sailed through the air. The .38 calibre bullet hit the butt of the Browning automatic on his hip and deflected into his upper arm, missing the bone and lodging in the muscle of his shoulder. His feet hit the embankment about halfway down the slope. The rain-slick grass was as slippery as ice as he jarred down on to his back, the impact jolting the wound in his arm with a numbing pain like the kick of a mule. He slid towards her like a bobsleigh as she raised the automatic with the classic one-handed posture of a duellist in an attempt at a second shot. Before she had time to squeeze the trigger, his feet hit her beneath the ribs on her right side and she catapulted into the river to join Lewis and the bearded man.

After that the fight went out of them. Lewis hauled himself

out of the water and picked up his Browning which was now lying by the edge of the stream. The man and woman clambered out and once more resumed their journey up the hill.

Finally they stood in the kitchen with the water that ran from them making pools around their feet on the tiles. The pool from the bearded man ran darker from the wounds in his buttocks. "Say nothing to them." He spoke in Arabic and Lewis noticed the look of contempt he gave him.

"Take off your clothes," Lewis said to them in the same language. "All of them."

Sandy entered the room with a bundle of possessions he had taken from the men in the field.

"Anything?" Lewis asked.

Sandy unwrapped the nylon jacket and dumped the stuff on the table. "Money, car keys, some identification, credit cards, no passports. All supposed to be students." He held up one of the credit cards. "That's what I like, a student with an American Express card. A Gold one, to boot." Sandy went to the canvas bags in the corner and produced some field-dressings. He examined Meredith's arm and then dressed the wound. "That's not bad," he said. "You'll be up and around in no time."

Meredith nodded his thanks. "I like your bedside manner. I'm already up and about – or hadn't you noticed."

Sandy handed two dressings to the woman who stood quite naked before them. "For your friend," he said, also in Arabic. The woman looked at the dressings but made no attempt to take them. Sandy shrugged and handed them to the bearded man who took them and started to bind up his own wounds.

"Get them a couple of blankets, Sandy," Lewis said and he handed the pistol to Meredith while he examined the clothes that the two had removed. They were all expensive and bought off-the-peg in Paris. Silk, wool and cashmere, the new uniform of the urban terrorist.

Sandy brought the blankets and draped them around their shoulders. The man pulled his around himself but the woman stood unmoved and made no effort to cover her nakedness.

170

"Take him to the other room," Lewis said to Meredith, as he lifted the telephone. Then he remembered that the line was down. "See if you can repair the line," he said to Sandy, who nodded and went back out into the rain.

Lewis stood in front of the woman and studied her face. There was no fear there, or shame for her nakedness. She watched him steadily, ready to use any opportunity to fight back. Her wet hair hung in jet-black coils framing her face. Lewis gathered it in to the nape of her neck so that he could study the bone structure more clearly. She moved imperceptibly and the blanket slid to the ground so that she was naked again. But Lewis did not alter the angle of the pistol he kept trained upon her.

He studied her body. There was a sexless quality about her. A total lack of femininity. She was like a pin-up in a porn magazine, flawless, but at the same time terribly flawed. To make love to her would be like eating bad junk food. After all the promise of the aroma and the appearance, all you really had was a mouthful of damp, flavourless sawdust. She read his thoughts and the look of hatred returned to her face. She stood defiant once again and he noticed the line of a scar beneath her right breast. It triggered something in his mind; he suddenly remembered who she was. "Pick up the blanket," he said, "and sit down." She did as he told her. "Are you going to talk?" he asked in a conversational tone. "People always do, you know." But as he spoke, he knew what he said was not always true. For the first time she smiled and Lewis knew she would welcome torture. She was the one who would relish suffering for her cause.

The jet ranger helicopter bucked and weaved through the storm as it headed west over Buckinghamshire towards Oxford. The land beneath them was a dull mass of sullen greys and greens. Charlie Mars directed the pilot, using the intercom, towards familiar landmarks until his own house was below them. They could see two police cars parked in the forecourt as they made their descent.

Charlie and Henderson sprinted from beneath the whirling blades and when they reached the gate to the paddock, they could see two uniformed policemen hurrying across the lawn towards them. Charlie recognised the taller of the two figures. It was the sergeant from the local village.

"Hello, Mr Mars, I'm glad you're here," the sergeant said.

"Hello, Bob, what's happened?"

"Mrs Patterson called us, sir. It seems she had to go into Oxford unexpectedly, being as her sister had the flu and she had no one to look after the kids. Anyway, when she got back just now, the door was open and there had been some sort of fight. She says the lady who was staying with you is gone and there's blood in the hallway."

They all walked towards the house and Charlie went into the kitchen where a distraught Mrs Patterson was sitting at the table drinking tea.

"Oh, Mr Mars," she said, jumping to her feet, "I'm so glad you're here. I've been worried to death."

Charlie calmed her down and patted the dogs, who seemed uncharacteristically subdued. "Will you get the chief constable on the telephone for me please, Bob," he asked and the sergeant went to do his bidding, glad to be able to find a useful task to perform amid the chaos. "Tell me what happened, Mrs Patterson," Charlie said in a calm voice.

"I don't know, sir. Mrs Mars left at about three o'clock. She said she wanted to do some shopping before she came to meet you. I was with the American lady and she seemed fine. Anyway, my brother-in-law phoned from work to say my sister was poorly and could I give him a hand. I didn't want to leave her here . . . the American lady, I mean . . . but she insisted I go. When I got back, I found the place like this, so I called Sergeant Crossley."

Charlie put a hand on her shoulder. "Don't worry, Mrs Patterson, you've been very brave. You did the right thing. Thank you."

He walked into the living room and Sergeant Crossley held out the telephone. "It's the chief constable, sir."

"Thank you, Bob," Charlie said and took the receiver. "Hello, Bertrand, Charlie Mars. We've got a bit of a problem here. It's a job for the Special Branch. Yes, at my home. Yes, we're perfectly all right, thank you. Can you get them here . . . and for God's sake, put out a block on anyone talking to the press. Sergeant Crossley will give you what details we have. I'll speak to you soon." He handed the telephone back to the sergeant and walked into the hallway.

Claude Henderson was studying the polished floor. "Dr Pearce appeared to put up some opposition," he said.

"How do you know?" Charlie asked.

Henderson pointed to the floor nearest the wall. A small table was overturned and there was blood on the floor; some was also smeared on the wood-panelling on the wall. Charlie looked around and could see there was really little disturbance at all. It was extraordinary how just a few things out of their familiar places could give such an impression of disorder. The carpet was rucked and the umbrella-stand had been turned over so that the walking sticks were strewn across the floor. But that was all.

"See those marks," Claude said and he pointed to some long scratches in the polished floor. "Someone dragged Dr Pearce across here from the kitchen. Her high heels made these marks. Whoever it was knocked over the table and broke the crystal vase which he fell on and cut his hand rather badly."

Charlie had not seen this side of Henderson before. He was rather impressed. "How do you know it was his hand that he cut?" Charlie asked, looking down at the remains of the crystal vase. It had been a wedding present from one of Sybil's family.

"Here," Claude replied, pointing to the wall. "There's a handprint and you can see where the blood flowed from the cut. He was about average height, judging from the size of the print."

Charlie looked around and felt a moment of guilt as he thanked God that Sybil and the girls had not been at home. "Come on, Claude," he said, "I think we'd better get to Upper Farm."

Sandy came back into the kitchen. "Sorry, chief," he said. "They've done too much damage . . . What did they use?"

"An Ingram," Lewis said.

Sandy nodded. "I suppose they only use pliers on people's fingernails."

The blanket had slipped from the woman again. Sandy wrapped it around her shoulders. "There you are, love, we don't want you catching your death." She looked at him with the intense stare of hatred. Lewis beckoned him to the far corner of the kitchen where they were out of earshot and held a muttered conversation for a few minutes; then they returned to her side.

"Clear the table," Lewis ordered and produced a coil of rope from their equipment. He then cut four lengths and they tied her by her ankles and wrists so that she was spreadeagled on the tabletop. She was smiling now, almost sensually. Lewis looked around the kitchen. The same thoughts that he had were communicated to Sandy.

"It looks as if we're going to make a porno film," Sandy said. "I hope Lady Brockwood doesn't walk in."

Lewis looked down at her face and spoke in Arabic, "Are you hoping this will cleanse you for the Pilgrims of Haifa?"

For the first time there was a flicker of uncertainty on her face. She swung her head away from him and shouted, "I will tell you nothing . . ."

"Let's go and see the man," Lewis said.

They left the two doors between the kitchen and the living room open. The bearded man looked up and his gaze continued on to the woman he could see behind them.

Lewis realised that this was the first time he had seen the living room. It would be a good place to spend a winter afternoon, he thought, as he looked around at the walls, which were covered with bookshelves. Behind the sofa, against the window, was a Georgian oval table with four chairs. In the centre of the table a silver rosebowl was filled with yellow roses from the front garden. The bearded man sat in the chair that faced the open door, the blanket huddled around him for protection.

Meredith, his arm in a sling, leaned against the back of the sofa. "I put some newspapers under him so that the blood wouldn't stain the chair," he said.

Sandy slowly pushed the living-room door shut and drew the knife from his shoulder-sheath. He held it so that the bearded man could see the blade. The prisoner looked away and began to study the bowl of roses on the table before him intently. His face was covered in a damp sheen but it did not come from the river or the rain. Sandy walked to the man and held his head back. He took the knife and to demonstrate the condition of its edge, shaved a small part of the beard from his cheek. He turned to Lewis and spoke in English. "Let's start with him. If I cut off his left bollock, he'll start to talk."

Lewis shook his head. "No," he said after a moment's consideration. "I think we will do better with the woman."

Sandy held his hands out and said in a matter-of-fact voice, "How far can I go with her?"

"I want her alive . . . understand that . . . hurt her but don't let her die."

Sandy nodded and smiled broadly as he left the room.

"Does he speak English?" Lewis asked, nodding to the bearded man.

Meredith shrugged, and stuck his Browning under the man's chin forcing his head back. "Do you understand English?" he asked in a slow, menacing voice.

"I do not speak your language," the man said in perfect French.

It was obvious to them that he understood English as well. From the kitchen came the sound of a low moaning. Lewis and Meredith exchanged glances.

"Are you sure he'll keep her alive?" Meredith asked in English.

Lewis walked to the fireplace and began to study the painting. There were cows in the pasture behind the house and sheep grazed where Lady Brockwood kept her garden. "He's the best," Lewis said without turning around. "He knows what he's doing."

The only sound to be heard was the hypnotic tapping of a rose branch against the window and a gentle flurry of rain. Then there was a long piercing scream from the other room.

Lewis walked to the hi-fi equipment. "Let's have some

175

music," he said in a stiff voice. The Brockwoods' choice of records was extensive. He took a long-player from the shelf devoted to musicals and put the record on the turntable. The sound of Frank Sinatra singing 'My Funny Valentine' filled the room. Above it, they could just hear another scream followed by a choking sob.

"Shall I go in?" Meredith asked in a low voice.

Lewis shook his head. "It's not our responsibility," he said. "If she dies, she dies. If they want us to work with butchers, they must expect the consequences."

The bearded man kept his head in the same position but his eyes flickered nervously between Lewis and Meredith. From the kitchen there came another series of moaning sobs culminating in a final dying scream.

Meredith started for the door. "For God's sake, Lewis," he said.

Lewis moved swiftly across the room and threw Meredith back into the room. "Leave him," he said angrily. "Leave him, he's doing what he has to do."

As Meredith collided with the edge of the sofa and sprawled on to the carpet before the fireplace, the door smashed open. Sandy Patch stood before them, stripped to the waist, his forearms covered in blood up to the elbows. There were splashes on his trousers and flecks on his face, which was distorted into a mask of animal rage.

The bearded man looked up at him, transfixed with horror. Sandy walked towards him and knocked aside the Georgian chair that was angled across his path. "She wouldn't talk," he said in a whisper.

"What have you done?" Meredith shouted and he tried to stop Sandy who lunged towards the bearded man.

"The bitch is dead," he said to the man, who was transfixed with fear. Slowly Sandy took the knife and started to slash through the blanket the man held before him. He jerked his arms away as the knife slid towards them. Sandy stood with his legs each side of the man whose eyes were rolling in fear, and slowly pushed the point of the knife about a quarter of an inch into the man's stomach just below the navel. Blood began to trickle from the wound.

"Who are you working for?" Lewis shouted in Arabic. The man was gasping for breath and saliva dribbled from his mouth. "Who are you working for?" The question was shouted louder.

"Kronstadt," the man gasped out.

11

"For I promise you both, gentlemen, I will not stand tamely
by, and see any violence put on the will of my pretty kins-
woman."

The Black Dwarf
SIR WALTER SCOTT

Sandy stood at the sink in the kitchen and scrubbed his arms
vigorously with a scouring pad. "What is this stuff, boss?" he
said to Lewis, who picked up one of the children's tubes of
paint and studied the label.

"It's acrylic paint . . . Why?"

Sandy held up his arms which were still red in parts.
"Because it's a right bastard to get off. Still, I thought it
added a nice touch. I don't think it would have worked with
her. She's much tougher than her companion."

"She would be," Lewis said. "That's Petra ben Azziz."

Sandy whistled. "The one who chopped all those people in
Haifa?"

Lewis nodded. "Chopped is the word. They cut them to
pieces. I read a Special Branch report stating that she might
be in the country. They were right."

"Your screams were particularly good, I thought," Meredith
said, "especially the last one."

Sandy looked around. "That last one was her."

"How on earth did you manage that?" Meredith asked.

"I didn't. I was moaning and groaning and it was knocking
hell out of my throat. I had my hand over her mouth in case
she shouted out, when the ginger cat came in. It saw her tied
to the table and went and sat on her chest. She took one look

at the cat and let out that scream . . . it frightened the bloody life out of me."

"How extraordinary," Meredith said. "I suppose her concept of hell would be a roomful of cats, which is exactly my Aunt Lucy's idea of heaven."

Lewis briefly wondered what his hell would be like. Permanent take-off probably.

Then, as if to complement his thoughts on aviation, they heard Charlie's helicopter approaching. Lewis and Sandy took up their submachine-guns and waited for it to land. The clattering sound settled behind the house and they looked through the rear window.

"Good Lord . . . the God of War," Meredith said. "And he's got Claude Henderson with him."

Lewis opened the back door and waved to them as they hurried towards the farmhouse through squalls of rain.

"How are things here?" Charlie asked as they entered the kitchen.

"Meredith has a wound; nothing serious. Why?" Lewis answered. He could see the anxiety on Charlie's face.

Charlie slumped down on one of the kitchen chairs, his head buried in the turned-up collar of his crumpled raincoat. "We've lost Dr Pearce. They raided my house and snatched her."

Lewis felt a new kind of fear, different to any he had ever experienced before. For a moment it opened like a yawning chasm of darkness, then he slammed it shut. "You've been back to your house?"

"Yes," Henderson said. "We've just arrived from there."

"Were Brockwood and Lowell waiting for you?" But Lewis knew the answer anyway.

"No," Charlie and Claude said together.

Lewis looked out of the window at the helicopter. He couldn't bear to think of Hanna.

"Things are really bad. They must have all three of them," Claude said as he sat down in the chair next to Charlie. He was wearing an ill-fitting green nylon anorak that he had obviously borrowed from one of the staff at Gower Street. His normally immaculate hair was ruffled and his once highly polished shoes were dull and muddy. He looked thoroughly miserable, like a dishevelled garden gnome.

"We've got one thing," Lewis said. Charlie and Henderson looked up at him. "We know who the opposition are working for."

"Who is it?" Charlie asked.

"Kronstadt."

"How did you find out," Charlie asked. "Judging from the bodies in the field outside, I thought you had killed them all."

"One of them is a civilian," Sandy said. "I think they shot him for a bit of target practice."

"Come and see who we have next door," Lewis said. He led them into the living room where the man and woman were securely trussed.

"That's an ingenious arrangement," Charlie said looking at the way they were tied. If they struggled too much they would throttle themselves.

"Old Bedouin technique," Sandy said. "I thought they might appreciate it . . . being Arabs, I mean."

Charlie recognised the woman immediately. "Well, the Special Branch will be glad to see these two," he said when they got back to the kitchen.

Lewis, Sandy and Meredith changed from their combat equipment back into civilian clothes. Henderson stood watching them as they packed their weapons away. "I see you still use an automatic despite my constant warnings," he said in a resigned voice.

"Why don't you have a long talk with Sergeant Patch about it on the way back to London," Lewis said. "I'm going to need your seat in the helicopter, so he can drive you."

"Why is it more important that you should get back to London before me?" Claude asked huffily.

"Because I've got to find Kronstadt and I know where to look," Lewis said.

"How do you know?" Henderson said, his voice full of doubt.

"We were friends at Oxford, Claude. Of course, he used to be a Tory then."

Henderson looked from Lewis to Charlie Mars. Charlie nodded. "Yes, I know him too."

Claude's face flushed and he ran his hand through his ruffled hair so that it lay upon his head in even greater disorder. "And you had the audacity to challenge me about traitors at Cambridge?" he said in a choking voice.

The lorry swung into a concrete wasteland to the south of the Thames. It had been ground flat by monstrous machines so that only the imprint of buildings remained, giving the effect of a great patchwork quilt of tarmac, concrete and rubble. Indentations in the surface had allowed the rain to form lakes of shallow water that reflected the distant lights of tower blocks. The lorry bumped over the surface and headed for a building that stood by the riverside like a solitary blackened tooth. The driver slowed down to a crawl and two men were revealed standing on a loading ramp. They both carried submachine-guns which they trained on the tail-gate of the lorry as it backed towards them. The driver got down from the cab and threw a bunch of keys to one of the men with the guns. He unlocked the doors and shone a torch into the interior of the lorry. Hanna, Brockwood and Curtis blinked into the powerful beam. All of them had their hands hand-cuffed behind their backs.

"Out," the man with the torch barked. They got up awkwardly and walked out on to the loading ramp.

"Up there," the man said, indicating a flight of steps with the torch beam.

They found themselves in a huge dark room. The iron-framed windows that overlooked the vast interior had lost their glass which they now crunched underfoot. The only light came from a hurricane lamp that stood on a plastic milk-crate. There was nothing else in the room. The whole place oozed a smell of decay: wet crumbling plaster, rotting wood, rusting iron and more than a century of accumulated dust and dirt from distant parts of the world. Once the building had known cargoes from the Orient: then, no doubt, the building had smelt of spices, but the great ships no longer came to the dead wharves. Even the rats had emigrated.

181

"Where are we?" Hanna asked as they looked down on the group below, who stood in the lights of the lorry that had brought them in captivity from Oxfordshire.

They had opened a great pair of doors so that the lorry could drive into the warehouse.

"These are the London docks," Lord Brockwood said. "There are miles of them."

Then they saw one of the group break away to climb the staircase that led from the interior of the warehouse to the room upstairs. Moments later he entered the room, accompanied by another youth who had been standing guard outside the door, and leaned against the wall.

He was young: Curtis judged him to be in his early twenties, with thick dark blond hair and almost angelic features. He smiled to expose teeth that were china-white. Everything about him spoke of wealth and privilege. He looked as if he should be at the bar of the best hotel in Switzerland's most fashionable ski resort, with a long cocktail in his hand instead of the Star Model 28.9 millimetre automatic he produced and let dangle casually by his side. He spoke excellent English with a pronounced German accent. "Someone will be coming to question you soon. Please don't waste his time by lying. He is very important and you will be insulting his intelligence if you imagine you can trick him in any way." As he turned to leave the room Curtis spoke angrily.

"Can you please tell us what is going on here and give us some explanation for this outrageous treatment? I am a citizen of the United States and work as a commercial attaché at the American Embassy. My Government will take this incident as a serious breach of international behaviour if we are not released immediately."

The young man sighed and held out the pistol to his companion. "If this gentleman tries anything at all, shoot him in the knee." He then walked swiftly up to Curtis and punched him expertly in the stomach. Curtis crumpled to the floor with a slight groan. The young man looked down at him. "You are Captain Curtis Lowell of the American Special Forces, so I suggest that you stop this ridiculous charade immediately. Your behaviour is exactly the kind I warned you against. Now please get up, Captain, I know you are hardly hurt and Klaus is most anxious to shoot you."

They left the room and Curtis slowly got to his feet.

"Why did you provoke him?" Hanna said. "It was obvious he would hit you."

Curtis shrugged. "I wanted to see if I could get him to tell us anything."

"But you didn't learn a thing. You just got yourself punched."

Curtis shook his head. "No, not quite. He told me how much he knew about me . . . which is everything."

Hanna, still standing at the window, looked around the gloomy room. "Do you think they've got this place bugged?" she asked.

Curtis scraped a patch of floor clear of broken glass with his foot and sat down. "No. I don't think they would bother," he answered. "They will make Lord Brockwood talk quite easily when they come to question us."

"What makes you so sure of that eventuality?" Brockwood asked angrily.

"They will demonstrate their ruthlessness in some way and then threaten to torture Dr Pearce," Curtis said bluntly. "You won't think the information you possess worth keeping silent for. It isn't a question of courage."

Brockwood nodded agreement while Hanna continued to look down at the group around the lorry. Three of them were girls. They didn't look menacing at all, despite the weapons they carried. "Do you think they will kill us?" she asked in a flat voice.

"I don't think so. We probably have a considerable hostage value to them. When you tell them about the Black Dwarf, Lord Brockwood, say that you know the one way in and that you will need Hanna to search through the documents because she is a qualified scientist. That's all we can do to buy time."

"What about you, Captain Lowell?" Brockwood asked. "There doesn't seem to be a role for you in this scheme of things."

Curtis smiled up at him. "Don't worry, old soldiers never die," he said.

Lewis locked the door of the car and walked towards the house he had not visited in ten years. The rain had stopped and the pavements were nearly dry. Far across in the darkness of Regent's Park one of the big cats roared. It was a strange, primitive noise to hear in the heart of London. Odd that most people called lions the king of the jungle, Lewis thought, when they lived in grassland and desert. They were creatures of open spaces. Lewis was a creature of the jungle. He remembered it well, the warm, close wetness of it, and how the bravest men could be defeated by the desire to fight that alien world instead of pulling it about you and existing like the other survivors.

Shaking off these melancholic thoughts, he looked up at the great white house. It was the same, even after ten years. Maybe the magnolia tree was taller. He rang the bell

The man who answered the door spoke with an unusual accent. Lewis guessed that he was from one of the remoter parts of Spain. "Yes, sir?" the foreigner said.

"My name is Lewis Horne. I would like to speak to Mrs Alberici, please."

"Are you a friend of the family?" the man asked politely.

"Mrs Alberici knows me," Lewis said. "Tell her it is important that I speak to her."

The butler looked at him for a moment. "Mr Lewis Horne?" he repeated.

"Yes," Lewis replied. "I'll wait here."

The door closed and Lewis turned to look back into the roadway. Then the door opened and the butler reappeared. "Would you follow me please, sir."

Lewis knew the way. And when he entered the drawing room he thought that Helen Alberici had hardly changed. She wore a black evening gown generously trimmed in silver and the pale rich decoration of the room contrasted with the darkness of her dress. She stood before a bookcase holding a glass in her hand. There was laughter coming from behind the closed doors that led to the dining room. As Lewis got closer, he saw that she had changed a great deal. Time and alcohol had not been gentle with her. She had remained slim, but that was all. He calculated that she would be in her early fifties now. Finally he noticed that she had the characteristic nodding sway of the seasoned alcoholic.

"Well, Lewis. It has been a long time." Helen Alberici still spoke in the voice that theatre-goers had once cherished. When she had last played at Stratford with Sir John Gielgud a critic had called her voice a bell to his cello.

"I would like to see Susan, please." The request was made formally, almost stiffly.

"And what makes you think she is here?"

There was a gust of laughter from the dining room. Lewis glanced towards the doors that had been closed against him. "A mutual acquaintance told me she was in the country. It is very important that I see her."

She looked towards the butler who had stayed in the room behind Lewis. "Mrs Armstrong is resting in her room. Will you tell her that Mr Horne is here, Alphonse." She looked to Lewis again. "Now if you will excuse me, I must return to my guests." Then she made good her exit, taking her hatred for him into the other room.

Once he was alone he could not hold the memories back. He wished he could tell Hanna what it had been like. Oxford, ten years ago. A few minutes later the door opened and Susan came into the room. "Hello, Lewis. It has been a long time," she said in a voice obviously inherited from her mother.

"That's what Helen said. You must have been reading for the same part," Lewis said and immediately regretted the sharpness of his reply.

She walked towards him and he took the hand she held out. "We don't have much in common anymore, except my father. He has been very ill, you know."

Lewis nodded. "Yes, I read about it. He's recovering from a heart attack, isn't he?"

Susan stood close to him so that he could smell her expensive perfume. Obviously, being married to one of Britain's premier revolutionaries didn't stop her buying the odd bourgeois luxury.

"No," she said. "It was a severe stroke, but there has been a lot of improvement. He's starting to talk and he can move his arm again."

Lewis nodded. It was hard to imagine Mark Alberici stricken in any way. He had been surprised when he had first met him. They had been the same height. Lewis had expected someone much taller. But he and his wife had been as striking a couple as had ever graced the gossip columns: Mark Alberici, the financier who looked like a Renaissance merchant prince, with his wife Helen, with the Slavic cheek-bones and oriental eyes. And together they had produced Susan, the perfect English rose. A girl for Henley and Royal Ascot. For country houses and the London season and definitely not for Lewis Horne, whose social position as the son of a major in the British army was, to them, roughly on a par with that of the doorman at Claridge's.

But Lewis's friend was the right stuff. Patrick Armitage was the very thing: grandson of a Duke, the heir to an old fortune. All doors opened for Patrick, even as he walked away from them. And the Albericis' door was no exception. Lewis could remember reading about the wedding that had taken place in Caxton Hall. He had stood on the bank of the Cherwell and thrown the paper into the river after briefly contemplating going in with it. Now, all this time later, he recognised the other sensation he had experienced that day beside anger – and was amazed to know that it had been relief.

Susan sat down on a sofa and held out a hand for Lewis to sit beside her. "You look thin," she said. "Have you been unwell?"

"I'm fine, Susan."

"You didn't stay at Oxford, did you? Everyone expected you to teach."

"No. I joined the army but I'm a writer now. That's what I'm here for. I want to contact Patrick. A friend of mine is starting a left-wing magazine and desperately wants me to interview him."

She smiled down at his hand which she still held. For a moment he thought of Hanna on the plane.

"And I thought you wanted to see me. I don't suppose you've thought about me at all."

Lewis shook his head. "On the contrary, I think about you often, Susan. I was talking about you to a friend just the other evening in fact."

Susan glanced up at him and then lowered her eyes so that he could see the long sweep of her eyelashes upon her cheeks. "What did you tell him about us?" she asked in a soft voice.

Lewis realised that she really hadn't changed in the years he had not seen her and he knew, suddenly, that she never would. The same wilful, selfish little girl. He shrugged. "I told him you were living in California."

"Why did you say that?" she said.

Lewis looked into her eyes. "I suppose it was easier than telling the truth."

Susan let go of his hand and clasped both of hers in her lap. "We did live in California for a time. We've lived in lots of places since then." She looked up at him and he could see a faint cluster of lines around her eyes.

"Where is he now, Susan?" he asked gently.

She turned her head. "He's not here. They're watching the house you know."

Lewis feigned surprise. "How can you tell?"

She shrugged. "You get used to spotting them. There was a man walking a dog when you arrived. I saw him from the window upstairs. It must be the most boring job in the whole world." She stood up and folded her arms, her shoulders hunched.

"Where can I get in touch with him? It is very important."

"I can give you a telephone number," she said quietly. "But you can't ring from here; this number is tapped."

She went to a writing desk and wrote down a number which she handed to him. She started to walk to the door with him when she stopped and reached out. He took her in his arms and she held him very tightly. "Oh, Lewis . . . I'm so tired, so weary of having no home." She rested her head on his shoulder and he could feel her fingers dig into his back. "You did love me, Lewis. Didn't you?"

187

He held the back of her head in his hand. "Yes, Susan . . . very much."

She continued to hold on to him. "Be careful, he'll kill you if he thinks you are any danger to him."

Lewis stroked her hair. "I just want to write about him."

She held his upper arms and looked into his face: "No, you don't. You're still a soldier. I can tell. I met an American recently. He felt like you – another soldier."

Then the door of the dining room opened and Susan's mother entered. She saw the two of them holding each other and her features twisted in loathing. "Going so soon, Lewis?" she said in that theatrical tone which manages to imply deeper meaning to the most mundane sentence.

"Thank you for your time, Mrs Alberici."

"Thank you for your time," she mimicked as she took three steps towards Lewis and tripped on the train of her gown. She fell on to her knees and he moved forward to help her. She looked up at him, her face contorted with hatred. "Don't you dare touch me," she said. Lewis stood still, numbed by the emotion she showed towards him. Susan helped her mother to her feet. "Get out," Helen Alberici choked out at him.

"I think they're coming for us," Brockwood said as he watched three of the group below break away and start up the stairs.

The young German stood in the doorway and gestured for them to come out on to the landing. Hanna looked down on the group as she descended the staircase. None of them appeared to be fanatical or dangerous. To her they looked like the sort of young people you would find in any expensive discotheque in the world: healthy, clean, well-dressed. Despite all evidence to the contrary it was still hard to visualise them as ruthless killers.

Hanna, Curtis and Brockwood were escorted to a row of chairs that faced a table lit by three hurricane lamps. It was like a makeshift setting for a revolutionary court. Hanna looked around the great rotting hulk of the warehouse and then at the bright eager faces surrounding them and knew that they wanted to play this game to the very end.

"Open up," the German said and four of the group swung open a great creaking door on to the waterfront. "Switch on the headlights," he said and the lorry's lights cut across the thin mist on the river's surface. They could hear the throbbing of an engine and a large cabin-cruiser slowly edged to the dockside. From somewhere on the river came the soft moan of a ship's horn.

A solitary figure stepped from the boat and walked from the dock into the lights from the lorry. Hanna was expecting someone devilish; instead she was confronted by a slim figure of average height with longish, sun-streaked hair that hung low over his forehead. He wore tight blue jeans and a pale grey open-necked silk shirt with a herring-bone tweed jacket. They looked like casual clothes from the previous decade, something Robert Redford or Dustin Hoffman would have worn as street clothes in New York. Lewis would have recognised him still. He kept tossing his head back to keep the hair out of his eyes as he walked towards her.

In the light from the hurricane lamps he was not sinister at all. When he spoke, his voice was low and cultivated. The effect on his followers was obvious. He was a superstar and Hanna could feel the excitement radiating from them. "Good evening. I'm sorry to have kept you waiting," he said as he leaned against the table that faced them. He smiled and the features were very attractive. Hanna felt very frightened by his charm.

"You are all intelligent people," Armitage said in an easy reassuring voice. "So I will explain my problem to you." He reached into his pocket and produced a packet of thin cigars. He lit one with a disposable lighter and waved the smoke away with his hand before continuing. "I want to know what Operation Hermann was and how our organisation can use it to our maximum advantage. I know from my own sources that you, Dr Pearce, and you, Lord Brockwood, can help me. My worry is that you will believe I am too civilised to cause you any real harm. Therefore, so that we can dispense with the preliminaries as swiftly as possible, I will demonstrate

189

my resolve to you." He turned to the German and spoke in a low conversational tone. "Tell Klaus to use the drill on Captain Lowell." He then spoke to Curtis in the same tone. "Remember, you are completely disposable."

Two men seized the American and pulled him to the table. They unlocked his handcuffs and forced him to his knees. Curtis felt the uneven concrete digging into his kneecaps.

Armitage smiled at them again. "You see, I really do not have any feelings for you at all. Klaus! Drill through his hand."

Lewis stopped in at the communications room when he got to Gower Street. He handed the telephone number to the duty officer. "Get me a trace on that number and call me right away. I'll be in Charlie Mars's room."

When he entered Charlie was sitting in his usual place on the Chesterfield. "How have you done?" he asked Lewis impatiently.

"I might have something. I saw Susan Armitage."

Charlie looked up, eyebrows raised. "How is that grotesque family?"

Lewis shrugged. "Helen seems to have kept her good opinion of me. How's Meredith?"

Charlie thrust his hands into his trouser pockets. "He's at Harley Street. The medical term is 'comfortable'. The Chief Constable of Oxfordshire is sweeping bodies from the countryside. We have a guard on the Brockwood family. Claude has gone to organise some food and Mr Patch is asleep in the chair over there."

"Only dozing, boss," a voice said from a darkened corner of the room.

The telephone rang and Lewis said, "That's probably for me." Charlie gestured him to answer it. "Hello . . . Yes . . . I see . . . Look, get someone from Special Branch to stake it out . . . They're using it as an exchange . . . Okay." Lewis put down the telephone. "I've got the number to call. It's a public phone box in King's Cross station." He dialled the number; it was engaged. He slammed down the receiver and folded his arms, took some deep breaths and waited, then

190

dialled again. This time there was an answer. He nodded an affirmative to Charlie and Sandy came out of his dark corner to listen. "Hello, my name is Lewis Horne, repeat Lewis Horne. It is most urgent that I contact Kronstadt."

There was a pause and a voice with a London accent said, "Give me a telephone number."

Lewis gave Charlie's number and then rang off.

Sergeant Hillary came into the room with a long printout. "This is the information on Patrick Armitage you requested, sir," he said and marched off again.

Charlie began to study it and Lewis went back in the corner to talk to Sandy. After a brief conversation, Sandy left and Charlie passed the first sheet of the printout to Lewis. "This reads like the synopsis for a horror film," Charlie said as he handed the second sheet of printout to Lewis. "Did he ever betray any symptoms of this kind of behaviour when you two were friends?"

Lewis sat down in an easy chair and glanced at the piece of paper. It was a grim catalogue of murder, kidnapping and terrorism. "At Oxford?" Lewis said thoughtfully. "No. In fact, he always struck me as being rather timid. If he had any political opinions at all, they were conventionally Conservative."

"Who was conventionally Conservative?" Claude Henderson said as he entered the room with his arms full of a large brown paper bag.

"Kronstadt, Claude," Charlie replied. "Lewis says he was conventional at Oxford."

Claude put the bag down on the table and took out a selection of sandwiches wrapped in clingfilm. Lewis unwrapped a ham and cheese. When he bit into it the texture was pulpy and there was no flavour at all.

Claude chose a liverwurst and chewed slowly with a growing expression of disgust. "Why is it civil servants always bring back coffee and sandwiches when you ask them for food at night? It must have been those bloody late-night talks the Labour Party was always having with the unions. Did you know him in his second year?" Claude said to Lewis.

"Who? Kronstadt? No, we only got to know each other in our third. He left without taking a degree."

Claude munched on. "Did you see a lot of him?"

Lewis thought. "A fair amount but not all of the time. Why?"

Claude sipped some coffee. "We found when we were looking into the Burgess, Maclean business that the long-term moles saw a lot of each other in their second year and then made new friends in the third year. Quite natural, you know, how people take up new friends and drop old ones."

They sat eating in silence for a few minutes. Henderson looked around. "Where's Sergeant Patch?"

"He's gone back to the Regiment to re-equip. I only borrowed him, you know," Lewis replied.

"Good sort, that," Henderson said as he started on a ham and cucumber. "He drove me back to London in his van. Do you know he's something of an expert on pistol shooting?"

Lewis nodded. "One of the best."

"Olympic standard, would you think?" Claude asked.

Lewis took another swallow of coffee. "If they were allowed to shoot at each other, I've no doubt he'd be a gold medallist."

Charlie picked up the telephone. "Sergeant Hillary, bring your notebook in."

Hillary appeared almost instantly and stood while Charlie dictated.

"'To all Intelligence Agency Heads: Please supply any information on Patrick Armitage, also known as Kronstadt, for years 1970–71. This has Prime Ministerial clearance. Code One.' That's all."

Hillary went to carry out the instruction and Charlie looked up at the ceiling, quoting Milton:

> "Thousands at his bidding speed
> And post o'er Land and Ocean without rest:
> They also serve who only stand and wait."

Time passed slowly. Henderson had taken Sandy's place and now slept in the darkened corner while Charlie sat with his feet up on the Chesterfield reading an ancient paperback entitled *The Public School Murder Mystery*. Lewis pretended to watch the late-night movie, his mind on Hanna.

He had been trained to identify problems and categorise them into those that could be solved immediately, those that were insoluble and those that could only be tackled after a passage of time. Hanna was most certainly a passage of time problem but that could not stop her intruding into his present.

The telephone rang. Henderson came to and they stared at the instrument for a moment before Lewis snatched it up. It was the voice with the London accent. He listened to the instructions and replied curtly that he had understood. Charlie and Claude waited as he hung up. Lewis looked at his watch. "Armitage wants me to meet him in thirty minutes; he knows I'm involved. He says if I take Petra ben Azziz with me they'll make an exchange for Hanna." Lewis looked at Charlie. "Can we do that?"

Charlie nodded. "I've got a Code One from the Prime Minister. That gives us the all-clear. Claude, you go and collect her from Scotland Yard; I'll make the necessary calls. Pick up Lewis here and drive them to the rendezvous."

He turned to Lewis. "Will there be any chance to tail them after the swop?"

Lewis shook his head. "It would be easy to spot."

Charlie reached for the telephone. "Well, at least we can be grateful that he has a weakness for Ms ben Azziz."

Lewis looked up as they passed the Old Bailey. Ragged snatches of cloud scudded across the bright night sky and it was warm again. Two City of London policemen glanced at the car with professional interest as they passed by and turned left up Ludgate Hill towards St Paul's. There was no other traffic. The buildings stood empty about them. They parked and Claude Henderson stayed with the girl as Lewis crossed St Paul's Churchyard, stood on the first step before the cathedral and turned to look down the hill towards Fleet Street.

He didn't have to wait long. A car came from the direction

of Cannon Street and stopped over to his left. Patrick Armitage got out and walked towards him. "You're looking fit, Lewis. The years have not wearied you. I suppose it's all that marching about. Square-bashing it's called . . . isn't it?"

"That's rather out of date, Patrick. It's a modern army now. We call ourselves The Professionals. Haven't you seen the advertisements?"

Armitage stood next to him and they both looked to the west.

"I'm not in England much these days. Forgive me if I seem out of touch with your ways."

"Don't you consider yourself English anymore?" Lewis asked.

Armitage paused before he answered and looked over his shoulder at St Paul's. "One of my ancestors was in charge there, you know."

Lewis shrugged. "At one time or another, one of your ancestors was in charge of everything in this country."

"Time changes. You know what Tom Paine said: 'My country is the world.'"

Lewis glanced at the profile next to him. "Is that why you chose the name Kronstadt?"

"What do you know about Kronstadt, Lewis? What could you possibly know about anything?"

Lewis shook his head. "I know what Kronstadt is – a naval fort in the Gulf of Finland. The Tsar put down a rising there and then Trotsky did the same a second time with the Red Army. They named you after a two-time loser, Patrick, but then history was never your strong point."

Armitage stiffened visibly. "Stop patronising me, you middle-class lackey. An Oxford degree and a soldier's suit don't give you that right."

But Lewis continued to goad him. "I should be more careful with your terminology; bourgeois is the word you were looking for and you're using the wrong quotation from Tom Paine – that one goes on to say: 'My religion is to do good.' Unless you consider mass murder doing good. Stick to lecturing your lost boys, Kronstadt. Grown-ups will take you for what you really are."

194

Two bright spots of colour appeared on Armitage's cheeks where the flesh stretched, taut across the cheekbones. Lewis could tell how angry he was but he also knew that Armitage had another card to play.

"Shall we make the exchange?" he said finally. "I'm bored with our conversation."

Lewis turned and waved to Henderson who got out of the car with the girl. Armitage made his signal and Lewis could see Hanna and a guard get out and stand by their car. Slowly they began to walk towards each other. Lewis held his breath and gripped the Browning in his mackintosh pocket. An exchange was always supercharged with tension and this was the moment of maximum danger; any odd or erratic movement and both sides could start shooting.

Henderson and the guard exchanged the women and both walked back to their respective cars at the same pace.

Armitage nodded his satisfaction and turned to Lewis. He spoke in a conversational tone with all traces of anger gone from his voice. "Just in case you are thinking of following us to the Black Dwarf I have taken out some extra insurance." He reached up to the top pocket of his jacket and casually took out a squarish piece of card which he handed to Lewis. "You won't do anything silly now, will you?"

Lewis turned over the piece of card. It was a polaroid photograph taken with a flashlight. The features of the two people were bleached white by the harsh lighting but there was no mistaking Brockwood and Lewis's sister Janet.

12

"Our information," said Earnscliff, "is positive; we are seeking goods which have been forcibly carried off, to a great amount."

"And a young woman, that's been cruelly made prisoner, that's worth mair than a' the gear, twice told," said Hobbie.

The Black Dwarf
Sir Walter Scott

Janet had suspected nothing: the voice was so English, so reliable. And when it told her to meet her brother in Rotherhithe she had willingly taken the taxi to the rendez-vous – and walked straight into the trap. Even now it did not seem real to her. She looked around the echoing warehouse and willed herself to believe that it was all some elaborate practical joke despite the handcuffs that now encircled her wrists.

Standing against the wall she could see Curtis Lowell and an elderly man with white hair. Both of them were handcuffed as well. Lowell had a bloodsoaked handkerchief tied around his left hand. His face was waxen but he tried a ghostly smile.

"What's happening? Where's Lewis?" She tried to keep her voice firm but there was a slight tremble when she spoke.

"Don't talk," one of the guards said in a flat voice: it was somehow more sinister than a shouted order.

"Can I go to the toilet?" Curtis asked. Klaus nodded to one of the others who prodded him with a revolver and waved towards the far end of the warehouse. Away from the hurri-cane lamps, they picked their way across the rubbish that littered the concrete floor into the darkness.

It was so gloomy that Curtis and the guard could hardly see each other. When they reached the door to the toilet, the escort reached in and operated the switch so that a shaft of light revealed another door; Curtis guessed it led on to the waterfront.

The guard waved him into the wretched room. Curtis shut the door behind him and looked round. It was small in there and flooded with water; sodden newspapers littered the floor and it was lit by a single naked bulb. Quickly Curtis removed the cover from an ancient brass light switch and smashed the bakelite interior so that the wiring was exposed. Then he stood on the lavatory seat, unscrewed the light bulb, shouted "Damn" and let out a long moan.

The guard opened the door and automatically put out his hand to the light switch as Curtis had anticipated. The shock jolted him back and he slammed against the wall. There was just enough dim light for Curtis to kick him in the throat. The gun skittered from his hand and Curtis scooped it up, stepped swiftly to the other door and ran his hand down in the darkness until he located the Yale lock.

He placed the muzzle of the revolver against it and fired two shots. The door gave a little but the lock was jammed. He fired twice more and then it gave with a splintering sound. He hurled himself out on to the jetty that ran the length of the warehouse, and jumped down into the soft black mud that was waiting for the rising tide. Behind him he heard shouting as he waded through the glue-like ooze towards the water's edge. The shoes were sucked from his feet as finally he waded into the dark Thames. The handcuffs made swimming difficult so he rolled on to his back and threshed vigorously with his feet. As he swam he realised that he had finally shot open a door, something he had wanted to do for years.

Curtis tried to remember the name of the artist who had illustrated the huge, leather-bound copies of Charles Dickens's novels that his late grandfather had kept in the library at his home in Boston. I suppose Uncle Ben has them now, he thought, as he looked around at a scene that could have come from one of those massive volumes. Bodies lay huddled around him in piles of rags and cardboard boxes; some were wrecks of winos or tramps, others were part of the army of young people who were adrift in the great cities of England looking for some kind of future. Now they had reached the bottom of the heap. They camped around oil-drum fires by the riverside in the heart of one of the world's richest cities.

His hands were still handcuffed together so that his right hand lay in his lap with his gold Rolex watch exposed. Now a nearby figure crouched watching him with the intensity an addict shows towards the needle. He was young but all of the youth had drained from him. His face was thin and bony, as if there was no flesh between skin and skull. He moved in a slow crawling motion towards Curtis, his eyes never leaving the gold wristwatch. As he drew close, he smiled, revealing a set of teeth that looked like broken crockery. Curtis had one effort left in him. As the scavenger reached out for the watch, Curtis caught him with a kick that sent waves of agony through his hand. The would-be thief rolled away, making a choking gurgle and blundered into some of the sleepers who mumbled and cursed as they squirmed in the squalor of their ragged nests.

Two policemen on their rounds looked over the huddled bodies. It was grim thankless work which they performed with a certain gruff compassion, like medical orderlies on a battlefield. Finally their torch light flickered over Curtis and rested on the handcuffs on his wrists. He could hear one of them talking into the radio that was attached to the lapel of his tunic, and knew that salvation was at hand.

Lewis and Charlie parked the car and were directed by one of the policemen.

"Here," Curtis called out in a weary voice when he saw them.

They crouched down beside him. "Can you make it to the car?" Lewis asked softly.

Curtis managed a weak smile. "You can tie me to a horse just as long as you get me out of here."

Lewis drove and Curtis talked as best he could. "Brockwood told them you can only enter the Black Dwarf at dawn. That English guy is crazy: I think he'll hurt Janet if you follow too close."

Charlie looked out of the window. "They must have gone by boat. The warehouse was empty when we got there."

Fifteen minutes later they arrived at Harley Street. Charlie checked the road for anyone watching, then Lewis buzzed a doorbell. The entryphone buzzed back at him and Lewis said, "Achilles." Then the lock clicked open.

The duty sister recognised Lewis immediately. "You again," she said with the usual brisk cheerfulness of her profession. "Well, at least you're walking."

"Not me, Molly. We've got another customer for you."

They got Curtis into the hallway. His face was grey and there were shadows of pale blue to his features. After a short wait the duty doctor arrived yawning in his pyjamas and they took Curtis away.

Lewis waited in the car while Charlie had a word about Meredith. Eventually he joined him and they looked down Harley Street into the pre-dawn darkness. "What do you think?" Charlie asked finally.

Lewis was bone weary. He rubbed his face with the back of his hands and kneaded his aching eyes with his knuckles. Charlie yawned in sympathy and wound down the window to let in the night air. He reached for a packet of cigarettes on the dashboard shelf.

"This is my second cigarette in two years," Charlie said reflectively as he put one to his lips. "I suppose Harley Street is as good a place to start again as anywhere."

Lewis massaged the muscles at the back of his neck before he spoke. "They're definitely heading for the Black Dwarf. Armitage boasted that he was taking them there. He never could resist telling you anything if goaded. That's why I took the risk. They're crossing by boat. They'll probably pick up transport on the other side and go by road. Our problem is that they've got plenty of time and can take any one of a hundred routes, so we cannot make plans to intercept. What we know for certain is that they will be at the Dwarf at dawn tomorrow morning . . . and that's where I shall meet them."

Charlie flicked the cigarette out of the window as Lewis eased the car away along the street, touched by dawn's early light.

Janet and Brockwood dozed fitfully in the cabin of the motorcruiser. Janet rested her head on Brockwood's shoulder and listened to the powerful drumming of the diesel engines that powered them through the calm waters of the Channel. The dawn light yellowed the lamps in the cabin. On the bench opposite them Klaus sat with a revolver stuck in his belt. He took occasional pulls from a cardboard container of orange juice until he shook it empty, turned it upside down so the last of the liquid dribbled on to the chart table between them, and threw the carton aside. The cabin was filthy. Plastic and cardboard containers with the remains of rotting food were littered everywhere. There was the sickly sweet smell of sewage and disinfectant from a chemical lavatory that had overflowed and slopped into the carpeted cabin. The boat was obviously very expensive but it lacked the care of a real owner. The brass fittings were green and tarnished and the heavy leather upholstery was cracked and dry and covered with cigarette burns. Janet felt contaminated by the surroundings. Nothing repulsed her as much as unnecessary squalor.

The engine cut and there was silence. Without forward motion the boat began to rock gently from side to side. Janet raised her head and glanced at Klaus. She did not like the way he looked at her. It was not sexual; more the attitude of a particularly savage dog regarding a piece of meat he wasn't yet allowed to eat. Brockwood began to speak to him very clearly in German, the way one does to somebody who is very stupid. "This boat is filthy. If you do not clean it you will catch a disease. Dirt is very dangerous. Would you like me to list all the illnesses it causes?"

Klaus's heavy features formed a familiar expression: the universal face of the bully confronted with a victim who refuses to be dominated. He pulled the pistol from his belt and pointed it at them. "Get up," he shouted, although they were no more than six feet from him. He indicated that they should go up on deck. They did so and Janet took deep grateful breaths of the fresh dawn air. There was a crystal clarity about the morning. They could see a low coastline ahead of the motorcruiser. "Over there," Klaus ordered and they went to the side where there was a black rubber boat with an outboard engine, tied next to the cruiser.

Armitage already sat in the prow. With him was Petra ben Azziz and the German who had hit Lowell. They now knew his name was Manfred.

"Get in," Klaus ordered and they climbed down the short ladder into the rubber boat.

Armitage spoke into a walkie-talkie. There was a crackle of static and then a voice replied, "All clear." He spoke to Klaus, who had sat in the stern and started the engine: "Head inshore."

As they got closer to the coastline, they could see a single figure waiting on the otherwise deserted beach. Far to the right was the smudge of a town. Klaus ran the rubber boat on to the beach and they stepped ashore.

"The car is over there on the road behind the dunes," the young man who had greeted them said.

Armitage nodded and they walked, single file, through the rough grassy hummocks behind the beach to a narrow road where a Mercedes was parked.

"This looks like the Dunkirk area," Brockwood said to Janet in a soft voice, but Armitage overheard him.

"Correct, Lord Brockwood," he said as he waved the rubber dinghy away. "And once more a little boat plays its part in history."

Armitage got into the front of the car with the driver, a young man who wore a dark blue suit, and the Arab girl. Janet and Brockwood were ordered to get into the back with Klaus and Manfred. They noticed that the car was brand-new but already, like the boat, the ashtrays overflowed and there were old newspapers and crumpled bags that had contained junk food scattered around the interior.

Armitage began to fondle the girl next to him and looked in the mirror to see if Janet was watching. Janet closed her eyes, wedged herself into a corner, and tried to find a comfortable position for her head. Brockwood looked around at the latest squalors and reflected that if these people ever came to found a new world order it would probably be wiped out by typhoid.

The car drove at a moderate speed and Janet occasionally opened her eyes to look out of the window, as they passed fields, villages and small towns. Eventually they joined an autoroute. She noticed a sign for Lille before she drifted back into sleep.

Brockwood let his mind keep time with the monotonous boredom of the autoroute. Flashes of light would bounce from the surrounding traffic and gleam from the cheap alloy surface of a St Christopher medallion that dangled from the car's dashboard. Each time it flashed, he thought of Madge, as he had so long ago on his first journey to the Black Dwarf. Then the engine noise altered as they passed through the concrete canyons cut through the countryside. How the Führer would have approved of these roads, he thought sadly.

Charlie Mars climbed the staircase to his flat. On each landing the names of lawyers flanked the doorway, neatly lettered in Roman script on mahogany panels. Sybil had inherited the chambers from her maternal grandfather when they had married and they had spent their honeymoon night there.

He opened the door as quietly as possible but he knew that he would wake Sybil. The smell of leather, old books and furniture polish wafted out to greet him. He went into the small kitchen, the only room that had been modernised since electricity was installed in 1923, and opened the refrigerator.

Sybil found him drinking milk from the bottle when she came in some minutes later. She put her arms around his waist and leaned her head upon his shoulder. He kissed her on the crown of her head. "A long night," he said looking through the window on to the treetops of Lincoln's Inn Fields.

"Come to bed," Sybil said, "unless you'd like a hot drink?"

Charlie thought for a moment. "Do you know, I think I would like a cup of cocoa. Have we got any?"

Sybil went to the cupboard and took out a tin of drinking chocolate. "I heard about Victor and Marjorie," she said gently. "Sergeant Hillary told me. I'm so sorry, Charlie."

He closed the door of the refrigerator and she took the bottle of milk from his hand. "You didn't know them very well, did you?" he said. "They were good people. The very best. I shall miss them."

Sybil nodded. "Go and get into bed. I'll bring the drink in to you."

Charlie walked towards the living room. "I still have a call to make." He flipped through the address book next to the telephone and dialled the number that was entered under the name of a florist's. On the third ring it was answered by a voice full of sleep. "Richard . . . It's Charlie Mars here . . . Yes, of course I know the time . . . Yes, it is very important . . . Code One . . . I need maps and reconnaissance photographs of an area in southern Germany . . . I can give you the details . . . Hang on." Charlie reached inside his pocket and took out a piece of paper, while Air Vice-Marshal Richard Rose went and got a pencil. Charlie read out the co-ordinates that Lewis had given him and the Air Vice-Marshal repeated them. "Thanks, Richard, it really is important to give us everything you've got on the area. Send it straight to Gower Street. Goodnight to you – or good morning if you prefer." Then Charlie reached out and took the mug of chocolate Sybil held out to him.

Sybil pulled the dressing-gown around her, sat down next to Charlie on the sofa and rested against him. "Do you ever wish we were back at Oxford, Charlie?" she asked wistfully.

He drank some of the chocolate before he answered. "I did, I suppose, because I missed the certainty of teaching. And up till now this was all a game, abstract, without conviction. That changed with the deaths of Victor and Marjorie. Now it has become a question of morality. Good and bad. Our side has got to win. The centre must hold."

Across Holborn, Lewis sat at his desk in the corner of his living room in Lamb's Conduit Street. He reached out for the model of the soldier and placed the figure on the desk in front of him. He studied the stern features of the little man with his bold moustache and mutton-chop whiskers, the dark green uniform and the black webbing. He knew a lot about these men: what they carried in their knapsacks; how far they could march in a day; how fast they could load and fire their rifles. And the victories they had carried by the point of their bayonets.

His mind ran over the events of the last twenty-four hours and he searched to isolate something he could have done better. But all that remained sharp and clear was the image of Janet in the photograph. He told himself it was pointless to brood over the events that had led to her capture. Instead he stripped away the clutter in his mind and concentrated on what he had to do. Logic told him he must sleep. He made for the bedroom, leaving the soldier bathed in the bright light of morning.

Beneath him in Janet's flat Hanna Pearce slept on, guarded by two men from Charlie's department.

It was quite a small castle but the rich lands that surrounded it had supported the family in great comfort for over a thousand years. Each generation of men had left the work of the estate to faithful stewards while they pursued the family hobby of making war. Down the ages, from Charlemagne to Hitler, they had fought and killed for Germany until the present Baron had landed his ME109 for the last time on an airfield in the American zone in April 1945. Pausing for a brief period to go through the tedious business of de-Nazification, he had returned to the estate from where he had developed an electronics empire.

The Mercedes crossed a small bridge and into a narrow courtyard deep in shadow. Brockwood noted the time on the dashboard clock; it was twelve forty-seven. Klaus, Armitage and the Arab girl got out of the car to be greeted by a slight blonde girl in a cream shirt and grey flannel slacks. The girl clung to Armitage until he had to take hold of her arms and release himself. Klaus gestured for Janet and Brockwood to get out and told the driver to park at the far end of the courtyard.

They followed Armitage and the blonde girl into the medieval hall. Janet looked at the battleflags, armour and high stone walls covered in the geometric patterns of weapons. Then they climbed stairs and walked through corridors panelled in black wood which were relieved with the delicate paintings from the German Renaissance. The blonde girl stopped and pointed. "You may use this place," she said and Janet entered the room she had been allocated.

Small mullioned windows looked down on to the neatly patterned countryside. There was an ancient carved four-poster bed and a dressing-table in the octagonal shaped room. On the bed were a selection of casual clothes. Janet looked into the adjoining bathroom and immediately turned on the bath taps. She added liberal selections of bath salts and stripped off her clothes, easing herself into the hot water. After soaking for fifteen minutes she wrapped two great fluffy towels around her body and returned to the bedroom. Armitage was there, sitting at the dressing-table, smoking a thin cigar. As she entered, he dropped the cigar on to the pale fawn fitted carpet and ground it out with the heel of his shoe. Janet walked across the room, without showing any surprise at his presence, picked up the cigar butt and placed it in a wastepaper basket next to the dressing-table. "Now I see who is responsible for the disgusting state of that boat," she said and turned away to dry her hair.

Armitage stood close to her and ran a hand along her naked arm. Janet wanted to flinch away but knew that it would be a mistake. Instead she looked at him with contempt. "You're a disgusting kind of person, Mr Armitage. You just want to turn the entire world into a sty, but even pigs like fresh mud when they can get it."

Armitage continued to stroke her arm. "The reverence for possessions has destroyed the brotherhood of man," he said in a half-serious voice. "Why should I care about luxurious surroundings when more than half the world lives in hovels?"

Janet willed herself to stay still; instead she put a hard edge on her voice. "Somehow I find myself strangely immune to your charm. So if you intend to do anything, you'd better call for a couple of your nasty boys to hold me down."

Armitage laughed and she could see that she had won. "I don't need a frigid woman," he said and closed the door quickly before she could reply.

Once he had gone Janet went to the bathroom and vigorously washed the place where he had touched her.

When she had dressed in clean clothes she left the bedroom and found Klaus waiting for her outside the door. He led her to a dining room that was set for a banquet, the table heavy with crystal and silver. Klaus and the driver sat at one end with Manfred, while Armitage, Petra ben Azziz and Brockwood sat at the other. Janet placed herself next to Brockwood who helped her to some cold meat from a salver before them. The Mad Hatter's tea party, he thought as he poured himself a glass of white wine. Then the blonde girl came into the room and sat down beside Armitage. The party was now complete with Alice, Brockwood noted sadly. Then he thought of Carl and the entrance to the Black Dwarf.

"Magda, pour my guests some of your father's excellent wine," Armitage said pompously. "The Baron is away in South America at the moment, no doubt paying his respects to some old comrades, but Magda is here to uphold the family reputation for hospitality." Armitage held up a goblet that was beautifully engraved and chased with silver. "Do you see this glass? It was one of a pair made for one of Magda's ancestors to commemorate a particularly bloody victory during the eighteenth century. The King of Prussia gave it to the family. It is unique and quite priceless." He turned to Magda. "What do you think of it, my dear?"

Magda looked at him and picked up the matching glass in front of her. She hurled it across the room at the fireplace where it shattered into tiny pieces. Armitage looked at Janet's expression and laughed. "Please don't think this demonstration has only been due to my influence. Magda's forebears tended to behave in a similar fashion in most of the countries of Europe and for a time, during the Crusades, in North Africa as well."

Janet had no appetite. She asked if she could return to her room. Armitage nodded and Klaus escorted her. Brockwood refused the offer of brandy but agreed to an invitation to walk on the battlements with Armitage. Escorted by Manfred, they made their way up a spiral stone staircase and stood looking over the rich farmlands below.

"Just think, Lord Brockwood," Armitage said as he rested his arms on the stone parapet. "All this for the benefit of the Russians."

"I'm sorry, I don't follow you," Brockwood said.

Armitage gestured towards the view. "This is dairy country. All the produce goes towards the Common Market butter mountain which is sold at giveaway prices to the Soviet Union. No wonder the farmers of Europe are so solidly conservative: imagine how horrible life would be for them if they had to compete in a free market."

Armitage turned his back to the breeze and lit one of his small cigars.

"What do you want with me?" Brockwood asked.

Armitage flicked his match over the parapet. "I intend to use you."

Brockwood shrugged. "What use am I?"

Armitage blew a stream of smoke into the breeze. "That very much depends on what we find at the Black Dwarf. If we can still get inside and find the evidence you tell us is there, we intend to hold a press conference when you will tell the world how Churchill sent you to stab the Russians in the back. That should give the Russian hawks sufficient excuse to call off the peace talks."

Brockwood shook his head. "I still fail to see what advantage you will gain."

Armitage studied his cigar for a moment. "Capitalism is a very simple system. I intend to exploit that simplicity."

Brockwood could see he wanted to boast. "Why should you, as a revolutionary, wish to exploit capitalism?" he asked.

Armitage smiled. "Revolution is an expensive business. We have an organisation in every country in the West and we need to sustain each one. There is only so much money and we do not have limitless resources. But after tomorrow, our movement will be one of the richest organisations in the world."

"How will you achieve this?" Brockwood asked with genuine interest.

"If you examine the shares of the great companies that hold defence contracts, you will find that the prices have been badly depressed in recent weeks by the dreadful possibility that peace might break out in the world. Tomorrow, the President of the United States and the Prime Minister of Great Britain are both due to make speeches dedicated to the arms freeze and a planned reduction in the stockpiles of existing weapons. This will further depress the price of the stocks in the companies I have mentioned. We shall then buy massive amounts of those shares, courtesy of some of our wealthy supporters, so that when we present the world with the evidence from the Black Dwarf, the Soviets will withdraw from the peace talks and the shares of the industries we have bought into will soar in price. The profits made will be unimaginable." Armitage's face was transformed. He looked like a glutton confronted by a table loaded with food.

"Will you release us then?" Brockwood asked.

Armitage turned on him with glittering eyes. "Oh no. We shall still need both of you. Our plan is that you shall produce a slimming pill from the research that you contributed to so ably during the war. And Janet. Well, she can be our insurance."

"But that will take years to get on to the market: so far it has only been tested on laboratory animals. It may never be safe for human beings."

Armitage smiled. "My dear Brockwood, how much do you think heroin would cost if you could buy it in a chemist's shop? As you know, it is about as expensive and difficult to produce as a plate of beans on toast. Human nature being what it is, surely you can see the attraction of buying an illegal slimming pill, one that allows you to eat what you want? Look what Prohibition did for alcohol in America."

"No one would believe me," Brockwood said. "They would laugh at my story as a fantasy."

Armitage flicked the remains of his cigar in a high arc, so that it curved and fell into the courtyard below. He spoke lightly, but with a sinister conviction. "In that case, we shall have to assassinate the President and the Prime Minister which would have the same effect on the stock exchanges and you and Janet will be our guests for even longer while you produce the pill."

Brockwood studied the fields below, saying nothing. He knew there was a terrible logic in what Armitage had just said.

Sandy Patch stood on the edge of the common with his wife Jean and watched while their son, Andrew, dribbled a football around their border collie.

"How long have you got?" Jean asked in her soft Hereford accent.

Sandy looked at his watch. "Better get going now." He raised two fingers to his mouth and let out a piercing whistle. The boy turned and kicked the ball towards his parents and they raced towards them together. Sandy ran forward and took the ball from the boy, kicked it for a few yards and let the boy take it again. Finally Sandy scooped up the ball and held it above their heads. "Come on," he said. "You'd better drop me off at the station."

They walked to the Mini Metro and Jean got into the driver's seat. The dog and the boy got into the back and began to wrestle. "Pack it in," Sandy said. "Your mother can't concentrate."

Jean pulled into the line of traffic and spoke to Sandy as she watched the road. "So what's this girl of Lewis's like?" she asked, her voice full of curiosity.

"Oh, you know, nice," Sandy replied with infuriating vagueness.

Jean sighed. "Is she tall, short, fat, thin or what?"

Sandy smiled. "She's terrific. I think he said she's a doctor but she looks more like a model."

Jean pursed her lips. "So you fancy her, then?"

Sandy smiled again. "You know me," he said. "I only fancy blondes."

Jean shook her short fair hair and grinned as she pulled into the kerb by Clapham Common Underground station.

Sandy leaned over and kissed her. "See you soon," he said.

Jean held him for a moment. "Take care of yourself," she said as he got out of the car. "And give my love to Lewis."

He waved goodbye to them and went into the station where he bought a ticket to Goodge Street.

Lewis stood in the doorway of his living room, adjusted the lengths of his tie, and straightened his jacket. The morning sunshine had passed from the room and now the soldier on the desk stood in shadow. While he was away, Roland had installed the battered piano in the flat. Lewis raised the lid and played the opening bars of 'East Side, West Side' then he walked to the window and looked up into the blue sky. Stay clear, he prayed as he put the soldier back on the shelf. Stay clear.

The bell rang. He opened the door on to the gloomy landing and found Curtis Lowell and Hanna waiting silently; he stood aside and let them enter. Curtis looked around the room. "You live here?" he said in an incredulous voice. Lewis nodded. "It reminds me of a hotel room I had in Buffalo once." Somehow he made it sound like a suburb of Hell.

"Well, when do we go?" Hanna said, her chin jutting out in a determined fashion.

"You don't," Lewis said in a flat voice.

"Now look," Curtis interjected as he gestured with his bandaged hand – which gave Lewis the chance to reach out and slap the hand hard to make his point.

"Was that necessary?" Hanna said in a shocked voice.

"Yes," Lewis said. "Very necessary. He knows better than to want to come. I can't take somebody who's crippled. I might think about it when I should be concentrating on more important things."

Hanna's voice changed. "Are we really that useless to you?"

"Yes." He shrugged. "I admire your bravery but I need someone who's worked with me before. Sandy and I move at the same time; it's habit." He looked at her for a few moments. "We don't know each other's habits," he said

210

softly. And in the silence that followed he crossed the room and let himself out of the flat.

Curtis and Hanna said nothing for a while and then Hanna walked to the shelf and looked at the model soldier. Without turning around she spoke. "The Pearce Corporation has a Lear jet. Do you fancy a trip to Innsbruck?"

"Let's go," Curtis said casually.

Charlie Mars came out of the entrance of Lincoln's Inn and crossed the roadway to Lincoln's Inn Fields. Two tennis players on the hard court flailed at each other with a ferocity that nevertheless did nothing to disguise their lack of skill. Both players were overweight. Rolls of fat bulged over their shorts and their faces, suffused with blood, glowed like over-ripe fruit.

As he headed for the road that led from the corner nearest to Holborn, Charlie skirted a netball match played by vigorous young girls from the surrounding offices. As ever, there was a fringe of male spectators, standing in mute appreciation of the firm young bodies that dashed and pounced with such dedication. Charlie passed by, his long legs carrying him at a deceptively fast pace.

"Charles, Charles." He heard a voice calling behind him and he turned around to see Claude Henderson hurrying to catch up with him. Charlie slowed down and they walked together through Holborn towards Gower Street. "Where have you been?" Charlie asked as they crossed High Holborn and cut up towards the British Museum.

"To the firm's solicitors," Henderson said. "I'm an executor of Victor Smight's will. I've just been going over things with Crawford. A depressing business."

Charlie looked down almost on to the top of Henderson's head. "I didn't know you were Victor's executor."

Claude nodded. "Yes, we were friends – although we hadn't seen much of them in recent years. He was very good to me when I first came into the service." They walked in silence for some time. As they passed the gates of the British Museum Claude spoke again. "What's going to happen, Charles? Can we do anything?"

Charlie looked at the façade of the museum. "It's up to Lewis and Sandy Patch now. They're both going to Germany. I thought I'd go part of the way with them," he said finally.

Henderson stopped and took Charlie Mars by the arm. "I would like to come as well. I owe you an apology, Charles. I now realise that Lewis Horne's presence is necessary at Gower Street. Our world has changed a great deal."

As they walked on Charlie thought for a moment about Victor and Marjorie. "Has it really changed, Claude? Surely people were killed in the past?"

"Hardly ever," Claude said. "Oh, in the war, yes, but in peacetime it used to be a kind of game. Half the time we didn't know what side the people we used were on. Espionage was just an extension of diplomacy. Now . . ." Claude shrugged. "The barbarians are at the gates and I have never fired my pistol at anything except a paper target and a lavatory bowl. It's a ridiculous situation."

As they arrived at the entrance at Gower Street a car drew up before them and a civil service messenger got out and hurried up the steps with a brown paper package. As they crossed the entrance hall Sergeant Major Watts called out, "Mr Mars, sir. This is an urgent package, just arrived for you."

Charlie took the parcel and asked if Lewis and Sandy had arrived.

"They both went up a few minutes ago, sir," Sergeant Major Watts said as Charlie and Claude hurried up the staircase.

Lewis and Sandy were waiting in the room when they entered. "This has arrived from our friends in the RAF," Charlie said, holding up the package.

Lewis and Sandy cleared the books from a large desk at the end of the room and switched on a big angle-poise lamp that flooded the table in a bright light. Charlie tore open the package and spread the contents on the table. There was a letter, a large-scale map, a huge photographic montage of aerial photos that had been calibrated to correspond with the map and a shabby manila envelope encrusted with dust and dated November 20th 1942. He opened the letter and read aloud:

"Dear Charlie,
Here is the map you requested and a patch-up from satellite photographs our people have put together. Beautiful job, isn't it? You asked for everything we have so I also enclose a file which seems to indicate some sort of activity in the area during the war.
Hoping this is what you need,
Yours ever,
Richard"

Charlie took the contents from the dusty envelope and laid them on the table. There were three creased maps, three flight plans and a wad of debriefing reports.

Lewis unfolded one of the maps and studied the lines drawn by a navigator so many years ago. He read the flight plans and finally a selection of the debriefing reports.

"It seems that on the night of November 20th 1942, Squadron Leader Victor Linsey took three specially equipped Lancaster bombers on a raid on Stuttgart. They left the main stream of bombers and continued to southern Germany where they dropped seventy-five parachutists at 02.47 hours. Here." Lewis pointed to an area on the large-scale map, then traced the same spot on the aerial montage. "We can assume that it was Fitzpatrick's force and they landed on Alpine pasture to the north of the Black Dwarf. They must have force-marched over the mountains at night."

Charlie and Claude studied the point on the map that Lewis indicated. "Where will you drop?" Charlie asked.

Lewis shifted his finger to another spot on the photograph. "Right here, on the wishing-well of the Black Dwarf."

13

"He is at present tame, quiet, and domesticated, for lack of opportunity to exercise his inborn propensities; but let the trumpet of war sound – let the young blood-hound snuff blood, he will be as ferocious as the wildest of his Border ancestors."

The Black Dwarf
Sir Walter Scott

The Mercedes stayed with the endless boredom of the European motorway system until Armitage ordered the driver to turn off near the town of Offenburg in southern Germany. Still in the outskirts of the town they drove into a massive car park between great walls of giant transporters where they came upon two heavy-duty safari trucks loaded with equipment. Five young men stood by them. Brockwood and Janet were ordered into the back of the first truck and had to squeeze along a narrow bench to avoid banging their knees on the equipment that jutted up from the floor. Armitage and Klaus joined them in the truck and Manfred took command of the other vehicle. Then they set off in convoy into the night.

Brockwood looked out into the countryside and remembered the last time he had made the journey. Then the towns and villages had been blacked out and the headlights of all vehicles had been cut to a glimmer. Now Germany glittered brightly with lights – as if the economic miracle was represented in neon. Against the sky they could see mountains that rose spectacularly, without foothills, from a flat plain.

The driver switched on the radio and tuned to a station that was playing rock music. As the record thundered to a climax the announcer explained that they were listening to a

214

programme of Sixties nostalgia. Brockwood felt very old. I suppose that's the definition of old age, he thought, when even your nostalgia is out of date.

Gradually they began to wind through mountain roads and it was well past midnight when they reached the village of Vosbach which lay in a valley separated by a stream that was fed by the high snows. No lights shone from the windows but the moon was bright enough to show every detail of the buildings.

The two vehicles passed over the cobbled street and the inn and the church flashed by. Brockwood noticed that the place had hardly changed at all. Then they came to the start of the road that led to the Black Dwarf.

"How long will it take from here?" Armitage asked.

"About twenty minutes . . . maybe fifteen," Brockwood replied.

"In that case we will camp here. Your description of the Dwarf sounds rather uninviting. I think we can wait until dawn to see it."

The headlights revealed a way into the pastureland to the right of the road. Armitage told the driver to stop and open the gate and the vehicles bumped over the grassy slopes to park under a fringe of pine trees. He had already told Manfred to go and reconnoitre the Black Dwarf and they could hear his truck fading away as it climbed the side of the mountain.

The air was fresh and cool in the meadow and scented by the pine trees. Brockwood's own tiredness seemed to pass but he could see that Janet was exhausted. Klaus handcuffed them together and attached a chain to the cuffs which he then locked to the truck. Another of the men handed them sleeping bags and Janet fell asleep immediately while Brockwood fidgeted restlessly. About fifteen minutes later he heard the other truck return and the muttered conversation between Manfred and Armitage: the road to the Dwarf was still open. His ordeal, it seemed, had only just begun.

Lewis and Sandy sat at the desk in Charlie's room all afternoon, studying the photographic montage until they could

215

close their eyes and see every detail printed on their minds. When they finally folded all the material away, Charlie poured them all a drink. "I think a Last Supper is called for," he said. "My treat."

They put their bags in the duty office along with the packet of maps and gave instructions for the driver to pick them up when he collected them from the restaurant. Then they strolled through the summer evening to Charlotte Street where Charlie had booked a table at Bertorelli's. The bustle of the long rooms and the cheerful directness of the black-clad waitresses lifted their spirits and Charlie made sure to keep the conversation light-hearted until they had finished eating.

"The aircraft will take us on to Innsbruck," he said as he raised a glass of brandy. "We have a car standing by for us there. Claude calculates that we should arrive at Vosbach no later than seven o'clock tomorrow morning."

Lewis looked around the mirrored room. The bentwood chairs and the white tablecloths put him in mind of the restaurant in Brooklyn and suddenly he remembered Hanna.

"The driver should be outside," Claude said. "Shall we go?"

Charlie put down his glass "Northolt here we come," he said. "It seems a suitably prosaic place to begin a venture like this."

When they reached the pavement, Charlie took a last draw on his cigar and dropped it into the gutter before getting into the waiting car. Fifty minutes later they were on the runway at RAF Northolt. Charlie and Claude watched as Lewis and Sandy stowed their gear aboard the huge Hercules transporter between the massive packing cases that made up the rest of the aircraft's cargo.

"What do you think the load is?" asked Claude.

"Home comforts for the British army of the Rhine I would imagine," Charlie replied as he watched Lewis going over the map of the dropping zone with the captain of the aircraft. There was a competence about their discussion that pleased him. Charlie liked to see any job done well.

Claude buckled himself into the seat next to Charlie. "It's been a long time since I flew in an aircraft with propellers," he said. "Odd, isn't it? One forgets there are still aircraft like this in existence. I suppose it is flying everywhere in civilian jets. What's it called?"

"It's a Hercules," Lewis said as he and Sandy joined them. "Very useful for jumping out of – much easier than a jumbo jet. We've never had one to ourselves before, have we, Sandy."

Sandy Patch grinned as he strapped himself into one of the light canvas seats that ran in a row against the side of the aircraft. "Maybe they'll let us keep this one, boss," he said as the co-pilot came back to speak to them.

"Everything okay? . . . Good. We shall take about three hours for the first hop. I'm afraid we aren't British Airways, so I should keep yourselves strapped in. First stop we shall be on the ground about an hour while we unload and refuel. It's a fine night for flying so enjoy your trip, gentlemen. See you in Germany."

Lewis had no time for his usual take-off nerves.

At 02.35 hours Greenwich Mean Time, the Hercules flew at a height of twenty-five thousand feet through the thin, crystal-clear air above the mountains of southern Germany. Charlie Mars and Claude Henderson sat wearing oxygen masks and watched Lewis and Sandy as they made their final preparations. To Charlie they looked remarkably like medieval knights. Their faces beneath the jump helmets were goggled and masked with breathing equipment. Packs and weapons were strapped to their bodies with instruments secured to their chests to record time, altitude and direction. Dressed and equipped in matt black, they were fearsome apparitions. The ramp lowered as the Hercules flew into the wind and the two figures raised their hands in a salute before turning to launch themselves into space like dark angels.

Lewis spread his arms and legs to form a star and con-trolled his glide as he hurtled towards the earth. Beneath him the pattern of the snow-capped mountains was as familiar as the face of an old friend. Carefully he reached up with his hand and wiped the frost from his goggles. It was an act that had to be performed with infinite care in case he should upset the aerodynamics of his glide and begin to tumble out of control. He located the pale speck that he could identify as the wishing-well of the Black Dwarf and altered the position of his arms so that he could line his approach.

The abstract pattern began to alter and take on the recognisable features of the land beneath him. He could see the village and the road on the mountain emerge.

At a certain altitude his parachute opened automatically and his body jerked like a puppet as his hurtling descent was checked. The squarish canopy responded to his directions as he took the lines and guided the final part of his fall. The mountains rose each side of him as he rushed towards the wishing well and he gathered a slack in the lines so that he released them at the last moment and his feet touched the edge of the mountain-top. Then he slapped the release button on his harness as the canopy of his parachute collapsed into the water of the Alpine lake.

Sandy landed within seconds of him and they both quickly gathered in the great squares of nylon. Working swiftly they removed their harnesses, helmets and breathing equipment and checked their weapons. Lewis walked to the edge of the lake and dabbled his hand in the water. As Brockwood had told him, it was warm. "Come on," he said to Sandy. "Dawn's coming soon."

They found the pathway and started a slow descent, checking the pathway at every turn. It soon became evident that no one had used the path in years as some parts were almost totally grown over with brush and fern. They reached a section that was overhung with rock and Lewis thought it corresponded to the description Brockwood had given to the part where the chimney led to the passageway into the Dwarf.

"Hang on," Lewis said and he searched for the recess. He found it and quickly climbed to the ledge and worked his way along until he found the entrance. Just inside was a rough wall of concrete. He rejoined Sandy on the pathway. "It's sealed," he said. "We won't be able to wait for them inside."

Sandy nodded. "Nothing's ever easy in this bloody life," he said as they made their way to the base of the Dwarf.

218

It was a melancholy place. They made their way through the decaying carcases of three lorries, rusting tangles of barbed wire, heaps of rubble and ancient oil drums. The old tarmac was seamed with fissures. By the light of the moon they walked to the spot where Whitehaven had first seen the figure of the Dwarf and studied it in turn. It bore no resemblance to the description they had been given. The mass of rock that had once formed the head and arms had been blown to conceal the entrance and the pillbox. The Dwarf was no more.

"Fitzpatrick seems to have left his mark," Lewis said softly. "Let's get to work."

Brockwood lay awake in his sleeping bag and watched as Klaus and Manfred woke the rest of the camp. He reached out and gently shook Janet's shoulder and she turned and jerked against the handcuff. "They're coming for us," he said in a low voice as she blinked in the fresh pre-dawn air.

"Inside," Klaus said as he unlocked the chain and pointed to the open rear door of the truck.

The lights cut across the meadow as they jolted back to the gateway and started their climb along the mountain road. There the truck slowed to a crawl as they negotiated the final yards past the great rockfall.

"Where to?" Armitage asked and Brockwood directed the driver to the edge of the precipice where he had first stumbled upon the entrance.

The sky was beginning to lighten and was gradually turning from indigo to light pinkish-blue. Armitage ordered them to hurry as they unloaded the equipment from the trucks. He took a large aluminium cylinder from one of the men and quickly assembled a telescope mounted on a tripod. The first spikes of the sun's rays blazed over the mountain-tops. "Locate the entrance if you please," Armitage said to Brockwood, who crouched behind the telescope as the sun's full splendour struck the side of the mountain and the three ribs on the side shone like gold in the first light.

"There," Brockwood said, standing back from the telescope.

Armitage pushed him aside and peered through the lens. "I'm glad your memory serves you so well," he said as he looked at the entrance to the passageway. He turned to one of the other men. "Otto, take a walkie-talkie and I will direct you from here." Armitage straightened up and slapped Brockwood heavily across the face with the back of his hand. Brockwood swayed but did not fall down. "There was no need for this charade. You could have led us straight to the entrance," Armitage said in a quiet voice.

"I was last here ten years before you were born," Brockwood said. "I couldn't be sure I would remember."

Armitage turned to one of his men. "Joachim, get on to the roof of the truck." The youth did as he was told. "Can you see the road from the village?"

"Part of it," he replied.

"Keep looking," Armitage said. "Otto will stay outside the passage. If you see anyone, relay the message to us. Petra, bring the harness."

The Arab girl produced an old-fashioned shoulder holster and strapped Janet into it, then she produced a British army hand-grenade.

"Set the fuse for five seconds," Armitage said.

She did as she was told and handed the fused grenade to Armitage who attached it to the straps of the empty holster. He then produced a piece of cord about seven feet in length and tied one end to the pin. "Simple, isn't it?" he said to Janet. "But I can hear you thinking, If he pulls the cord he could be hurt as well. Petra . . . the jacket please."

The girl reached into the kit in the truck and pulled out a standard NATO flak jacket which Armitage fitted over the shoulder holster. He patted it like a tailor who was proud of the suit he had just made. "There," he said to Janet. "Now you're just a danger to yourself. All you and Lord Brockwood have to remember is not to make me angry."

"Otto is at the pathway," Petra said.

Armitage handed her the cord and took a walkie-talkie from Manfred. He turned to the telescope. "Go on another hundred paces." They waited until Otto did as he was told. "Good . . . you're directly under the entrance. Go forward about fifteen metres and look for a recess . . . Found it? Good! Go up and find the entrance."

Otto scrambled clumsily on to the ledge and worked his way to the entrance. His voice came over the radio. "The entrance is blocked."

"A rockfall?" Armitage asked.

"No . . . manmade . . . it's concrete."

Armitage turned questioningly to Brockwood who shrugged. "It must have been done after we left."

"Luckily we have brought explosives," Armitage said. He looked up at Joachim. "Stay alert. The rest of you load the equipment into the other vehicle."

Concealed beneath a pile of rubble, a few feet from the truck Joachim stood upon, Lewis watched as Janet was led, like a dog on a lead, across the perimeter. Three times he had come close to killing Armitage but each time someone had obscured the shot. Now he waited as the group reached the rock overhang that led to the entrance. While Armitage stood holding Janet on the lead, the others unloaded the equipment. They produced folding ladders and two of the group went up to join Otto on the ledge. They laid an explosive charge against the concrete wall and played out a cable from it back to where the others stood under the overhang. Armitage gave the signal and they detonated the charge. The boom from the explosion echoed around the surrounding mountains while a great cloud of dust billowed from the entrance. At the moment of explosion Lewis broke from his cover and seized the youth on top of the truck by the ankles and jerked them from under him. The youth crashed down smashing his chin on the edge of the vehicle's roof before tumbling to the ground.

Lewis stripped off the boy's light blue nylon jacket, put it on and climbed swiftly on to the roof of the truck before the echoes of the explosion died and the dust settled.

On the pathway Armitage ordered the two back into the passage. After a few minutes they re-emerged.

"There is another wall, and a body," one of them called down.

221

"Blow it as well, and get a move on," Armitage said.

After a few minutes there was another explosion. Again the mountain bounced the noise back but this time there was also a great boom from inside, like a giant drum being struck inside the rock. They all climbed the ladder to the entrance. Armitage followed last. When he and Janet were on the ledge he looked back at the tiny figure in the blue jacket who stood guard on the roof of the truck. Armitage pointed towards the figure and spoke to Otto. "If he warns you that anything is coming, come into the tunnel and fire one shot."

Otto nodded.

Armitage switched on a powerful torch and entered the passageway with Janet. They picked their way carefully over the remains of the concrete wall and worked along the passage where they found Brockwood. He was standing in front of a mummified body that had been crucified on a rough wooden cross. Around the neck was a metal plaque on a chain with an inscription. Armitage shone the torch on to the plaque and read the words aloud: "I am a traitor to the Third Reich."

"You knew him?" Armitage asked.

"It's Willie Keuen," Brockwood said. "He first showed me this tunnel. We used to swim together in the lake."

Armitage shone the torch on to the face. "Why hasn't the body decomposed?" he asked.

"It happens under certain circumstances," Brockwood replied. "The dryness of the atmosphere dehydrates the body."

Armitage examined the plaque again. "Metal. They must have wanted this to last for a thousand years."

From his position on top of the truck Lewis snapped on his own radio set. "Sandy, can you see the one they've left on guard at the entrance?"

"Clearly," Sandy replied.

"Can you get him?"

"There's about twenty feet of exposed ground between us. But I can hit him easily from here."

"No, I want you to take him quietly," Lewis said. "I'll distract him. Wait till I say go."

"Okay, boss."

Lewis reached into his overalls and produced a small square of polished steel. He caught the reflected light of the sun and watched the bright dot of light on the rock wall of the mountain as he moved it to the guard's face.

"Now," Lewis said as he hit Otto with the dazzling light.

Sandy broke cover from the carcase of one of the trucks and sprinted silently to the footpath.

"What the hell is that?" Otto said over the radio. He spoke in French.

"What was what?" Lewis replied, thankful that Armitage led an international team.

"The light shining in my eyes."

"I was drinking from a can of Coke. The bottom must have caught the sun."

Sandy had worked his way up the pathway until he stood under Otto's ledge. Sandy gently lay down his submachine-gun, unclipped a hand-grenade and defused it, weighed it in his hand for a moment, and made a scratching noise on the pathway. As he anticipated, Otto's head peered over the ledge and he threw the grenade with all his might into the face. It struck Otto between the eyes and he pitched forward on to the pathway at Sandy's feet.

Lewis was about to leap from the roof of the truck when he saw movement on the section of the road from the village. It was a blue car travelling at speed. Quickly he made a holding signal to Sandy and ran to the great pile of rock where the car had to slow down to enter the perimeter. The Porsche edged around the obstruction and Lewis raised the Heckler and Koch. Sunlight reflected from the car's windows so that he could not see the occupants and his finger lightly touched the trigger. The slightest pressure and fifteen rounds of nine-millimetre ammunition would enter the car in precisely one second. Then the sunlight slid from the window and Lewis could see Hanna quite clearly. He lowered the submachine-gun and felt his anger mounting.

Hanna got out of the car carrying a square leather briefcase and stood surveying the area. She looked capable and resolute and despite his first stab of anger Lewis was glad to see her.

"Over here," Lewis said softly and raised his ski mask so she could see his face. She turned around quickly and when she saw him she held up the case.

"Medical officer reporting for duty."

Lewis leaned against the rocks and beckoned her over. When she stood close he held up his right hand and she stiffened as if expecting a blow. But instead he gently held the side of her face in his cupped hand.

"Dr Pearce, you are a very difficult woman," he said quietly. She raised her own hand and covered his.

"Where's Lowell?"

Hanna looked around. "I don't know. The louse double-crossed me. I brought him here last night. We stayed in the village, then he ran out on me. When I woke up this morning he'd left me a note saying I should stay at the hotel."

"Was he armed?" Lewis said.

Hanna nodded. "With a Winchester pump-action shotgun. He stole it off some guy at Innsbruck airport who was going on a hunting trip."

Lewis looked around the surrounding mountains and then back at Hanna. Something was wrong. The kaleidoscope whirled once again, but refused to settle into a pattern.

He took Hanna by the shoulders, shook her gently and looked into her eyes. "If there was an outbreak of the bubonic plague, I would put myself under your instructions and obey every order you gave me." Hanna nodded while Lewis continued, "I ask you to do the same."

"Every order?" Hanna asked with a flicker of doubt in her voice.

"Every one," Lewis said with conviction.

"Suppose that I can't give that undertaking?"

"Then I will have to immobilise you."

"Immobilise me! That's a euphemism for knocking me out, isn't it?"

Lewis smiled. "That's right."

For a moment they studied one another, each testing their will power. Hanna could see he meant it. "Okay," she said finally, holding out her hand. "You're in charge." He smiled.

"But only until there's an outbreak of bubonic plague," she added.

They joined Sandy at the pathway and Hanna made a quick examination of Otto who lay at Sandy's feet.

"He'll live," she said. "But I wouldn't like the headache he's going to have."

Lewis unbuckled Otto's belt and strapped his hands behind his back, then the three scaled the ladders the others had left and entered the passageway. By the light of torches they made their way through the twists and turns of the tunnel and paused for a moment to examine the crucified figure. At the final turn of the passage, they could see light on the wall ahead. They switched off their torches and edged forward to the opening. The sight revealed to them was awesome.

The battery-operated arc lights that Armitage's men had brought with them illuminated great areas of the cavern – and a sight that Lewis would always be able to remember. A battlefield lay below them, frozen in time. The bodies, preserved in the great sealed tomb, told the story to Lewis of the action that had been fought.

"What happened here?" Hanna whispered and Lewis began to explain in a soft voice.

"This was a wartime British commando raid led by Colonel Fitzpatrick," Lewis said. "They descended from the top of the mountain by ropes into the entrance when a convoy was entering the hall. See those two tankers inside and the lorry half-buried by the rockfall? The SS regiment counter-attacked to retake the gates and Fitzpatrick blew down the mountainside to seal all of them inside the Dwarf. Both sides seem to have fought to the last man. In the final stages the fighting was hand-to-hand."

"How do you know?" Hanna said.

"See where the field-grey and khaki uniforms lie together?" Lewis said.

"They did all right," Sandy said softly.

Lewis nodded. "Come on," he said and they climbed down the ladder on to the gantry that ran around the dome.

★

Inside the maze of tunnels Brockwood stood in front of the room where Werner had shown him the film so many years before. They entered and a quick search along the shelves soon revealed the canister that Brockwood had brought from England so long ago.

"I would like to see the faces of our Soviet friends when they get this," Armitage said as he tapped the canister.

"Do you really think they'll care?" Janet asked.

"Obviously you have never visited the Soviet Union," Armitage said. "The Great Patriotic War, as they call it, is still very much a part of their lives. Most of the people who run the country remember it as though it were yesterday. Believe me, this will have a profound effect on the way they regard the West." Armitage placed the canister in a leather satchel that was slung from his shoulder and tugged gently on the cord attached to Janet. "Come along, we have more work to do," he said. "Lead us to the records room, if you please."

Brockwood took the party through the maze of narrow corridors until they reached the file room. When the door was forced clouds of dust rose into the air and hung like fog in the harsh light from the arc lamp that Armitage had ordered one of the men to set up. Brockwood was set to work to gut the files. Armitage told the four men to explore the rest of the complex for anything of value, while he and the Arab girl watched Janet and Brockwood. One of the men stayed as a guard.

Lewis, Hanna and Sandy had descended from the gantry and were exploring the area of the great dome when the flicker of torches told them that the four men were returning. They concealed themselves by the simple process of hiding among the dead and watched the four as they skirted the battlefield and made their way to the north-eastern section where the army quarters had been.

"Stay here," Lewis whispered to Sandy and Hanna. "I'm going to take a look at the others."

He worked his way through the corridors until he could see the light from the records room. The door was open inwards and light flooded across the narrow corridor. Lewis took his steel mirror and extended it so that he could see the room reflected on the shining metal. Armitage sat at a table, his right hand holding the cord connected to the grenade next to Janet's heart. Janet and Brockwood were loading files into two canvas airline bags. The guard stood against the wall next to the arc lamp, holding a machine-pistol. Petra ben Azziz stood as close as she could to Armitage, resting one hand on his shoulder.

Brockwood had opened the last filing cabinet and was studying a document intently.

"What is it?" Armitage asked.

Brockwood turned to face him. "This is the last record of Operation Hermann," he said. "The experiment ended in catastrophe. When we escaped, Himmler ordered Carl Raeder's second-in-command, Frederic Dorf, to experiment on the rest of the scientists. It was the first time the drug had been used on human beings. They all died of malnutrition in eighteen days. This is a document recording their deaths prepared by the medical officer of the Regiment. The process accelerated at an incredible rate. It was a terrible way to die.

"This rather alters your plans to produce a pill to sell on the black market, doesn't it?" Brockwood continued. "You might get one batch of customers but they would soon set rather an unfortunate example to other potential buyers."

Armitage was about to reply when there were two long bursts of submachine-gun fire from the dome. He handed the cord to the guard. "Kill them if they try anything. I'm going to take a look. Come on," he said to the Arab girl and both of them started for the sound of the gunfire.

Sandy Patch and Hanna lay on the concrete floor of the domed hall between the mummified bodies of two Waffen SS privates. Hanna's eyes were inches away from the collar insignia on one of the field-grey uniforms. A few feet away Armitage's four men sprayed the roof of the dome with random bursts of fire from the Schmeisser machine-pistols they all carried.

Armitage shouted at them as he emerged from the corridor. "What the hell are you doing . . . stop firing." From the corner of his eye Sandy could see the giant shadow Armitage threw against the dome as he came in front of the arc light. The others were like boys on bonfire night, intoxicated by the explosion they were causing.

"Kronstadt," one of them said in an excited voice, "we found the armoury. There are hundreds of these," he said holding out the machine-pistol. "And thousands of rounds of ammunition. All sorts of weapons."

Armitage took the gun which was factory-new. As he examined it, the cracking boom of a grenade exploding rolled into the dome.

Lewis had moved back down the corridor and slipped into the next room as Armitage and Petra moved down the corridor, and when he judged that they were far enough away, took the same position by the door again. He checked in the mirror and found that the guard was sitting at the table as Armitage had done. He had the cord wound around his right hand and was facing both Janet and Brockwood across the table.

Lewis put down his submachine-gun and took the knife from his shoulder sheath. He held it in his left hand, blade down, took one step sideways into the light and leaped into the room. The movement of his body caused the dust to whirl into the air once again. He landed next to the guard who hardly moved his head before Lewis stabbed the knife down through his hand and pinned it to the wooden table. The man stared in shock as Lewis let go of the knife handle and drove his arm back so that his elbow smashed into the man's face just below the nose. The guard crashed back and then sprawled unconscious over the table. Janet edged away in terror from the frightening apparition, his face obscured by a ski mask. Lewis watched hopelessly as the cord, wound around the guard's hand that was still fixed to the table, tightened and then grew slack as the pin was pulled from the grenade. He vaulted the table and seized his sister, tore open the flak jacket, grabbed the grenade, turned and threw it out of the open door.

In the confined space the noise was shattering. It echoed

into the great dome which caught the sound and held it with a mighty resonance.

In the records room Lewis pulled off his mask.

"You almost frightened me to death," Janet said angrily.

A literal truth, Lewis noted, as he turned to Brockwood.

"Where is the film canister?"

"The Arab girl has it. It's in a leather satchel she's got slung over her shoulder."

Lewis picked up the automatic pistol the guard had dropped. It was a Walther. He checked the magazine, released the safety catch and cocked the weapon. "If you want to fire, just point and pull the trigger but keep your finger off it till then." He handed the pistol to Brockwood. "Armitage and his thugs will be here in a moment. Can you get us into the main hall again by a different route?"

Brockwood picked up the torch from the table. "This way," he said.

Lewis and Janet followed as he led them through the labyrinth of passages. Janet watched the flickering figures ahead of her as they passed through the endless turnings of rock and steel and moved in and out of the blinding white light of the torches. Eventually Brockwood stopped. They were at the edge of the great space within the dome. Lewis went forward and checked. It seemed to be empty. He made a curious clicking sound and Sandy and Hanna rose up from among the dead and joined him.

Hanna could see that Lewis was holding his left shoulder at an odd angle.

"What's that?" she whispered.

"Grenade splinter," he whispered back.

She took hold of his left arm and raised it above shoulder-level. He winced with pain.

"How's that?" she muttered urgently.

"It hurts like hell," he said.

"You're supposed to say it's only a scratch."

"Why?"

"There's not much blood loss and you can still move your arm."

"Okay. Let's go."

Lewis looked towards the labyrinth beyond the dome. He could see there were four possible ways Armitage and his group could come at them, too many for he and Sandy to defend the others.

He pointed up at the gantry. "Take them out, Lord Brockwood," he said. "We'll cover you." They could hear the sound of Armitage's group returning. "Go," Lewis said. Hanna looked at him. "Go," he said gently and Brockwood took Janet and Hanna and gently pushed them forward. They started to run for the staircase.

Lewis looked towards the open ground from the edge of the battleground to the entrances Armitage had to come from. Two arc lights illuminated the area. Lewis began to search the edge of the old battlefield, scavenging for equipment until he found what he was looking for – a Verey pistol and a box of cartridges. He stuck the pistol in his belt and a handful of flares into his pocket.

"Here they are, Lew," Sandy said and Lewis looked up to see Armitage and his group come out of the complex.

"Over there," Armitage shouted and they began firing at Janet, Hanna and Brockwood who were still on the iron gantry.

"Kronstadt," Lewis bellowed as he shot out the two arc lamps.

The beam of the torches carried by the men began to stab towards Lewis and Sandy but one remained trained on Hanna and Brockwood. Sandy fired a burst at the light and it wavered before clattering to the ground. The other torches were switched off, leaving the dome in total darkness.

Lewis could hear the minute noises that the others made as they advanced towards them. The dome acted like a whispering gallery and magnified the scraping of feet and the clink of arms. He muttered an order to Sandy and they both sank down among the petrified bodies. Then he fired the Verey pistol into the dome and watched the four guards as they moved ahead of Armitage and Petra ben Azziz.

The ball of green fire hung in the great dome. Lewis concentrated on Armitage and Petra, and when the flame was extinguished the image remained on his retina. He moved forward silently towards the negative imprint that Petra had formed: by the light of the flare Lewis had seen that she was carrying the satchel.

When he judged that he was very close to her he took a grenade from his webbing and spoke gently in Arabic. "I am here."

"Where?" she said, suddenly startled. With that Lewis reached out and felt her shoulder: it was enough to guide his fist holding the grenade to her chin and knock her out. The satchel was slung across her body. Lewis leaned foward and let her fall across his shoulder. Then he pulled the pin and hurled the grenade along the clear area of concrete. He turned his back as he heard the clattering noise it made. The bomb exploded and illuminated the dome like a flash of lightning to enable Lewis to make for the staircase that led to the gantry. When he reached the gantry he lay Petra down and waited in the pitch blackness for Kronstadt.

"Light," Armitage screamed. "Light." And two of the powerful torches illuminated them. In his frenzy Armitage seized Lewis by the front of his smock and swung him against the wall like a rag doll. The light from the torches showed him raising the machine-pistol to bring it down on his opponent's head. Lewis took his submachine-gun in both hands and brought it up to break the grip and block the descending pistol. He then swung it into Armitage's face. It knocked him against the rough wall of the dome and Lewis hit him twice each side of the throat.

Armitage went down and gunfire began to explode around him, ricocheting from the metal gantry and the surrounding rock. Lewis threw himself down beside the bodies of Petra and Armitage and the firing ceased. There was a deep quiet in the dome and Lewis waited for the ringing in his ears to settle. Moments later he heard the sound he had been praying for: the splashing noise of liquid gushing on to the floor of the dome. Sandy had opened the stop-cocks on the two tankers and the strong smell of petrol fumes filled the dome.

Sandy groped his way through the darkness across the battlefield holding his submachine-gun in front of him as a blind man would a white stick. Occasionally he stumbled over the long-dead bodies but eventually he found the great mass of rock that Fitzpatrick's men had brought down into the entrance so many years before.

Desperately he groped along the rocks until he located one of the ropes the original raiding party had descended on. He tested it with all his weight and it held. Swiftly he began to climb to the gantry.

While he waited for Sandy Lewis rolled on to his back and loaded another cartridge into the Verey pistol.

"Lew," he heard Sandy call as he rolled back on to his stomach.

"Here," he replied and masking the torch he quickly flashed the dim light on to Armitage and Petra. Armitage was regaining consciousness.

"Get up the ladder and I'll send him up to you when he comes around."

"Okay," Sandy whispered and Lewis drew his Browning and stuck it into Armitage's open mouth.

"Can you hear me?" he said in the velvet darkness. A gurgling sound came from Armitage and he began to move slowly. "I'm going to give you a chance to live," Lewis said in a low and gentle voice. He took Armitage's hand and placed it on the ladder to the entrance.

"There is a friend of mine waiting for you at the top of this ladder. Try anything and he will not hesitate to kill you, understand?" The gurgling sound came again. "Now stand up slowly and remember the gun in your mouth has a hair trigger."

Armitage did as he was told and when they both were standing Lewis transferred the Browning from Armitage's mouth to the small of his back. "Now climb," he said and gave a gentle jab, then he leaned down and scooped up the inert form of the Arab girl. As he lifted her on to his shoulders he remembered the forced marches of his training across the Brecon Beacons. At least it's not raining in here, he thought, as he started to climb the ladder. When he had mounted the second rung a voice suddenly called from the floor of the dome. "Kronstadt."

Armitage, who had reached the safety of the entrance to the passageway, called back, "I'm here – open fire!"

The beams of the torches carried by the men on the floor below framed Lewis and the automatic fire began to explode around him again. Holding on to the ladder with one hand and with the Arab girl over his shoulder he half-turned and with his free hand he fired the Verey pistol into the void behind him.

The green ball of intense light curved gracefully through space, bathing the men below in the eerie glow.

The four stopped firing and watched as it began its descent. Just before it touched the ground a massive fireball erupted as the fuel from the tankers ignited. Lewis could feel the searing heat as he turned and resumed his climb towards the entrance.

14

> "I would pamper him with wealth and power to inflame his evil passions, and to fulfil his evil designs; he should lack no means of vice and villainy; he should be the centre of a whirlpool that itself should know neither rest nor peace."
>
> *The Black Dwarf*
> Sir Walter Scott

As Lewis stumbled through the twists and turns of the narrow passageway he could feel the hot wind of the fire blasting behind him. Ahead he could see Sandy holding his gun to Armitage's head.

Suddenly the mountain was shaken by a great booming explosion and a curious ripping noise. The shudder that rocked through the Black Dwarf caused Lewis to stumble and lean against the wall of the passage to regain his balance. As he did so he could feel the Arab girl scrabbling for his Browning.

He unloaded her from his shoulder and pushed her ahead of him. They emerged into blinding daylight and Lewis held up his arm to shade his eyes. To the left of the entrance Brockwood, Hanna and Janet stood facing the wall with their arms raised. Sandy lay unconscious at their feet. Armitage was taking his weapons. Petra scuttled forward to join him. Lewis half-crouched and began to swing his submachine-gun up into the line of fire.

"No, Lewis."

At that moment he felt the pressure of a gun barrel on the back of his neck.

"Put your weapons on the ground in front of you. Slowly!" the familiar voice commanded and Lewis did as he was told. "Now turn around."

Curtis Lowell stood nursing a pump-action Winchester shotgun. "Step back, please," he ordered. The brutal-looking weapon was pointed at Lewis's chest, where the satchel containing the film canister now hung.

"I take it you two are friends," Lewis muttered.

"You could say he's a close friend of the family," Armitage replied. "He and Susan had a summer romance in Berlin last year. That's where we got to know each other."

"I don't understand," Janet said. "Why did they torture you in London if they are your friends?"

"To convince you of his reliability when he escaped," Armitage said. "Even my people didn't know we were working together. Every organisation has its traitors."

"What are you?" Lewis said to Lowell. "A traitor or just a plain crook?"

Lowell shook his head. "You British, Jesus, when are you going to wake up? When the Russians are changing the guard at Buckingham Palace? Your universities, trade unions – even the House of Commons – are full of people who think you've only got to hold hands with the Soviets and the world's going to change into Sunnybrook Farm. You and I know the Russians want to win and that's exactly what you've lost, Lewis, the will to win."

"So you're a traitor," Lewis said. "I just wanted to be sure."

"That's garbage," Lowell replied. "The winners decide who the traitors are. The next men in the White House will probably make me a general."

"You're a long way from Appomattox."

"It's a different kind of war, Lew."

Lewis gestured towards Armitage and the Arab girl. "What about these . . . your soldiers?"

Curtis followed his glare. "They're just retarded children; murderous too, perhaps, but nothing more. And they did come in useful." He looked at Petra who stood now as if she were posing for a revolutionary poster, her head thrown back in proud defiance. How easy to show defiance, Lewis thought, when you had all the weapons.

"Did you have Victor Smight and his wife killed?" he asked Curtis.

"That was us," Petra said with unmistakable pride.

"Step aside, Lewis," Curtis said in the same easy voice. He did so and Lowell shot Armitage and Petra, his action on the Winchester so swift that the two explosions sounded almost as one. Petra's body was thrown from the ledge by the force of buckshot hitting her and Armitage sprawled back across the body of Sandy Patch.

"Spring cleaning," Lowell said in answer to the shocked expressions on the faces of the others.

"Are you going to kill us all?" Hanna asked.

"I don't want to, believe me."

"But the end justifies the means." Lewis finished the sentence for him.

Curtis clicked his fingers and held out his hand. "The satchel please."

As he spoke a great rumbling started from deep inside the Dwarf and the ledge began to tremble. As if in protest at the shattering explosions within, the mountain groaned and a great fissure opened up beneath the wishing-well. The Alpine lake poured into the hollow mountain like a mighty flood-tide, thrusting the manmade detritus before it. In moments the tidal wave smashed against the passageway and the pressure caused the water to hose through the tunnel and come crashing out as a great waterfall where it hurtled down the mountainside.

The geyser erupted a few feet behind Lowell. Lewis knew this would be the only chance he would get. He threw himself forward, and gained a fleeting impression of moisture upon a black wall as their bodies collided and they both catapulted into the water. Curtis shouted out and the half-human cry was borne back to the ears of the others as the gushing torrent carried both of them down the mountainside.

Lewis felt his body battered as the raging water hurled him from rock to rock until a final blow brought oblivion. He was aware of peace and a great sense of calm. But Hanna called him from the deep rest and slowly and with reluctance he returned. First there was her voice accompanied by the sound of rushing water, and he thought for a moment they were back on the bridge at The Trout. He smiled until he became aware of the pain, a pain that seemed to engulf his entire body. Then he felt firm hands methodically feeling him and he knew that nothing serious was broken. Finally he opened his eyes and looked up at Hanna who knelt beside him.

Lewis eased himself to his elbows and saw the others who stood around him in a semicircle.

"How did I make it?" he said.

"You got caught in the barbed wire, boss. At the cliff edge."

Lewis looked towards the torrent of water that still spurted from the mountain and cascaded over the precipice.

"What about Lowell?"

Sandy shook his head. "No sign. He must have gone over."

With great effort Lewis got to his feet and supported by Sandy and Hanna looked up at the ruined outline of the Black Dwarf. From somewhere within, air trapped by the rising water forced its way through a fissure and the mountain seemed to let out a great final sigh.

Hanna carried her bag towards Lewis's room in Charlie Mars's house at Oxford. She knocked briskly on the door and entered. Lewis lay on the bed. He was wearing evening trousers but no shirt.

"People are supposed to wait until they're asked to come in," he said as she beckoned him from his lying position.

"Shut up, I'm a doctor," Hanna replied as she ripped the dressing from his shoulder.

"Did you notice I didn't flinch," he said as he tried to encircle her with his free arm.

"Cut that out," Hanna said, "or I'll report you to the British Medical Association." She took the arm and lifted it up and down before applying a new dressing. "You're doing too much with it. Try and rest it for a few days." She took the dress shirt that hung from behind the door and held it out to him. "Hurry. They're waiting for us. You and Charlie are going to drop Sybil and I off for our own dinner before you go on to your college."

237

"You're very cool," Lewis said as he struggled into the shirt.

"That's because I'm working. I've seen you in your professional capacity, too, remember. You tend to be short of charm when you're about your business."

Lewis got into his jacket while Hanna went to the dressing-table and picked up his black silk pocket handkerchief. She folded it and tucked it into his top pocket. But before he could reach for her again she opened the door.

"Get moving, Captain. We're late," she said lightly.

As they reached the top of the stairs Lewis spoke to the back of her head. "Did you enjoy our walk this afternoon?"

"Yes," she said in a matter-of-fact voice.

"What did you like most about it?"

Hanna paused for a moment on the stairs. "It was nice that nobody shot at us," she said finally.

As the Latin prayer came to an end the Provost rapped twice with his gavel and there was a scraping of benches and chairs on the stone flagged floor as the diners sat down.

At High Table Lewis looked past Charlie Mars who sat opposite him, resplendent in academic finery, and into the body of the hall where the undergraduates were beginning their humbler meal. Nothing had changed much since he had sat with them. There was a sprinkling of women now but the blackness of the gowns tended to preserve the sameness of the scene, just as they had throughout the centuries.

"Extraordinary business with Brockwood," said the Provost, who sat to Lewis's right at the head of the table.

"Yes," Lewis replied.

The Provost put down the glass of wine he had been examining with a careful eye, pushed some pâté on to his toast and began to munch reflectively.

"Did you discover who was passing on information from Gower Street?"

Lewis glanced to his left. A Bishop sat morosely chasing his food around the plate trying to hide scraps of it beneath some limp lettuce leaves. Lewis had already discovered he was stone deaf. He looked across the table. Next to Charlie

Mars sat the Dean, deeply engrossed in conversation with the multinational industrialist. The Dean was busy explaining how a few millions willed to the college could guarantee immortality. Lewis turned back to the Provost. "I'm afraid it was me."

"You?" the Provost said in a puzzled voice.

Charlie raised a hand. "As often happens, the unvarnished truth is misleading. The guilty party was one of our American friends."

"An *American* traitor. How unfashionable," the Provost said with only a hint of mischief. "What was his name?"

"Lowell, Curtis Lowell."

The Provost raised his head so that the candlelit silver on the table before them danced in the reflection of his spectacles.

"Lowell? A common enough name in Massachusetts."

"One of his ancestors was a general with Grant when Lee surrendered at Appomattox," Lewis said.

"Oh, *that* Lowell," the Provost remarked, tapping the table before him. "Captain Ephraim's brother."

"I thought Ephraim canned beans," Lewis said.

"He owned a canning factory, certainly, but during the war between the states he was a blockade-runner for the Confederates. He brought so many guns from England that Union troops began referring to a wound as an Ephraim."

Lewis took a sip of the college wine.

"Tell me," the Provost continued, "what was his motive? Greed?"

Lewis shook his head.

"Why then?" Charlie Mars asked.

Lewis shrugged. "I think he was a patriot of sorts. He was a genuine soldier. And they don't often turn out to be traitors."

The Provost nodded. "Difficult types. Useful in wars but awkward in these piping times of peace. But how about Bellingford? I didn't think he was the right material for his latest promotion but the Prime Minister regards him as something of a blue-eyed boy. I understand he is getting the credit for a brilliant piece of work that is all hush-hush."

"Do you know him well, Provost?" Lewis asked as he dipped into the butter dish.

"I wouldn't say well. As you know he wasn't at this college, but he saw a lot of Patrick Armitage during his second year, so he was about the place. Personally I thought little of them both, but evidently I was wrong. How do you judge him, Charlie?"

Charlie Mars looked up. "I'm sorry, I was concentrating on the wine. German, isn't it?"

"Yes. Do you approve?"

Charlie raised his glass in Lewis's direction and took another sip. "Yes, I rather think I do."

As Lewis raised his glass to acknowledge the salute the Bishop jogged his arm and some of the wine spilt on to the table. He looked down and his napkin had slipped from his lap to the floor. It meant reaching down with his wounded shoulder, so Lewis pulled the silk handkerchief from his breast pocket. And as he did so, three buttercups fluttered down on to the table before him.